Dylan's Chase

TOM FAUSTMAN

Blue Sky Ventures
175 Tryon Street
Glastonbury, CT 06073

This book is a work of fiction. Names, characters, places and incidents either are products of the author's imagination or are used fictionally. Any resemblance to actual events or locales or persons, living or dead, is entirely coincidental.

Cover Design by expertsubjects

Manufactured in the United States of America

DEDICATION

To my incredible "Drexel Hill Courts" friends—Fran, Kutch, Michael, Dunph, Gator, Blade, Bird, Jimmer, LTL, Paul, Hank and Eddie who were the inspiration for Dylan's unshakeable joy and optimism. Friends for life.

PECULIAR FRIENDS

As I walked down Shady Lane on the mild November day in 1966, I was troubled by thoughts of changes in my friends Nut and Truck. Bobby Carr didn't become Truck till his growth spurt after freshman year. He not only got tall, he got thick through the chest and shoulders. Until that point, not a natural athlete or overly aggressive, Truck became a ferocious competitor and great basketball player in the last couple years. Not just a tough player like Nut and me, Truck would cream anyone in his way. Most times he did it within the rules; sometimes he flat kicked his opponent's ass. The new meanness bothered me. When I brought it up, he said, "Dylan, in this world it's eat or be eaten."

I raised my eyebrows, "Truck, then you've got one hell of an appetite." He chuckled, didn't argue.

John O'Hanlon had been "Nut" since grade school. He earned the title when he climbed the flagpole outside St Tim's in 7th grade and refused to get down. It was his way of protesting what he thought was an overly harsh punishment for putting a dog turd in Jane Dolgerts's lunch pail. All the kid's in the recess yard chanted his name. Finally, Sister Agnes came out to check on the noise, spotted him, "John, get down from there. People will think you're some kind of nut!" A star was born. I was the mastermind of the turd caper but Sister Agnes accused Nut and he accepted blame. When I told Sister Agnes I was the fecal culprit, she punished Nut anyway for not telling the truth, ratting me out. We have been inseparable since.

My mother liked all my friends but noted they were mostly peculiar. Her theory was, "My Dylan likes to collect stray pets, the ones nobody wants." My real name was Tommy but even my parents called me Dylan. I got the name as homage to the scraggly folk singer. Jimmer Keilmann was an older kid, and responsible for most nicknames in our neighborhood. Since I was neat and clean-cut, Jimmer saw an ironic way to pay tribute to his favorite singer. Jimmer's exact words were, "Frazier, you look like an altar boy with that wavy black hair, jet blue eyes and stick-up-your ass posture. You are the polar opposite of Bob Dylan." That's how Tommy Frazier became Dylan.

Another thing really eating at me lately was doubt about the Catholic religion. My mother Kate went to church every day, spent every free second helping others and worried she wasn't doing enough. She was born dirt poor, was abandoned by her drunken, philandering father and yet considered herself the luckiest person on earth. Kate always had a smile on her face; never yelled at me but somehow maintained total control. I would do anything to help my mother. I truly believed she was a saint from heaven. But I had so many doubts about Catholic doctrine, was the type who questioned everything and rarely heard a sensible answer to satisfy me. The nuns used to tell my mother, "Your Tommy has a wee bit of the devil in him."

My mom always had the same response, "He's my get-into-heaven-free card." I had her sense of humor, why didn't I have her faith?

Since I was being introspective, I had to admit a quirk of poking in other people's business. It was an irresistible draw. It wasn't just curiosity, more a compulsion to find out what was right. More accurately, what I viewed was right. Not from a religious sense or anything spiritual, it was more an intolerance for bullshit. I was that way from an early age. It wasn't like the quirk just came with puberty or some striking experience. Apparently I was born with a micro-sensitive bullshit detector. My parents told the story of me at age five arguing about going to kindergarten on the bus. Allegedly, I told my mom, "There's no way I'm going to school; I'm too little." She laughed, told me to hop aboard, waved as I began the one-mile trek through busy suburban Baltimore. I remembered looking out the bus window, memorizing the route. When we got to school, I blended into the playground chaos, slipped away, walked home. Apparently, there was a major highway or two that I traversed. When I walked in, saw my mom sweeping the kitchen floor, I waved, "Told ya." She rode the bus with me for the next few days until I relented from the protest.

♦

My flashbacks stopped as I neared the cyclone fence that separated me from "the courts." Since 6th grade, I had thoughtlessly vaulted this fence and entered a different, much simpler world. As I trudged over the beat up softball field, I remembered back when Jimmer Keilmann and I watched the courts being paved, even then knowing something was wrong. Jimmer had turned to me,

exclaimed, "Frazier, the dumb asses forgot to level it, it'll be like playing on a God-damned ski slope."
Unexplainably, this slanted mis-creation had become the basketball Mecca of suburban basketball in Philadelphia.

Early on, Jimmer became the self appointed "Commissioner of the Courts." His rationale was: "It may seem too structured to have a commissioner but we need to avoid chaos. Trust me; the shit will fly if there's no order." At the time, no one argued because no one cared. But in hindsight, it was an act of genius. The courts got so popular that his distinction as arbitrator of disagreements became all-powerful. Jimmer used obscure rules whenever there was any argument over playing time. I saw Jimmer randomly prohibit kids from playing because:

- They sucked
- They had ass breath (his judgment)
- Wore hats with propellers or feathers
- Were judged not serious about basketball (and sucked)
- Wore bad shoes (sandals, hush puppies, Flagg Flyers etc.)
- Had weird clothes (argyle socks, corduroy pants, anything pink)
- They irritated Jimmer

The best part of the summer was when Jimmer stepped into disagreements, imposed one of the above rules. I can remember one fool arguing his dismissal, being told: "Look pal, I'm doing you a favor. It can get rough out there sometime and I'd hate to see your culottes get twisted up."

And then the kid said, "They're not culottes, they're clam diggers."

Jimmer then turned to the horde of watching players, looked horrified: "See guys, the poor guy must have made a wrong turn. He thinks he's at the Jersey Shore with all the other shell collectors." Over time, no one argued with Jimmer.

I chuckled as I recalled that funny day. But it was now Thanksgiving vacation of my senior year at Monsignor Conner. We were odds-on favorites to win the city basketball championship, barely losing in the semi-final last year. We had the whole team back and we had Truck. If we had Nut on the team, we would have won last year. His cheap father, Digger, wouldn't spring for the meager tuition, sent him to Upper Derby, the local public school. That was where Nut discovered wrestling, so the move worked out for him. He was the reigning state heavyweight champ since sophomore year. Nut was a legend in wrestling circles, considered a future Olympic champion. But Nut had other plans. That's what ate at me.

DIGGER

James "Digger" O'Hanlon was a savagely brutal man. He was the spitting image of his father, James Sr., who was alcoholic and viciously abusive. Born in County Kerry, Digger was moved at age six to West Philadelphia, an Irish enclave in a beat down section bordering the southern end of the City of Brotherly Love. Things only got worse for the O'Hanlon family in the "Land of Hope and Dreams," work was scarce, the family scrapped by. And the worse they struggled to make ends meet, the worse the beatings by James Sr.

As strict Catholics, the family marched into St Barnabas every Sunday, sat quietly and robotically followed their parents to the Communion rail to receive the Holy Eucharist. They were the perfect Catholic family. But the pastor, Father Bell, spotted the signs on the bedraggled kids. One Sunday he approached the senior O'Hanlon, "Don't be overdoing the discipline, James. Your family looks a little worse for wear."

James, Sr. looked Father Bell straight in the eye, "Spare the rod, spoil the child is how I see it." They never went to St Barnabas again.

So perhaps Digger was another helpless victim of his brutal childhood environment. Or was he just born mean? He learned over time he had some special qualities. He could take a licking without crying, ever. As Digger grew into adolescence he became a gifted boxer, unusually strong for his slight build. He won the prestigious Golden Gloves contest in Philly as a scrappy twelve year old. What he lacked in weight he made up with savagery. And using an entirely different talent set, he could display any emotion at will; convince others of his intentions without an ounce of sincerity: A born actor. And lastly, with no prior training, he became a great mortician while serving in World War II. Because of this last gift, he avoided the front lines, turned this talent into a lucrative profession when he returned home. Digger knew that life was random. Instead of becoming a hopeless drunk like his father, he had become a pillar of the community, the most influential parishioner at St Timothy in Drexel Heights.

Now 50 years old, Digger sat in his comfortable funeral home and finished working on his deceased customer, Mr. Kessler. Digger mused aloud, "Kessler, sounds German. I wonder if his relatives were Nazis? He has that superior look about him." He thought wordlessly for a few moments: Anyway, his family has money, paid 50% upfront without blinking an eye. They said they heard I could work miracles.

He laughed at that: If they only knew his secret. When he prepared dead soldiers after the Normandy Invasion, most of them were horribly mutilated. Since the brass just looked at the face, he experimented on ways to make them more life-like. Puffing up their cheeks and adding color was his magic. Since he had meager cosmetic supplies, he used what was at hand. Who would ever know that blood would be such great rouge? All you needed was to mix a dose of motor oil for a lasting scarlet tinge. And stuffing spare skin and muscle did the trick inside the mouth. The cheeks became plump and rosy. He never cared how gruesome this was. That he was defiling these brave heroes never bothered him. No one would ever know.

These macabre practices continued as he began his funeral business in West Philadelphia. He grinned: Wouldn't the Kessler's be shocked at his secret formula?

As Digger laughed aloud, suddenly his thoughts shifted to Mary. He married Mary Flaherty shortly after returning from the war. Mary was a beautiful and popular girl in West Cathedral High School. Digger used his considerable acting skills to convince her he was "a catch," that she was lucky to snare him. Before he made his move, Digger stalked her, studying her likes and dislikes. Mary was a daily churchgoer so he became a regular at six o'clock morning mass. Mary always chatted amiably with the elderly woman afterward. He mimicked the friendliness. Digger outdid himself by helping the octogenarians up and down the steep steps at St Bernadette, a true gentleman.

Pretty soon Mary wondered: Who is this sweet boy? By then Digger had her schedule down pat. And he discovered her weakness: Mary Flaherty had a heart of gold. After six months of stalking, Digger finally made his move. He asked Mary shyly after mass, "Would you help me start a visitation program for the sick parishioners? Some of them can't make it to mass and the priests can't always get them communion. There must be a better way." Mary Flaherty was hooked. She and James O'Hanlon became inseparable, dated all through senior year and got engaged before he was drafted into the Army. Mary never knew she married a sadist until shortly after their wedding.

Digger stopped his musings and walked to his black

Buick, opened the glove compartment. He pulled out his worn set of lightweight performance boxing gloves. And then thought: The only thing I ever learned from my piece of shit for a dad; how to hide a pummeling.

He remembered the day long ago when Father Bell challenged dad for beating his family. Good old dad wasn't about to stop the thrashings. His dad went to an Army Navy store and bought a used set of boxing gloves to mask the damage. Digger sat back in the car seat and visualized his boyhood terror of dad putting on those gloves. Even today, that vision made him shiver. But rather than reversing the cycle of violence when he married, he brought family discipline to new levels of pain.

Digger slid the gloves into his black briefcase, started home. He smiled as he planned the evening. Mary would be alone. John had a wrestling meet and wouldn't be there to interfere. Thinking of John got Digger worked up. He used to beat John senseless until he grew into a formidable young man, not only big but a champion wrestler.

His son got the nickname "Nut" because of his fearlessness. And then John started to protect his mother. Digger's rage grew as he recalled when John had broken his arm a couple years ago, sending him to the hospital after teaching Mary a lesson in obedience.

Shaking off that sour memory, Digger reached into the briefcase, fondled the gloves, got a contented look. He wouldn't leave a scratch on Mary. He'd hammer her torso. He'd only hit the sides of her head, careful to let her hair cover the bruises. Digger smiled for the first time that day. He'd show Mary he was still the boss.

TRUCK

While I ambled to the courts on that mild November day, Truck sat in his bedroom, stared at the letter that just arrived. All it said was, "Robbie, it is a joy to see you become a great basketball player. I'm so proud of you." There was no signature. Not knowing why, the letter disturbed him, just as the others had. Truck received many fan letters since being named to the Philadelphia All City basketball first team as a junior. He had his pick of college scholarships. But many of his fan letters were taunting, probably from rival teams he thrashed. The taunts made him laugh. He tossed them away mindlessly. He knew the way he played pissed people off. When he got on the basketball court he became a gladiator. "Last man alive," was his internal pep talk. That style won no friends. He was most at peace when playing basketball. No other voices haunted him while he played. But then the strange letters started arriving.

A loud noise shattered his daydream. His "cousin" Liz was always throwing things around in her room. Liz liked to rearrange according to her whim that month. She was back from college for Thanksgiving holiday. It both excited and disturbed him. Since moving in with "Aunt Sue," Liz had been a defining presence in his adolescence. Like her mother, Liz was a large girl but very pretty. Her breasts were huge. They had captivated Truck from the first. Liz knew of his fascination and took great pleasure in exciting him. From the very first, she kept her bedroom door open, walked around topless when she knew Truck would be around. Things got worse from there.

NUT

A few blocks away, Nut just finished lifting weights, was deciding whether to head to the courts or just go to the track and do sprints. When he walked up from the basement, he saw his mother hard at work preparing lunch. It bothered him when he saw how slumped she'd become. And that made him think of Digger and that made him angry. Nut walked over and put his powerful hands on the sagging shoulders, massaged his beleaguered mom. Mary O'Hanlon turned toward her youngest son, rested her head on his sculpted chest. Nut patted her head, whispered, "You're the best mom in the world."

The moment was broken as the black Buick rumbled up the driveway. Nut looked outside as his older brother shot hoops on the basket attached to the garage. Since they were little, the O'Hanlon boys scattered when Digger arrived. He always parked his car in the middle of the half-court, thereby ending the game. Today, Digger slowly opened the car door, growled, "Get inside and make yourself useful." Knowing this wasn't an idle command, his brother sprinted through the kitchen door. Nut watched him hurry upstairs, out of the line of fire. Digger followed shortly, looked at Nut's protective stance beside Mary. "Leave your mother be, John. She's got work to do." Digger O'Hanlon never used nicknames, was the only person that called Nut by his real name.

Digger never acknowledged Mary, went upstairs to change his clothes. That helped Nut make up his mind. "I'll just make a sandwich, Mom, got to get to the courts early. If I get on Jimmer's team with Dylan and Truck, we'll win all day."

You could see the disappointment on her face but she said, "Have fun, son, you're only young once. Tell Dylan and Truck to stop over sometime, I miss those boys."

Nut rubbed her head, went upstairs to change. Nut knew the sandwich would be waiting when he got back in a few minutes. Mary O'Hanlon ran a tight ship. Digger insisted on that.

THE COURTS

Most afternoons there would be fifty guys waiting to play on the slanted court. New guys would look at the angle and ask, "Why are we playing here? This place is fucked up." The court regulars had adjusted to the surface, grinned and shook their head smugly, knew the rookies would probably lose until they played here enough.

The unspoken grin meant, "More playing time for us." Through dumb luck, there happened to be a load of talented basketball players within a few blocks of the Drexel Heights courts, you could always find a game there. I grew up on the court and perfected the required alteration of uphill and downhill shooting. Depending on where you stood on the surface, there was a foot variation. Great shooters elsewhere became very mediocre on our court. It was fun watching the frustration and disbelief as the ball missed badly.

As I thought about that, I watched Truck and Nut drive up and park. I studied my closest friends as they approached. Truck was blond and blue-eyed, about 6'4" and weighed 225 lbs. He was muscular but his barrel chest and thick neck made him look shorter. Truck wasn't a great leaper but his balance, ferocity, fundamental skills and great hands made him special. If he got near a ball, it was his. Truck's dad was a butcher; he had helped lifting heavy slabs of beef in the shop since first grade. Truck's hands weren't just strong; they were weapons. If he punched you, you bled. And lately, he was punching too much.

I switched my gaze. Nut was 6'3", but his 220 lbs were all sinew and defined muscle. Even his face looked strong; his cheekbones bulged under pale blue eyes and a sandy-colored crew cut. But oddly, he didn't look his weight, was sleek like a cat. His wrestling coach said he could add another 30 pounds without losing quickness. Even when Nut moved, it was like an animal lope, a tiger stalking. But unlike Truck, Nut never fought unless provoked. And even then, Nut would quickly put the foolish opponent on the ground, pinned under his knee. I often wrestled with Nut, not because I enjoyed it, but just to let him try new moves. By default, I became a good wrestler and could handle myself against most people. But when it came to real fighting, I was no match for Truck or Nut.

From the far end of the court, Jimmer yelled, "Truck, Nut, Dylan, Smitty and me against you other guys." He pointed at the nearest opponent, "Call for first in."

He flipped a coin, we heard Jimmy Tordone foolishly yell "tails." Jimmer looked at the coin, quickly put it in his pocket without showing the actual outcome.

He threw me the ball, "Heads, you lose. Dylan, bring the ball in." Our team chuckled. None of us could ever remember Jimmer losing a coin flip. That's how most games started if Jimmer was around. He'd stack the sides, so he'd win all day. He always picked me so I never bitched. If someone complained, he'd stand looking completely dumfounded and say, "What do you think this is, a fucking democracy?"

As predicted, our team won all afternoon. A few college players showed up and eventually got to play. One of the kids starred for Temple, was a big guy, about 6'8". Kind of wiry but was a good athlete. You could see Truck getting worked up, competing against this older player. Early in the game, rebounding a missed shot, Truck blocked the taller guy so hard he fell over. Furious, the Temple kid came up swinging. Truck deftly ducked, punched him so hard in the cheek he collapsed. I watched him on the ground, bleeding from four of Truck's knuckles. Jimmer moved in fast. He looked at Truck, then at his fallen opponent, "Fights over. Get up and play ball. No more shit." The Temple player was useless the rest of the game, they lost badly. But all during the rest of the game, I was worried about Truck, silently made a promise.

During the last game, Hank Greenberg drove up, stopped to watch. Hank had become friends with Nut when they met at Upper Derby High School. Hank managed the wrestling team. He and I instantly hit it off. Nut didn't make friends easily so I knew Hank was solid. We learned Hank was called "Hesh" by his parents. The Greenberg's described themselves as "not so Jewy." And that cracked me up. Our gang was all Roman Catholic so that neutral religious arrangement worked out. I asked Mrs. Greenberg about the nickname for Hank. She smiled, "When Hank began to grow, he started to look like his uncle Herman so he's been Hesh ever since."

That made no sense so I looked at Hank for clarification. He grinned, "Now you know why I'm so confused."

I yelled over, "Hey Hank, what are you doing tonight?" He worked for Solomon's, a nearby drugstore, did shifts at night doing deliveries. "I'm off at 10, where will you be?"

Most summer nights or holidays during school we'd hang around after we played hoops. Usually hit the nearby DQ, hauled the goodies back to the courts and listened to Jimmer tell stories. I yelled, "We'll be here, just drop by." Watched Hank drive off, thought about how close we'd become. He even took religious classes with Nut, which was required by the church for Catholics who went to Upper Derby. Mrs. Greenberg loved Hank's new friends, never objected to his interest in Catholicism. That's where the famous "not so Jewy" phrase was first dropped.

Jimmer yelled from the other end of the court. "We're retiring undefeated, so anyone that didn't play yet can shoot fouls for our spots." Since there was about 5 minutes of daylight left, his generosity was greeted with silence. Soon everybody wandered to the edge of the court, sat down. Jimmer noticed no one was taking up his generous offer, shrugged to me, "That's why those guys never get in. They suck and do nothing about it. Remember how we used to scramble for playing time in the beginning? What happened to American drive and ingenuity?" He had a bewildered look on his face, totally serious. How do you answer that?

Nut sat down, said he had a date, he was only staying a few minutes. I asked, "How's it going with Reneé? Don't see you as much lately." Reneé Sandberg was one of the hot numbers at Upper Derby, had been Nut's steady for months. She was also one of my old flames so I was careful how I tread.

He looked at me squarely, reading my mind, "I think she latched onto me hoping to get back at you. But then we really clicked. I like her; she's interesting. Plus she's one of the few people that actually knows something about wrestling. Not many girls that look like her really care about sports. She's neat." And then added a rare quip. "Even though she used to have bad taste in boys."

Before I could spar back Truck weighed in, "You're gettin' whipped, Nut. Hell, you're the best wrestler in America. Play the field more! Reneé's too smart for a muscle head like you."

Nut was a serious guy, didn't laugh or joke much. But he knew Truck was just busting him so he got up, nodded and smiled. "Truck, when I want dating advice, you are not the most reliable source for good taste. What's your standard line with the girls, 'Give or get out?' Now that's a classy way to go."

With that, Nut patted Truck on the head, walked home. Truck turned to me, "Is he questioning my way with the ladies?"

I knew Truck didn't really want my opinion. But I put my hands up, "I think what Nut was trying to say was that smooth you ain't. Maybe that you epitomize the 'You can't get pearls from swine adage.'" I got a double bird as response.

Jimmer Keilmann broke in, asked if anyone wanted beer later that night. I said no, because basketball practice had started. But Truck nodded vigorously, "Two quarts, any kind'll do."

Jimmer looked at him, "It's not a great idea for wonder boy to be drinking during the season. If you get caught, you're ass is grass."

Truck looked at him with an innocent smile, "You offered, I just answered your question."

Jimmer wasn't exactly an altar boy but he knew Truck had a big-time future. He wagged his finger, "I was asking if any of these pathetic losers wanted beer." Jimmer waved his finger at the large group surrounding us. Finished with, "Not you or Dylan, guys that actually have a shot at pulling your head out of your ass."

With that, we broke for dinner, promising to re-huddle around 8 pm or so. Truck offered me a ride home. I agreed, wanting the opportunity to mention my concern about his roughness. As we got in the car, I asked if he wanted to come to dinner, told him my mom hadn't seen him for a while, was asking for him.

He grinned, "I'd come to your mom's house for dinner every night, that little lady can cook. Let me run over and tell Aunt Sue. I doubt she'll be back from the shop yet but Liz is probably there." Truck hadn't mentioned Liz being home before. He was usually pretty private about her. Watching Liz's huge knockers was one of the highlights of my early teens. But I kept that to myself, wanting to change the topic.

"So, Truck, I wanted to compliment you on using restraint when you pounded that Temple player. I mean the kid only bled from four spots. You missed a knuckle; most of your victims bleed from all five of your meat hooks. Worries me you might be going soft."

Truck cut his eyes at me, knowing I had some other message. "Being funny, Dylan?"

I pushed his shoulder. "Keep your eyes on the road." I continued. "Remember we learned in English class last week about irony. So, in case you were dosing off, my last comments were dripping with irony." Before he could protest, "Let me finish. Don't give me that bullshit about being a warrior. If you pull that shit in the Catholic League, you'll get kicked out. You'll screw up our season. Lots of people counting on us to win it all, big guy. So how about toning it down, huh?"

Truck didn't say anything. I could see my friend thinking. He pulled into his driveway and sat still, making no move to go inside. He turned, had a strange look. "Can I talk to you about something bothering me?" I nodded, saying nothing, prompting my private buddy to open up. "I've been getting some odd letters the past few months. At first I just blew them off, but the last one got me thinking. I can't shake this weird feeling." I asked what the letters said. "Nothing real unusual, just stuff about good luck this season, things like that."

I opened my hands, "So what's so odd about that? Maybe just another fan, you got lots of them, big boy."

I could see Truck squirming, uncomfortable about what to say next. Finally, "In all the letters, the person calls me Robbie. The only person that ever called me that was my mom." I never knew Truck's mom, she had died before he moved to St Tim's. In fact, his dad eventually moved from their old house to help get away from the memories, at least that's what I had pieced together. Before I could say anything, Truck started again. "And that got me thinking about my mom." He hesitated, "I really don't know how she died. Dad never talked about it, said it was 'too painful,' so I haven't asked about her for years." And then, "These letters got me thinking I'd like to know more about my mom. Does that make any sense?"

Before I could answer, Truck's head snapped up, seeming to notice something. He opened his door suddenly, hustled toward his house. I gazed up, saw the silhouette of an undressed girl at the window. But it quickly disappeared as the shades closed. Truck was already through the door, a few paces ahead of me. I followed him inside, was stunned to see Liz standing in the dining room ironing. Not stunned because she was lazy and didn't iron much. Stunned because she had nothing on but panties and a skimpy bra. Liz turned, looked surprised but giggled, "Stop staring, haven't you seen a girl in her undies before?" She scampered out of the room. Have to admit, I admired those luscious, bouncing melons every step of the way.

Truck turned to me, put his finger out. He had a fierce look in his eye. It was the look he had before he decked someone. "Stay there, Dylan." He started after Liz but spun around, "Matter a fact, wait outside. I'll be there soon." I went outside, leaned against Truck's old Chevy. It was hard to get the image of the sexy Liz out of my mind. I wasn't sure what to say to Truck when he came out. It turned out that wasn't a problem. I waited half an hour and my surly pal never showed. Rather than head back to the lion's den, I ambled home.

I shook off the vision of Liz, thought about Truck's mom. My mom was the core of my strength, how would it be to have no mom and know nothing about her. I resolved to help my troubled buddy.

♦

While Truck and I were having our heart to heart, Nut was getting changed for his date with Reneé. From his room, he heard his father and mother arguing in the kitchen. The harsh sounds of disagreement were a familiar part of the O'Hanlon house. Nut knew all too well that James "Digger" O'Hanlon was an intense man. He had learned from his mom that Digger was a second-generation Irish immigrant, raised in poverty, had fought for an education and oddly got attracted to the funeral business while serving in WWII. According to mom, after arriving in Normandy, through dumb luck, he got assigned to the Medical unit and prepared dead soldiers for shipment back to the States. He had a knack for making the badly wounded more "normal looking." That skill kept him behind the lines, away from the heavy action.

Nut inhaled, seemed to be fighting an unseen devil, thought about Digger O'Hanlon's other skill: boxing. Although a slight man, about 5'8', 150 lbs, Digger made up for his lack of size with quickness, skill and feral savagery. He rose to lightweight champ at Fort Dix before being shipped overseas and discovering his mortuary knack. But Digger never lost the desire to hit people. When he stopped competitive fighting because of a growing family, and lucrative funeral business, he kept in shape by beating his wife and kids. Nut got the worst of it being the youngest, the final target. Well, really his mom got that honor. Whether physically pounded or with abusive taunts, Mary O'Hanlon rarely had a peaceful week. Unknown to Nut, over time, Mary got used to the beating, had given up. Digger never hit her face. He preferred to pepper her arms, stomach, and chest. She was a walking bruise. No one could remember seeing Mary O'Hanlon in sleeveless, summer attire.

Those painful images of his father shot through Nut's subconscious as he now went to protect his mother. Like a graceful leopard, he raced downstairs. He saw Digger's hand in mom's face. Digger turned, fury in his eyes. "Your mother tells me you're going out with a Jew, haven't I taught you better than that? You can have any girl you want, big wrestling star, why a Jew?" Nut hesitated, not expecting Reneé being the cause of the fight.

He glared, "First of all, Dad, you haven't taught me anything I'm proud of except maybe how to fight. Second of all, Reneé is a nice girl, so don't call her names. And last of all, if I ever see you jabbing your finger at mom, I'm going to snap it off." Nut seethed, was ready to strike.

Digger was no fool. He stopped hitting Nut after the growth spurt. His son towered over him, had become a feared wrestler. Digger looked at his enraged son, decided to let things settle down. He backed away from his wife, asked Mary, "Tell him the Jews will never accept him. Tell him the girl's just using him because he's a hot shot." He looked at Nut; "I'm telling you John, you're playing with fire when you mix religions. What's Monsignor Pugh going to think when he hears this?" It then dawned on Nut how his father learned about Reneé. Monsignor Pugh gave the CCD classes, and got to know Reneé and Hank when they came along, expressing an interest in Catholicism.

Digger threw up his hands, stomped into the living room. Nut looked at his mother, making sure she was okay. Mary O'Hanlon loved her protective boy, smiled, "I'm okay, son. Your father's worried he'll get needled by the other men at church. Just let him simmer down. I told him you said she was a great girl; that we need to be open-minded. You know how your father is."

Nut didn't want to do anything that caused his mother more grief. So he added, "Mom, Reneé and I are going out. You may remember that Dylan also went out with her a couple years ago. Last time I looked, Dylan hasn't started growing horns."

Mary laughed. She came over, gave Nut a big hug. Looking up, "What would I do without you?" And that's exactly what worried Nut.

♦

Seconds after Nut left for his date, Digger put on the light boxing gloves and went for Mary. She was cleaning dishes, turned at the noise; was hit with a sharp jab to her left breast. As she slumped forward, Digger delivered an uppercut to her unprotected kidney. The pain shot to her brain before the nausea came. The punch to her stomach finished the fight. Mary vomited violently on her spotless floor. Digger jumped out of the way, barely avoiding the spew. Furious, he screamed, "You worthless slut, clean that mess up and get up to bed. I've got my needs." As he walked away, "And get a shower first. And put on that nice slip you wear to weddings." Mary slumped to the ground.

PRACTICE

We had basketball practice the Saturday after Thanksgiving. Nut called early, said he was going to watch practice; that we could walk there together. Coach Gallagher loved Nut, had tried relentlessly to convince Digger the tuition was an investment, that if our team won the city title the scholarships would pour in. Digger's response was vintage: "Let's see, coach, I pay nothing for Upper Derby but pay a grand a year at Conner." And then Digger raised each hand, pretending to weigh one with the other. And then looked at Coach Gallagher, grinned: "What a ya know, nothing wins!" Coach tried again before sophomore year but by then Nut was becoming the greatest wrestler in state history.

About halfway to Monsignor Conner High, Nut brought up the Green Beret topic he discussed with me over the summer. He never looked at me, just said, "Will you come to the Army recruitment office with me next week? I want another opinion on what the recruiter says. I want a guarantee that I get fast-tracked to the Special Forces training after Basic and then right to the Green Berets. I think the guy is saying that but you're an expert at drilling people for direct answers. I need your help." I let that sink in without answering. Nut was planning to go directly from high school into the Army and then become a Green Beret. Although he had talked about that since grade school, I had hoped he'd grow out of that crazy idea. The Vietnam War was raging. I didn't want my close friend going to Nam.

I turned to Nut. "Are you saying I have some special

skill for dealing with bull-shitters? Or are you trying to say that I'm an bullshit artist and I also have a unique talent for wading through bullshit and that you need to tap into my expertise? I'm just trying to see if this is a positive or a negative about me."

Nut never flinched, pointed his finger at me, "That's what I mean. Just do that."

I was the only person he had discussed this Green Beret plan with. He had pledged me to secrecy. So I added, "Have you told your parents yet?"

This time Nut came to a stop. He had an anguished expression, "I really need your help with that, telling mom." We continued silently to Conner, carrying this problem into practice.

♦

Our basketball team was a collection of unusual pieces. Nut, Fran Philips, Kevin (Drum) James, Edgar (Scoot) Smith and I played for St Tim's grade school, had won the Mid-Atlantic state title as 8th graders. When Truck was added to this group in high school, we were a force. Everyone had their roles and did them well. Our chemistry made us special, no glory hogs. Fran Philips did everything with seeming ease. I looked like I was running fast, but Fran flew past me, almost like he floated. I never saw him sweat or get nervous. He was a true natural. If he cared more, he might have been better than Truck.

But Scoot and Drum were equally vital parts. They never scored much and didn't fill the stat sheets. They just didn't lose. Scoot was short, barely 5'8", but quick, a sure ball handler, fierce driver and a huge pest on defense. Drum was 6'3", weighed about 215 and was the smartest kid in Monsignor Conner. But that didn't mean he was a good student, which was a source of endless frustration to the priests who saw the perfect college boards scores and knew his attitude needed adjusting. But on a basketball court, Drum saw every weakness in an opponent, was a walking scouting report after brief study. Coach Gallagher always took Drum to watch any team that might be a problem on our march to the city title.

The challenge for Coach Gallagher wasn't winning games. His challenge was keeping us out of trouble. We were all basically good kids. We just had mischievous sides, me being the worst. Early in my sophomore year, Coach pointed at me, "You look innocent Frazier, but I know you're the ringleader. I'm watching you."

My answer might have dug my hole deeper. "You got me wrong, Coach. I was the most valuable altar boy at St Tim's. Just ask Monsignor Stinky, er, I mean Pugh." Monsignor Seamus Pugh was the pastor of my parish, had been named "Shameless Poo" and eventually just "Stinky" by someone who resembled me a lot.

Coach Gallagher smiled, "Monsignor Pugh was the one who ratted you out."

Monsignor Conner High School was a basketball factory for college players in Philly but oddly had never won a city championship. Something always went wrong. Over time it became known as "the Conner jinx." We probably would have won the city title last year but Truck got in foul trouble right away, hardly played at all and angrily drilled an elbow for his final foul with almost a full quarter to play. Even without Truck, we only lost by 3 points. But Coach Gallagher wasn't taking anything for granted. He ran us hard in practice, making sure we were in better shape than our opponents. After running suicide drills for 20 minutes, Coach finally pointed at the first team, told us we could sit down. I dropped immediately to the floor, sprawled out, let out a big sigh. The other players laughed as they moved toward the bench. Coach Gallagher finally spotted me sprawled on the floor, fought back a grin, "Funny, Dylan, very funny."

I looked at him seriously, "Just following orders, Coach. Like a good soldier."

FRAN PHILIPS

Our teammate Fran Philips joined Nut and me on the walk home, so we never discussed the Green Berets. Fran lived across the street from the courts, was my pal since he moved in 5th grade from West Philly. His relaxed style on the court transferred to his personal life, he was easy to be around. He got this personality from his parents. Mr. and Mrs. Philips did not believe in yelling or strict discipline. They showered their kids with love and trust. But this casual background also got Fran in trouble at school. Fran could tell you Johnny Carson's monologue from the previous night verbatim but the Algebra homework never made the priority list. Despite being assigned tutoring from Coach Gallagher, Fran was on the edge of flunking off the team. On the walk, I brought up the worry, telling Fran we needed him eligible. He grinned, "Not to worry, Drum started doing my homework. Even if I fail all the tests, the homework grades will save the day." Nut and I almost choked laughing.

♦

When I got home, I called Truck to follow up on his search for information about his mom. I had been thinking about it, had a few ideas. I had an insatiable dose of curiosity and liked solving puzzles. That trait was the source of great personal pleasure but it also got me in trouble with authority. If you added my weird sense of humor, you had the makings for mayhem. Well, I also had an edge sometime, didn't like people pushing me too hard. "Irish temper," my mom called it. Others not so kind called it "being pissy." Mom and dad spotted my quirks early, had given up trying to tame me, thinking time would heal. As dear mom said, "In a house full of normal people, God gave us you to keep us on our toes."

My comical dad had an alternate view: "If I didn't know better, I'd swear gypsies switched you at birth." Oddly, my parents were my biggest fans.

Truck seemed agitated when he picked up the phone. I told him what I wanted, he got quiet and then said he'd be over soon. As he hung up, I heard the giggle of the voluptuous Liz in the background. Although I could still vividly picture her ironing, I also thought how odd it would be to have her walking around half naked. Liz was called a cousin but I never really got the full story. Truck got vague if you brought up Liz or Aunt Sue. While I waited for him, I wondered if Truck's sex maniac reputation had anything to do with what I had witnessed. If I got to look at those amazing boobs every day, wouldn't that make me hornier than a toad? Truck went after girls like Wilt Chamberlain going for rebounds. He was relentless.

I saw Truck pull up, decided to solve that problem another day. Time to find out about his mom. My large friend now seemed in a chipper mood so I asked if he had anything about his mom that might be useful in our search. He shook his head, "Squatola. I don't even remember the funeral or ever visiting the cemetery. I mean, dad just clammed up whenever I asked about her. The one line he always used was, 'Some things are best forgotten' and then he'd talk about something else." He raised his hands in exasperation, "Finally, I stopped asking." He already told me about his dad's reluctance so I said my idea of visiting Fitzmorris Hospital, seeing if they had something useful.

Fitzmorris Hospital was the only hospital in our area. It was also close to Truck's former neighborhood, so it was the likely place they would have taken his mom if she were really sick. The Fitzmorris family lived in Drexel Heights, their son Wally went to grade school with me. Wally was really smart, was destined to become a doctor, as was his father and grandfather who founded the hospital. I looked at Truck, "Wally and I are tight. I'll use that as my ace card if we get any shit at the hospital.

Truck grinned, "Isn't he the kid you called 'space-helmet head' and hates your guts?"

I let that sink in before adding, "You got a point. Maybe I should low-key that connection." We soon were parking, chuckling as we headed to "Information."

As we waited in line, I eyed the large woman who manned the desk. She answered people's questions briskly, didn't seem interested in idle chat. I nodded toward the lady, whispered to Truck, "All she needs is an 'I don't give a shit about you' sign on her head." He started belly laughing and unfortunately we suddenly became the next in line.

The mammoth lady glared at me. "What can I do for you two comedians?" And then she looked closer, "Aren't you Truck Carr?" And then she looked me up and down. "And you're Frazier. My son Bart is in the Conner pep band, we go to all the games. What can I do for you young men?" Sometimes you get lucky.

I apologized to the information lady for the laughter. I leaned in, "The guy in front of us broke wind while he was talking to you. Truck and I weren't sure whether to puke or run away, so we panicked and laughed. Sorry about that."

I heard Truck giggling behind me. But the lady didn't seem to mind, shook her head, "You wouldn't believe the things people do in this lobby. I tell my husband stories every night."

I shook my head in agreement. "Art Linkletter has it right, 'People do the darndest things.' " With that segue, I told the lady about Truck's situation, wondered if there was any records that might tell us what happened to her.

The big woman actually teared-up; took some notes, said, "You poor boy. Give me a few days and I'll research it for you. Can you drop back next Saturday?"

As we drove home, Truck was still laughing about the hospital. "You really do have a loose connection, Dylan. I mean, BS just rolls out of your mouth like water."

I didn't argue, knew he had a point. But added, "My mom always threatened to take me to Lourdes to dunk me in the holy waters. Early on, the nuns told her I might be one of those demonic possessions. That a trip to Lourdes might chase the devil from me. But you know my dad, too cheap to spring for airline tickets."

Truck smiled, turned back to the real issue, "What do

you think she'll find about my mom?" I had been waiting for that. Getting serious, "They'll probably find the cause of death and what funeral home they transferred her to for burial. I know when Nut works for Digger sometime, he has to drive to the hospitals to get the bodies." Truck's eyes blinked rapidly, was quiet. I mumbled, "Sorry buddy, but at least you'll know something about her."

THE O'HANLONS

I always walked to school. My dad Frank was notorious for never giving rides. If you asked about getting a lift, his standard line was, "So when did you break your legs?" If I pressed him, he'd give an elaborate explanation about how he was building up my legs for basketball. That one day I'd thank him. That caused me to wonder: Maybe it wasn't mom. Maybe dad was where the crazy genes came from? Anyway, Nut often walked with me, so I dropped by his house, waited for him to finish breakfast. When I gave Mrs. O'Hanlon a hello hug, I noticed her wince in pain. "Sorry, Mrs. O, didn't mean to squeeze so hard."

I watched her exhale, gathering herself, "It's nothing Dylan, not your fault. Just have a little soreness. Just getting old."

From the corner of my eye, I saw Nut's head pop up from the table. He rose quickly, came to his mom's side. "You okay mom?" He looked at her intently, "Has it started again?"

Mrs. O'Hanlon dropped her eyes, wordlessly moved to the sink. Without looking at him she said, "Just an accident, dear. Nothing for you to fret over." I could see Nut's color rise like it did when he was about to cream an opponent. He moved closer, whispered something to her; massaged her head.

While I watched the tender scene, I remembered my mother once said to me, "Mary O'Hanlon seems to have a lot of accidents." My mom wasn't being critical. She had another message that I didn't understand at the time.

Nut was quiet for the first few blocks. While he was thinking, I recalled Nut talking about the "scheduled beatings" at his house. At first I thought he was kidding but came to learn that each Saturday morning, Digger would line the kids up, review the list of chores and school problems from the past week. Even if you had a flawless record you got whacked for being "a do-gooder." Some weeks Nut was so sore he couldn't play football or basketball. He never talked about it much, just said it was good practice for when he got in the Green Berets. I never probed him too hard for details but I thought now might be the time.

I reached over, put my hand on his muscular shoulder, "Are you going to talk about it, or do I have to beat the shit out of you first?"

He turned, chuckled, "You really are a piece of work, Dylan." And then exhaled, "You asked for it." For the next half hour he told me of the abuse his family endured from a sadistic father. That it had seemed to stop after he had a knockdown fight with Digger after his sophomore year. I recalled Mr. O'Hanlon breaking an arm, wearing a sling for months. Now I knew why. Nut got quiet again but finally added, "My mom took the worst of it. When I learned to wrestle, I thought that might stop him." He looked at me intently. "But it didn't, it took me breaking his arm to do that."

We were getting close to Upper Derby. Nut concluded with, "My worry is that Digger will start all over again when I go in the Army. There won't be anyone there to protect my mom. My brothers already moved out, except for Jimmy and he'll be gone when he graduates from college this May. Digger won't screw with me anymore but I think he went after mom again. We had an argument the other night about me going out with Reneé. Or as he called her, "That bagel bending Jew."

I shook my head in wonder. Reneé Sandberg was a knock-out and a real nice girl so that description was ludicrous. I looked at Nut, "Your dad never had a way with words but I think his eyesight's going. Maybe the embalming fluid? Has he even seen Reneé?" But then I got to the point, "What can I do to help?" When he told me what he was thinking, I was stunned.

Before I could argue, he said, "Keep it between you and me. Our secret. Just think about it. We'll talk again soon." And then he was gone up the school steps.

START OF THE SEASON

We won our first couple games by wide margins but next came Roman Hall, game at their gym on Friday. Roman Hall's court was a pit. And no matter what the talent level, their team was almost impossible to beat at home. To give you an idea how weird the place was, the opposing team had to dress in the boiler room, entered the gym by the fire escape ladder and then through an open window. The first time I played there, I said to the freshman coach as we slumped through the window, "Maybe this is how they train to be cat burglars after graduation." The coach got a good laugh out of that but wasn't smiling when we left barely winning in overtime to their weaker squad.

In preparation, Coach Gallagher worked us hard that week. He piled chairs around the court, sat kids there from detention to taunt us. He wanted us to experience the close-up frenzy we were about to face. One imaginative kid kept yelling, "Truck, Truck, you suck. Look out for the big fat ugly Truck."

When Truck came over to the kid, Coach Gallagher stopped him. "Leave him alone, I wanted crazy and that kid's nothing to what you'll hear on Friday. Those Roman fans have imagination." Anyway, it was a creative move on Coach's part that worked. We ended up beating the hell out of them 68-40. It was the worst loss at home for Roman in 20 years. Next day, the Bulletin sport page headline read, "Can anyone stop the Conner Express?"

Truck and Fran Philips were averaging over 20

points, making it look easy. My job was to hit jump shots when the other team sagged on our stars. Against Roman I was 7 for 7 in the first half, so they had to play me tough the second half. That let Truck operate in the middle, and Fran could drive with abandon. They combined for 35 second-half points, we left the Roman fans nearly speechless. Scoot and Drum got no press but were almost perfect when they got an open shot. As we exited through the window at Roman, Drum looked at me, "We've got to push ourselves harder. We can't start believing our press clippings. Bad games are ahead when we won't hit shit."

I knew he had a point, nodded, "Just enjoy this for tonight, leave the gloom and doom for tomorrow." But I kept thinking about his message.

BACK TO THE HOSPITAL

We had the day off after the Roman game, so Truck and I went to Fitzmorris Hospital to check what the friendly nurse had found about Truck's mom. As we waited in line, I saw the glazed look on her face as she answered endless mundane questions. As we got to the front, she looked up, smiled as she placed us. Deadpan, I looked at her, "Before we start, you seem to have all the answers so I need your help with a medical question. Are they really called beriberi and agar agar or did the doctor who named them stutter?" Seeing her puzzled look, "Just kidding, you get so many stupid questions. I thought you needed a mental health break."

I got a delayed reaction; but then she grabbed her belly, laughed merrily. As she recovered, she added, "My son never told me you were so funny."

I nodded, "Don't spread it around. Coach Gallagher said I need an attitude tune-up, need to get my head out of my tail pipe, so to speak."

With that light start, she dug into her desk, riffled through a pile, pulled out Mrs. Carr's records. Asked us to move closer. She looked at Truck, "I'm sorry son, but it says your mom died from an overdose of medication. She died in the hospital when the ER staff was unable to awaken her. Sorry."

I heard my huge friend gulp. He started to swallow, trying to find words. I jumped in, "We really appreciate your help." I had expected sour information and was prepared for it. "Does it say what funeral home she went to or what cemetery was selected? He just wants to be able to visit the grave, say his goodbyes."

Truck looked at the nurse, "Sorry, I gotta go. Thanks for your help." I watched this tough guy walk off, clearly shaken. The nurse said to me, "There's nothing on a cemetery but here's the funeral home."

Outside I found Truck slumped against the car. Not knowing what else to do, I gave him a hug, told him I was sorry about his mom. He looked at me, "What does 'an overdose of medication' really mean? Did she have an accident or did she kill herself?" I could see anger rise in his face, "Why would she kill herself? I mean, that just makes no sense. Jesus, this really blows."

Remembering how my dad always handled tough situation with me, I said, "Let's not jump to conclusions before we have all the facts, Truck. Maybe the funeral home will have more information. Nut knows a lot about this stuff, with Digger's job and all. Let's talk to him, see what details we can get. Maybe that will help."

Truck seemed to compose himself, "You know what, Dylan? That might be the most sensible thing you ever said to me." And then he hugged me till it hurt.

THE COURTS

It remained a mild winter, so I told Truck to drop me at the courts. There were a few of the "little guys" hanging around, shooting the ball but mostly shooting the shit. Jimmer considered himself the founding father of the courts, named everyone not in his age group, "the little guys." It wasn't a term of respect. It was code for "they sucked," and were banned from games on the real court till they got better. Even though Truck, Nut and I were 4 years younger, we escaped this title because according to Jimmer, "we weren't total ass wipes." There was an 8-foot full court that ran parallel to our slanted regulation height court and "the little guys" played there until Jimmer ran short of players, gave them a shot with the big guys.

I joined into the bullshitting, fended off talk about us going undefeated, finally winning the big one for Conner High. "Lot of tough games ahead, boys, don't jinx us."

Fat Matt Kelley wouldn't back off, "You guys are the best team Conner ever had. You'd be the biggest choke artists ever if ya blow it." Fat Matt was only 5'8" but weighed about 280 lbs., built like a manatee. But his mouth was what really earned the name. Fat Matt woke up talking; never stopped all day except to stuff the pie hole.

I just smiled at him, not wanting to wind him up and listen to his relentless horseshit. But then I couldn't help myself, "Thanks for the pep talk, Matt, I'll tell Truck what you said. He'll probably tie you naked to a tree or something imaginative." Last summer Truck had tied him to a bicycle rack in the scorching summer heat when he got tired of his mouth. Fat Matt started to talk, remembered the incident, smartly shut up.

I grabbed a ball, dribbled to the empty side of the court. Between what Nut had confided about his family, and Truck's mom, I had some thinking to do. I shot jump shots from 20 feet, tried to catch any ball that missed before it hit the ground. And then I'd shoot the recovered ball immediately, trying to simulate game speed. If I made the shot, I'd go to another location, start the process over. Growing up, I'd do this for 2 hours at full speed. But after an hour, I'd reached some conclusions. First, stop at Nut's house and get some tips on what to look for at the funeral home that buried Truck's mom. I was hoping the cause of death would be something other than suicide. If we had a better ending on that Truck would be happy. Last, what to say to Truck if the news was lousy.

♦

Nut was walking home from wrestling practice, enjoying the quiet. It was his time to think. Part of the problem with being so good was finding someone to give him competition. Coach Leonard periodically brought in college wrestlers from nearby schools to prepare him for a big meet. Nut smiled as he thought about the big wrestler today from West Chester who growled at him, "I'm gonna tear yer face off, school boy." Usually, he toyed with opponents long enough to get decent exercise. Not today. When the huge kid came in fast, he went under his outstretched arms, hit hard at his mid-section, tossed him over his shoulder, slammed him down like a bag of door knobs and quickly pinned his shoulders for the required count, ending the match.

The stunned bruiser gulped for air, rolled over, dry-heaved on the mat. Nut had handed him a towel, leaned close, "Want another shot at my face?"

Although Nut had a good sense of humor, he rarely joked around. But that pompous jerk had it coming, was a nice distraction from his quandary about Digger. He worried he shouldn't have told Dylan his plans. But he needed someone he trusted to help guide the right decision. He also needed help executing one of the complicated alternatives. Plus he might need an alibi. When Nut tested for Special Forces, he was shown to excel at planning. The testing Sergeant looked at his results, seemed to be puzzled. He stared at Nut, shaking his head, "I've administered this test for 5 years, no one got a perfect score, or even close. You've aced it son. God-damndest thing I've ever seen." That didn't really surprise Nut. He'd spent his whole life learning how to dodge his father and the beatings.

But Nut knew he could trust Dylan, even with his life. He had been vividly clear that his father's brutality started with his mother, onto his brothers, and then to him. Dylan's eyes were wide when he gave him details. "Remember in 8th grade when I missed four football games, told you I fell down the stairs? It was really Digger hitting me so bad he broke my ribs." And then, "Remember freshman year when my mom went to the hospital with the miscarriage? That was after a beating, they had to abort the baby. She would have finally had a girl." When Dylan didn't answer, "That's when I went out for wrestling and fortunately grew big. Remember Digger's broken arm, that wasn't an accident. I put a hammerlock on him so hard it snapped his radius and ulna. When I went to the hospital with him, I told him the next bone I'd snap was his neck."

Nut considered Dylan his brother. The only person closer was his mother. Truck was a close third, but Dylan's quirky sense of humor and calm family life was like a magnet. The Frazier house was a sanctuary for him. He always went there for the peacefulness. But he wondered if he went into too much detail with Dylan. He had planned his father's fate like an Army mission. These were the alternatives he discussed with Dylan:

- Cure him of the abusive behavior.
- Have him put in jail.
- Disable him, so he was harmless.
- Kill him.

He had considered the likelihood of Digger stopping his rages, knew that wasn't possible. Hours in the library made him an expert on abusive parents. Abusers were trying to exert power and control. Abused women and children commonly experienced shame and reluctance to seek help. The abuser relied on this sense of helplessness. But what scared Nut most was reading about the likelihood of extreme violence when the victims tried to escape or prosecute. He consistently read "many family violence cases end in homicide or suicide." The abuser will go into rage when their world order is threatened. The only cure was old age, when the abuser was no longer able to hurt people. He knew his mother was incapable of action. She was the classic case of self-blame and depression. It was up to him and he would act decisively.

Dylan spotted Nut as he walked down School Lane toward his house. Nut stood waiting when he saw me coming. He had a pensive look on his face. "You look troubled big boy, like you need a good dump. You been starving yourself to make weight? Try broccoli, my mom swears that would clean out the county jail."

Nut grinned but got down to business. "I'm worried about what I told you about Digger. That has to stay between us, you know that, right?"

I saw the concern on Nut's sculpted face. "It's in the vault, Nut. Only one I'd ever discuss that with is you." And then added, "It's not like anyone would even believe what you were thinking about. I mean knocking off your old man isn't exactly normal behavior for a high school kid." He didn't laugh.

Finally, Nut nodded but still looked worried so I switched gears. "Need your help with funeral parlor matters." I had gotten Truck's permission to tell Nut what was going on, so I told him what we got at the hospital, what funeral home she was sent to.

He thought awhile before offering, "You'll be able to see Mrs. Carr's birth certificate and death certificate. They have to keep those records, that's the law. Some places might be lax but I know Gabriel's runs a good funeral home." I had forgotten about the death certificate. Maybe that would solve the suicide question. Obviously, Truck had never seen it or he'd know how she died. And then I thought if roles were reversed I probably wouldn't have ever gone looking for my mother's death certificate. Too gruesome.

And then Nut told me he had an appointment with the Army recruiter's office on Monday. He knew I had that day off from practice, hoped I could come. We'd have to take a trolley and subway to 401 North Broad Street in downtown Philly. My dad took that route to work each day and he regaled me with many stories of the travails of public transportation. Dad referred to the other passengers as "the great unwashed." I had given him a nose clip as a joke last Christmas. When he looked puzzled, I clarified, "To make the great unwashed less noticeable on your daily commute." That ran through my deranged noggin as I agreed to the journey.

CCD

Sunday night was Confraternity of Christian Doctrine (CCD) class for Nut, Hank and Reneé. Catholic kids going to public school had to attend. Hank and Reneé were Jewish but went because of their friendship with Nut and a curiosity in his religion. I was intrigued with their participation, decided to be a surprise visitor. So many things about Catholic doctrine bothered me. Maybe this was an opportunity to clear things up. I walked into St Tim's small assembly hall, got funny looks from my friends. But Monsignor Pugh was the most surprised. "Well look what we have here, one of my former crosses to bear. Dylan Frazier coming to religious class of his own accord. To what do we owe this miracle?"

I gave him a polite bow. "I heard you were talking about Purgatory tonight, wanted to get some pointers. Anyway to shave off a few years to my sentence is time well spent, don't you think Monsignor." He chuckled, told me to behave myself.

Despite being my former squeeze, Reneé and I had remained friends. We both realized it wasn't a good match. When she and Nut linked up it made it even more important to keep things smooth. Besides being beautiful, she was really smart, had a good sense of humor. We first met when I was at a summer dance at the local swimming club. I had told a couple cute Jewish girls from Drexel Heights Junior High that I was also Jewish. My buddies were momentarily perplexed but played along. As I used all my arcane knowledge of the Hebrew culture, Reneé had wandered by, overheard my spiel. When the girls went off to dance to a Bobby Darin song, Reneé lingered. "It's not often you meet a Jewish boy that goes to St Timothy. You must have really liberal parents."

That started an ill-fated relationship that lasted all summer and part of freshman year. Reneé was super popular, very verbal and used to having her own way. I was a gifted wiseass and used to doing what I wanted. The clashes were immediate but we were infatuated. I remember when she asked me to go swimming at her country club. I smirked, "Don't think so. Probably just some ploy to get me to caddy for your old man." Her father was an avid golfer and at that time of my life I thought golf was just about the lamest way anyone could spend time. What about real sports—like basketball? When I said that she giggled but I never went to her club.

The relationship faltered along as we went back to school. I was mildly well-known from basketball success, so I seemed to be a good match for the most popular girl at public school. Unknown to me she was dating upper classmen throughout our sporadic relationship. I found that out when I went to her house on Valentine's Day to give her a card I shelled out 50 cents for. I felt pretty cocky about that since all my previous girlfriends' cards cost a dime. Her mother answered the door. I saw a wall of flowers behind her. It looked like the church altar at a big-shot's funeral. Reneé's mother didn't seem to like me much, probably worried about Catholic mismatch; like maybe I was pushing her to switch teams. She took some pleasure telling me Reneé was out with Eddie Cash, getting a soda at Howard Johnson's. I mumbled something inane, left the fancy card.

She called later that night, thanked me for the beautiful card. I told her I was surprised she could find it amidst her floral forest. Reneé laughed hesitantly. I plowed ahead, "When were you going to tell me about all your other boyfriends?" She went into a calm explanation that, "her mother wanted her to date other boys and that they didn't mean anything to her."

I responded, "If they don't mean anything to you, stop going out with them. I'm not really a sharing-your-girlfriend kind of guy."

And then she made a mistake. "But I like you the most of all the boys I date. What's wrong with having other friends who happen to be boys?"

She didn't like my answer. "What you're saying is when you slice your popularity pie, I get two pieces and a dab of ice cream. The other guys only get one lousy piece? That's my big reward? What a lucky guy."

I thought it was a good line but she failed to see the wit. We split amiably but I was probably the only boy who ever broke up with her. We were cordial but she was clearly peeved. So when she started dating Nut last year, I went out of my way to mend fences. It took some doing but as her fondness for Nut blossomed, we settled in. I told Nut every detail of our past. He got a kick out of the stories of our turbulent relationship. I remember him looking at me, "If I had to pick two people least likely to go out, it would be you and Reneé. You both like to lead and have the last word." And then, "Plus Reneé s serious and you're not." He had me there.

The CCD class went along smoothly until Reneé's question on baptism. "Monsignor, you mean I have to go through the Baptismal ceremony to become a Catholic? Even at my age? I thought that just applied to babies."

He gave her the answer that always bugged me. "Yes, Reneé, Baptism is required before you can become Catholic and attain the eternal reward of heaven." My father wasn't Catholic but was a kind, delightful man. So the thought of him being denied heaven because he wasn't baptized or Catholic bewildered me. I had argued the point relentlessly with the nuns but was often banished to kneeling for the rest of the class period. Maybe that's why I have such good posture? A strong core from hours of punishment.

That was the hornet's nest Monsignor Pugh walked into. I raised my hand. "Yes, Dylan?"

"So, Monsignor, you're telling me that if Hank decided to become a Catholic, went through all the grueling study and was walking to church for the Baptism, when out of nowhere, St Tim's school bus swerved out of control and killed poor Hank. Are you telling me that he wouldn't go to heaven because he wasn't baptized?" Monsignor Pugh eyed me closely but said nothing. I continued, "Or same scenario with Reneé. But she was actually in church, leaning over the Baptismal fount when a lethal bolt of lightning tears through the roof and strikes her dead. I mean, is poor Reneé doomed to eternal damnation?"

The whole class was giggling. Even Monsignor Pugh had a smile on his face. He cleared his throat, "You might be surprised, Dylan, but in your extraordinary examples, both Hank and Reneé would be welcomed into heaven because they committed to the Catholic faith and had the intention of Baptism." He paused. "I know in the past, some ill-informed instructors failed to acknowledge this point of clarification. I hope that relieves your worry."

It actually did satisfy me. "Thanks for clearing that up. The thought of my friends going to all that effort and toasting in hell disturbed me. It would give me nightmares tonight."

Monsignor Pugh smiled, "Glad to help. And by the way, I'm not sure if hanging around with you is the best course for Hank and Reneé. Both your mother and I are not so sure even Baptism will get you through the pearly gates." He threw up his hands, as if apologetic. The class giggled agreement.

INDUCTION CENTER

Nut and I walked to the trolley stop after school on Monday. The trip downtown was usually uneventful but you never knew when you rode public transportation. With my father's commuting stories in my head, I told Nut to follow my lead. He frowned when I told him of my expertise in navigating Philly's transit system. "Never give up your seat, Nut, even to pregnant women." He looked at me funny. "My dad says most of them aren't pregnant, they stuff a pillow in to fake it, get seats all the way in. Works like a charm except on the savvy travelers. Weird stuff like that happens. Believe it."

Nut shook his head, "I always thought your dad was normal. Now I'm not so sure."

We boarded the trolley; it was mostly empty. I turned, "Wonder if we'll see Guy Valero? Jimmer said he rides the trolleys most afternoons. Going back and forth till dinnertime. Interesting, huh? I guess even crazy people get hungry, have to stop to eat."

Nut shook his head, "I hope not, Guy is one really odd kid. I sat behind him in church last Sunday. He was talking to himself the whole time. He kept singing after the hymns were over. It was kind of funny but he's off, no question." The Valero family was very wealthy, big benefactors at St Tim's. But the old man didn't do it out of the goodness of his heart. He wanted everyone to know he was a big deal. He liked the bragging rights. But God in his goodness got even. All the Valero kids were goofy, with Guy leading the freak parade.

Our ride into 69th Street was uneventful, no Guy sightings. Despite its suggestive name, 69th Street was the broken down, grimy junction of the suburban trolleys and buses that fed into the subway system for the City of Brotherly Love. To get to the subway section, you had to maneuver dirty tunnels cluttered with hotdog stands and donut shops. My dad's advice popped into my head, as Nut asked if I wanted a hotdog. "My dad says you'll shit like Niagara if you eat any of this junk. Still want to risk it? I'm out."

He shrugged, "I just lost my appetite. Do me a favor; keep your dad's advice to yourself the rest of the trip."

As we trudged to the subway, I had a thought. "Maybe that's what happened to Guy Valero." Nut look puzzled. "He ate too many hot dogs, pooped out his mind."

Nut didn't react. I think his stomach was doing flips. The subway system was elevated above the road, called The El until it went underground when you crossed deeper into Philly. Most of the early boarders were suburbanites, semi-normal looking. But it got more interesting as we got near the subterranean section. Three greasy looking characters, maybe 16 or 17 got on around 46th street. They eyed us menacingly as they moved through the car and sat behind a cute young girl with a long brown ponytail. As the El picked up speed, I watched the punks grab the girl's ponytail, start to untie it. She turned abruptly, surprised. The leader told her to relax; he just wanted to braid her beautiful hair. She pulled her hair away, didn't say anything to the punk, turned around.

And then it went downhill. The thug looked at his buddies, grabbed her hair forcefully, "Didn't ya hear me honey, trying to be nice. Just want ta make ya look sexy." He jerked her head back. She yelped in pain. Nut was in the aisle seat and moving before I could do anything. He was on the punk instantly, punched his ear with his huge palm. I saw the kid's eyes bulge out as the shock waves sailed through his feeble brain. Like picking up a rag doll, Nut lifted him from the seat, dropped him to the floor. He looked at his buddies, "Take your friend, move to another car. If I walk up there and find you messing with anyone else, I'll put you all in a world of hurt." The two guys stared at my massive friend who clearly wasn't bluffing. They picked up their shaken friend, shuffled off.

I had moved beside Nut but it was over in seconds. While he asked the young girl if she was okay, I looked anew at my childhood friend, understood why he was headed for the Green Berets. Not only was he big and tough, he had an intense hatred for bullies. And then I thought about Digger terrorizing his family till Nut grew into a fighting machine. Nut had been talking about the Green Berets since he was 10. It all made sense, Nut had declared war on bullies, he'd had enough. The girl moved beside us, clearly shook. Nut asked her where she was headed, learned it was our stop, told her we would stay with her and make sure the thugs didn't follow. The rest of the way was quiet.

We hoofed it to 401 North Broad St, entered the infamous Induction Center. Since Vietnam was raging, this address was one place no one entered happily. "Look at those poor saps."

I pointed to a row of new recruits being lectured by a bellowing Drill Sergeant. "Stand up straight you maggots. Mommy's not here anymore to wipe your ass." And then he grabbed a flabby kid, told him to drop down and give him ten.

The helpless kid sat on the ground, fumbled through his wallet, held up a five-dollar bill. "This is all I got, Sir." Everybody chuckled except the Drill Sergeant. He swung his fist, knocked the wallet away. He grabbed the kid, pushed him to the floor, yelled for him to do push-ups.

I looked at Nut, "Nice career decision."

In the corner of the ground floor, there was a decorated section with striking Army posters all over the walls. The furniture was impressive, richly stained mahogany wood that matched a magnificent burgundy Oriental carpet. The unspoken impression, "This is where real men work." An attractive woman in Army uniform welcomed us as we approached. "It's nice to see you back, Mr. O'Hanlon, we don't get recruits walking in here like you too often. Colonel Lynam will be glad to see you." And then she looked at me, "Did you bring another recruit for the Green Berets? He looks almost as fit as you."

I clicked my heels together, stood straight, said firmly, "Only if they promise that you and I are in the same platoon, Sir!"

She was obviously used to attention. "Not even the remotest chance that will ever happen, young man." She told us to have a seat, ignored me as I pretended to weep.

Colonel Lynam was an impressive man. Nut explained I was there to listen to the details of his enlistment, that he wanted my opinion. The Colonel nodded and then outlined how Nut would go to basic training and AIT at Fort Benning. But there was a special regiment for elite recruits. These special recruits would skip the normal drone of mindless training and immediately start training in fitness, hand-to-hand combat, airborne and weaponry. I raised my hand, "Colonel, Nut is already the best wrestler in the state, maybe the country, wouldn't the hand to hand be a waste? I mean Nut will beat the piss out of the other poor saps. They might run home to their mamas to get their ass wiped like the Drill Sergeant said." I smiled inanely.

He thought for a while before answering, like he was pondering whether to imprison me or tolerate me to keep Nut happy. He opted for the later. "The training will focus on judo and karate for those recruits already proficient in wrestling or boxing. We know John has unique talent, we will fast track him wherever we can."

I nodded sagely, like I really had a clue what he was talking about. Nut looked at me sternly, his expression telling me to stop fooling around. I looked back, crossed my eyes, started wiggling my ears. Nut cracked up. I looked at the Colonel, "Sorry, sir, I'm incorrigible. And paused before adding, "But I am personally responsible for Nut being the physical specimen you see before you. He's been tossing me around my back yard since we were eight years old. Without my help he might have been a pianist."

Colonel Lynam smartly ignored me, plowed on.

"After that, John will go to Ft Bragg. There he'll get more focus on weaponry, language, tactics, demolition, unconventional warfare, evasion and escape, withstanding torture and other covert operations skills."

He stopped talking, looking to see if I had any wiseass comments. But after listening to Nut's list of serious training, "No questions."

He shook his head, "John has the highest test scores we've ever seen, he could go in any direction for additional training. For instance, he has great aptitude for engineering. The Special Forces has great need for minds like John's. I can see you two have a great bond. But trust me, we won't waste your friend's talents. He was born to be a warrior. America needs him. These are very tough times for America." That took the wind from my sails.

On the ride back to Drexel Heights, I asked Nut about punching the punk in the ear. "Never saw that one, Nut, pretty neat trick."

He turned, "I almost did that to you when you said the other recruits would run to have their mama's wipe their ass." And then he chuckled, "I thought Colonel Lynam was going to spit out a tooth. He was pissed." And then he answered the question about the punch. "As you know, Jimmer is almost an expert in judo; I've been training with him when I have free time. I think it might give me an edge when wrestling starts. Both use balance and leverage, but maybe I can use a modified form of the striking techniques to stun the other guy." He shrugged, "I just have to figure a way to do it within the rules." I felt sorry for his opponents.

Nuts effort to improve his skill didn't surprise me. Over the past three years he practiced ways to beat each classic wrestling move. Usually, I was the practice dummy. By repetition, I had become a decent wrestler. One of Nut's early obsessions was learning how to break and counter the full nelson hold. In the past, if his opponent got this hold on him, it was a dogfight to avoid a pin. Nut found a way to not only break it, but to turn tables and quickly pin his adversary. Now he lured his opponent into getting the full nelson on him if he wanted to end the match fast. Once the full nelson was attempted, Nut would drop to the ground, using his weight to change the balance, grabbed his stunned adversary behind the head as he fell, flipped him over his head to the floor and immediately pinned him. He did it so fast no one could figure what happened. Except me, of course. He'd done it to me so many times. I could do it in my sleep.

I switched topics as we left the trolley, headed home. "Nut, can I go to your funeral home sometime soon, I want to look through the paperwork for a normal burial. When I go with Truck to check his mom's records, I want to be thorough, not miss anything. Okay?"

He hesitated, "We have to do it when Digger's not there. He doesn't let anyone—especially me—look at his records. He'll go crazy if he knows we did it." Before I could comment, he started to grin. "I kind of like the idea of doing something to piss him off. I might even tell him after we're done. Maybe he'll go after me." I could tell by the look on his face he was visualizing what he'd do to Digger. He told me he'd find the right time, let me know.

♦

That night I had a frightening dream about Vietnam. It was very vivid. Nut and I were together on the edge of a lush plateau. He was pointing to a muddy road carved through the jungle. The Army Corps of Engineers had used giant bulldozers to hack a trail through a place that didn't want to be entered. Nut nodded, "That's where we go tomorrow."

I looked at my massive friend who was dressed in camouflage gear. "You have to be shitting me, Nut. Why the hell would I go into that God forsaken place? I'm not crazy like you."

He had a sad look on his face as he said, "It's your destiny. There's nothing you can do about it." The next thing I knew, I was sitting up in my bed. Sweat was dripping. I exhaled deeply. Was I just disturbed by going with Nut to the Induction Center? I was the least likely kid to be in the Army. I never even played War as a kid. Thought it was stupid. Who wants to pretend you're out fighting other people? Nut always said I was a natural soldier, a born, if reluctant leader. I shivered, worried this was more than a dream. Was this a premonition of my future? I couldn't get back to sleep.

HOOPS

Coach Gallagher worked us relentlessly. You could tell he was feeling the pressure of an undefeated team expected to win it all. Our next game was in South Philly against a strong South Catholic team. Most of their players starred on the football team that won the Catholic League and City title. Their best player was Angelo Di Muzio. Angelo was a great athlete. He quarterbacked their team and was MVP in the Catholic League. He was a good basketball player but more importantly a great competitor. If he sensed hesitation, he'd nail you. My job was to guard him, to make sure he never touched the ball. Since he handled the ball for them, I was in for a long day.

I covered him last year and he had a big night. But we won. Coach Gallagher was telling me that I had to do a better job this time. "Dylan, Angelo ate your lunch last year. I don't need to remind you he'll remember that. What did you learn from last year?"

I looked at him deadpan, "I learned that if I were the coach, I wouldn't have me cover him again this year." Truck burst out laughing and Gallagher was about to explode when I added, "Just funnin' with you Coach. We played him in the Narberth League last summer. I realized he always goes right. He might fake it left, go that way for a few dribbles, but it always ends up back in his right hand. This year he's in trouble."

Coach Gallagher had regained his normal color. "That's a much better answer."

South Philly was heavily Italian. There were pockets of Irish and German but mostly the neighborhoods stayed with their own. If you wanted the best Italian cuisine in the city, you went to South Philly. Once a year my dad would truck us here and spring for a big meal. Knowing my personality, my dad always told me, "In the restaurant, pretend you're Italian. If anyone asks you a question in Italian, just scrunch your shoulders like you can't make up your mind. Point to what you want on the menu, no wise ass comments."

One year a waiter asked for my order in English, I scrunched my shoulders before saying, "No speaka da English. Wha da ya meana?"

When my mom stopped laughing, she looked at the waiter, "He's adopted."

With that memory as background, I walked up to Angelo Di Muzio as the game was about to start. "Say, your name is Angelo Di Muzio, right? Isn't that Irish?" Before he could react, the ref tossed the ball up, I intercepted the ball headed for Angelo, cruised in for an easy layup. That was the last points I scored all night but I held Angelo to 8 points, we won by 20. At every jump ball, I made some quip to Angelo about celebrating St Patty's Day or one day sharing a Guinness with him at O'Reilly's Pub. Plus I covered him so close he got frustrated and got a technical for throwing a punch at me. At the end of the game, we lined up to shake hands. He looked at me, "What are you retarded or something? What's with the Irish shit?"

I looked at him, scrunched my shoulders, "Na, I'm

66

just adopted." My mom and dad got a kick out of that
when I told them afterwards.

THE FUNERAL HOME

Nut called Sunday night, told me we could go to the funeral home next afternoon while Digger was at the cemetery. Nut always helped out when his father got busy with multiple funerals the same day. Nut said, "I'm calling from the funeral parlor, big Irish wake, have to help out with parking. I can't believe the jewelry their burying with Mrs. O'Callaghan. This big blue necklace, Digger said its topaz, what a waste." I heard Digger yelling in the background as Nut said, "Gotta go, the old man's hyped up." But then he added, "You ought to see Digger, dressed up in a tuxedo, oozing condolences. What a joke. If they only knew what he said about them when they left." And then he was gone.

O' Hanlon's Funeral Home was in West Philly, a polyglot of ethnic neighborhoods. Digger buried most of the Irish in the area, even faked an Irish brogue as needed. "He's a perfect mimic," Nut advised. There was no doubt he was a talented man. People in West Philly would be shocked to learn he was a sadist and wife beater. When Truck heard what we were doing, he wanted to be involved so he drove us there, would act as watchman for Digger showing up unannounced.

Truck looked at us as we entered the funeral home, assumed his guard post, "What do I do if he comes? What's the signal?"

I smiled, "That's easy, just blast out one of those monster farts you do at practice. No way we won't hear that." He punched at me.

We got to the back room where the bodies were stored before going to the cemetery. Nut pointed, "That's Mrs. O'Callaghan." I wandered over to look at the closed casket. Nut added, "She's being buried tomorrow morning."

I remembered what he'd said about her jewelry, "Do people usually get buried with their jewelry? I mean, what a stupid waste."

Nut nodded, "All the time, especially the Irish and Italians, they want to look good, make a good impression when they meet their maker."

I shrugged, "Not me, I won't go quietly, the only thing I'm going to do is have a one word message on my tombstone."

I didn't say anything else, finally Nut asked, "Okay, I'll bite; what will you have on your tombstone?"

I smiled, "Pissed." Nut laughed for the first time that day.

We left Mrs. O'Callaghan to herself, entered Digger's private office. Nut rifled through his side drawer, fished out a key magnetized to the top. And then he opened the lower drawer and pulled out a large black book. Nut pointed, "Digger's master file, he keeps meticulous notes, even does his own accounting work. You ought to see our chore schedule at home. He checks completed tasks off like it's a religious experience. The asshole keeps all the lists numerically, tracks our failures over the year. That used to get you a special beating if you won that contest."

He seemed lost in that thought but suddenly raised his eyebrows, "Only thing he ever gave to me worth a damn, his skill with numbers." In addition to his athletic prowess, Nut was a National Honor Society member, excelled at Math and Science. He had every Ivy League school after him. But he was going into the Green Berets after graduation. In my mind a colossal waste but he never wavered from that plan.

Nut showed me all the documentation for Mrs. O'Callaghan, since her records were the most recent. There was a copy of her birth and death certificates—she died of heart failure after a long fight with dementia. Nut looked at me, "Funny thing with many dementia victims, they don't seem to age much after they get it. Mrs. O'Callaghan is about 80 but only looks 60 or so. Digger said it's the lack of worry that keeps them young."

I grinned, "Maybe that's why Truck looks so young." Before Nut reacted, I saw the line item about the topaz. It said it was worth $5,000. "Do you see what that rock was worth? I don't even know what a topaz looks like. It must be huge."

Nut nodded, "It is, want to see it? It really is something."

I paused, "I really do, but is that too creepy?" Nut smiled for the second time that day.

We made our way to the adjoining room. I watched as Nut began to open the casket. While he was working, he explained the casket would be closed next morning at the ceremony. The family wanted to remember her as she appeared at the wake last night. Nut finally popped the lid. He was right, Mrs. O'Callaghan looked great. "Who does all that make-up?"

Nut grimaced, "Another of Digger's skills, that's what got him into the business to start. He was an artist at making dead people look terrific, sometimes even better than when they were alive."

While he was talking, I looked for the topaz. "Where's the big rock, Nut?"

He snapped his head forward, stared at her exposed neckline, then lifted her dress to see if it had slipped. He carefully combed the entire coffin, found nothing. He looked at me dumfounded, "Jesus, it's gone." He carefully closed and locked the coffin.

As we walked back to Digger's office, I looked at Nut, "Do you think the family changed their mind? I mean that's a lot of money to put in the ground."

Nut shook his head, "I heard the family talking about it last night, how happy she'd be to be buried with it. Apparently they're a rich family, seemed proud she would go with her prize possession. Plus, those things are in their wills, it would be illegal to tamper with their wishes."

We looked at Digger's ledger. The topaz item was clearly noted. "To be buried with the deceased." And at the end of that line there was a series of numbers, letters and an asterisk 609633-C-7058-19*. I looked at Nut, "What does that mean?" He was thinking, didn't answer.

I had enough information for Truck and didn't want to risk bumping into Digger. "Let's beat it, don't push our luck." As we put the ledger away, I spotted a blue gleaming light from a napkin in the corner of the drawer. It must have been dislodged as we took the ledger out. "What's that, Nut?"

He reached in, pulled out a beautiful blue gem. He looked at me funny, "That's Mrs. O'Callaghan's topaz."

We stood there, not saying anything. Finally, "How'd it get in Digger's locked drawer?"

Nut shook his head, gave me another odd look. After a minute or so, "I think Digger stole it." I just stared at him.

On the ride back, we filled Truck in. "Are you telling me that Digger rips off dead people's jewelry? I mean I know he's a sick puppy but that's really crazy."

Ever since Nut mentioned his suspicion, I'd been thinking. If Nut was right about Digger's obsession with lists, I had a feeling. "Do you think that group of numbers in Digger's ledger is some code for tracking what he steals? I've been thinking about my brother and his stamp collection. He trades stamps all the time, trying to get better ones he's missing. But he always keeps records of what he traded. Even though he doesn't own them, he likes to remember that he once had them. Digger sounds like that, maybe that code tells him that was from Mrs. O'Callaghan." I paused, "If not that exactly, something like that."

Truck laughed, "What are you Dylan, trying to play Boston Blackie?"

Nut was quiet for a while. "The only way we can find out is go back and look around in Digger's office. Dylan's right, Digger tracks everything. If he's stealing, he's got some record of what he took. You ought to see his closet. All shirts and ties with the same colors put together, lined-up just right. Shoes always polished daily. Even his underwear gets starched and pressed."

Truck still had his doubts. "You guys got wild imaginations. There might be a simple explanation." And then added, "I guess we can't ask him. We'd have to admit we snuck into his secret records while he was out burying some stiff." We rode quietly but ended up agreeing to take another trip when Digger wasn't around. While Nut and Truck were talking about the South Catholic game, I was working through a strange idea that popped into my head. I thought silently: It might work.

LIZ

When Truck got home he noticed his father's car was gone. Late night at the shop? He wondered if Aunt Sue was home. Liz had gone back to college, life had settled down. Although he never felt too close to Aunt Sue, he could see that his father loved her. Until the last couple months, that rankled Truck. How could he forget mom? But to make his father happy, he decided recently to make peace. He entered the quiet house and thought it would be nice to have a brother or sister. And then he thought about Liz. She was 15 when she moved in with her mom. Truck was 12. Things were normal for about 3 months. And then she started her "sex classes."

Aunt Sue came to work for Truck's dad after her divorce from a dead-beat. That's how things started. She ran the counter, organized all the deliveries. She was pretty and very friendly to the customers. Business picked up, Bob Carr Sr. knew Sue was the reason. He had been lonely for a long time. He began to look forward to going to work. Sue always got in early, had a cup of coffee and donut waiting for him. They fell into a comfortable routine and within a year were in love. He proposed to Sue but she said she wasn't ready, too soon after making that marriage decision incorrectly the first time. Bob was disappointed but he was patient. He planned to wear her down with kindness.

A year later, he asked her again. This time she said, "Yes, but only after we live with each other for awhile. I have to be sure. I love you, Bob. I just want to make sure you're as perfect as you seem. Plus you have little Bobbie

74

to think about. I can see he's still missing his mom. I don't want him to hate me. You know what I mean, stealing his mom's place." And that's how it had been for 6 years. Truck's father was infatuated and it was clear Aunt Sue loved him dearly. Neither dad nor Sue knew that Liz was a sexual predator. Apparently she inherited the deviant traits from her dead-beat dad. Unknown to her mother, Liz's dad had molested her as a child, left her damaged. Like many abused children, she continued the cycle with her new "cousin." Truck became her toy.

On some level Truck knew these sex games weren't right. But Liz made it clear that the pleasure would stop if he said anything to anybody. The sessions went on weekly for a couple years, till Liz got a serious boyfriend. Liz turned her considerable energy to the older, more mature playmate. Truck was beside himself. He had gotten used to the sexual escapades and became angry. He started looking for new outlets for his precocious skills. Some girls went along with heavy petting but few would go the distance. But then he became a basketball star and more choices came with the fame. He had acquired a reputation for "being fast" but the girls still came around. But Truck had become despondent, he wasn't happy. His Catholic upbringing pulled at him, he knew what he was doing was wrong. But how could he stop?

That's what Truck was thinking about as he sat alone; eating the meal Aunt Sue had left him. She was a great cook, made sure he had something to eat if they worked late. He got shivers as he thought about Liz. She tried to seduce him when home for Thanksgiving. Her trick of ironing in her bra and panties in front of Dylan had infuriated him. He tore into her calling her a slut, saying he'd tell Aunt Sue about her if she did that again. He could tell he'd scared Liz. It was the first time he ever saw her look worried. But she recovered quickly. "I'll deny it. Tell them you're a pervert, always sneaking around when I'm naked. Who do you think Mom's gonna believe?" Truck let it drop, pretty sure she was bluffing. He was proud he finally resisted her.

Ever since he started getting the mysterious letters, Truck had funny feelings. He wanted to turn his life around. He thought about discussing it with Dylan. Dylan was always needling him about being too rough, like he had a demon. Truck smiled, thought to himself: Dylan does it with a joke, but it's really his way of saying there's a problem. Truck finished dinner, washed and dried the dishes and put them away. He usually left them for Sue but maybe that would be his first step—be nicer to Sue, make his Dad happy, try to be like a real family. And then he thought about Liz.

CCD

I continued to go to CCD classes. Hank had gotten serious about Catholicism, asked me to be his sponsor, to help him better understand the doctrines I'd heard since 1st grade. I had to walk the fine line between encouraging Hank and getting my own concerns voiced. There were many aspects of my religion that troubled me. I used the CCD classes as a way to vent. You didn't dare do that in religion class at Conner, the priest would kick your butt for being a pagan sinner. I tried that once as a freshman, spent the rest of class with my head in the trash can. But Monsignor Pugh was a great guy, took my tirades in stride, actually seemed to enjoy the debates. Tonight I chose celibacy as the topic to grill. When Monsignor Pugh asked if we had any questions, I blurted out, "You can't tell me that Jesus really wanted you guys to stay single your whole life. My Dad said if he weren't married, he'd never have learned the true meaning of aggravation. That my Mom is a true expert on his faults. That nothing slips by her. I mean, who do you have as a priest to keep you on the straight and narrow?"

Monsignor Pugh chuckled, "I know your Dad well but I think the aggravation part came after you were born. Each year you get older I see him slumping a little lower."

And now the whole class was laughing. Undaunted, I continued. "How do we know that Jesus wasn't married. I mean, why wouldn't he try marriage out to get a better handle on all the stuff families go through? My dad goes to the Lutheran church once in awhile, said their minister just got married to a beautiful woman and never stops smiling. That he's truly like a different person now. Was cranky and unsociable before. Seems to me if priests got married, maybe they'd have better luck solving all the marriage problems. Like they were in the soup themselves, and learned how to cool it down."

Monsignor Pugh wasn't laughing now. I think he could tell I wasn't just horsing around, that there was a real question lurking. He breathed in, "Jesus wants priests celibate because that is making the ultimate sacrifice for his love. He wants priests to be able to withstand the greatest of all human temptations—the love of a woman. If a priest can't do that, how will he be able to hear your confessions and absolve you of your sins? Priests are humans, they are attracted to the same vices that you are. Instead of the love of a woman to guide them, they are married to the church and use the church as their strength against the evil that lurks in the world. Celibacy is a great sacrifice but it is the cornerstone of our love for Jesus and his church."

I was watching Monsignor Pugh closely as he spoke. His color rose as he voiced his beliefs. You could sense his sincerity and commitment. But his words did not allay my doubts. It wasn't the time for a witty reply, so I said simply, "I guess that's where my faith gets a little shaky."

Monsignor Pugh knew me well enough that he sensed my uncertainty. "Sometimes you just have to pray for faith, Dylan." He saw the doubt on my face. "Sometimes God doesn't answer your prayers. Sometimes you have to stay patient, put yourself in God's hands. And that's when you find out whether you have the strength to weather the storm. Sometimes you aren't ready for the truth or you just don't see it. Faith isn't easy, it's a rare gift."

Hank and I walked home that night. He brought up the celibacy question, mentioned the rabbi in his old synagogue was married. Hank grinned. "But he's a miserable putz to deal with, Dylan. My ma says he gives Jews a bad name. What I'm getting at is, I don't think being married is any magic cure. I kinda like Monsignor Pugh's angle."

I didn't answer right away. The celibacy question wasn't one of my top concerns. I was just warming up. "Hear you, Hank. I was curious about it, just wanted to keep Monsignor Pugh sharp. Want to make you sure you get the full scoop before you switch teams."

He grinned, "Reneé and I look forward to CCD. Kids that never show up are starting to come just to see what you're gonna say next. You're getting a following." I thought back to grade school when I peppered the nuns with questions. I spent lots of time kneeling in various positions of crucifixion after I got too exuberant. Instead I said, "Do you think Reneé is really interested in this?"

Hank shrugged, "I think she just wants to be with Nut. She said he's always talking about going into the Green Berets. I think she's worried he won't go to college, that she won't see him after this year."

Since I knew she was right, I switched direction. "It's nice to see them together. At first I didn't get it, but now I do. Both are serious but both happier when they're together. It just works."

Hank and I came to Highland Ave, where we split in different directions. My head hurt from thinking about mystical things like faith. Besides, something had been bugging me about Truck's mother. There was an idea that lurked in my sub-conscious that stayed murky, wouldn't get clear. Sometimes obvious things are hardest to see. When we were snooping around Digger's records, something popped up about Truck's mom but we got so absorbed with the missing necklace that I lost the thought. I usually did crossword puzzles when my mind was stuck. I got that trick from my dad who was an avid puzzler. "Just start on the puzzle and sometimes the blocked answer appears," was his advice. So I brought the Sunday puzzle up to my room, went at the arcane clues. The magic didn't work that night. I drifted asleep wondering what the difference was between a dugong and a manatee.

♦

Nut was in the Drexel Heights library doing research on poisons. Last summer he went to Parris Island to take a survival course. Colonel Lynam pulled some strings to get him in, because he wasn't military yet. After going through an intensive training course, you were dumped on a remote island, expected to not only survive but to avoid being caught by a platoon of experts. And if that wasn't bad enough, you had nothing but the clothes you wore, flint and a pocketknife. Your first order was to find water, make weapons and find food. Plus you had to avoid that pesky platoon. One of the training techniques was cutting small bamboo for spears, knives, blow-guns and darts. As if they weren't lethal enough, you looked for native poisons to make your weapons more deadly, bring down bigger prey quicker. With Nut's aptitude for science, he was a star.

Just as he was turning to the oleander section in his book, his brother Jimmy tapped him on the shoulder. "What cha doing Nut, becoming a gardener?" Jimmy was just about out of St Joseph College. He didn't have a job picked yet but was getting by helping Digger run the funeral home. Jimmy was the image of Digger, short and wiry, but fortunately had a gentle soul. He also had the shit kicked out of him as a kid but somehow internalized it, remained stoic and seemingly emotionally unscathed.

Nut closed the book so Jimmy wouldn't see the reference to poison. "Just brushing up on some botany questions, our advanced chemistry teacher likes to spring obscure questions."

Changing topics, "How's it going with Digger?"

Jimmy shrugged, "Funny as it seems, I think Digger actually likes having me there. It gives him more time to do Knights of Columbus work. Since he got elected president, that's all he wants to do. He's teaching me everything about the business. Remember how he used to hide all the embalming tricks from us, like it was his personal treasure? Well, now he's got me doing everything."

Nut looked at his big brother, smiled. "Sounds awful to me, Jimmy, I hate being around him, even when he's in a good mood."

Jimmy smiled back, "Damndest thing is, Nut, I kinda

like the work. Digger leaves me alone." With that, he patted Nut on the shoulder, left the library with his book on mortuary science.

Nut flipped open his book, began reading the oleander section intently. "Oleander poisoning can occur from sucking the nectar from the flowers, eating the leaves, ingesting the sap from the stems or breathing smoke from burning branches. There have even been mild cases of poisoning when eating honey from bees that used oleander for nectar." There was wild oleander growing on Parris Island and Nut had become expert at milking the nectar to poison his spears and darts. White tail deer would die quickly after being impaled from his spear thrown from the tree stand Nut had expertly devised. He always targeted the neck and then rapidly removed the spear so the poison didn't spoil the meat.

Nut's house was near Carlington Cemetery, which had a huge garden area for growing plants. One of the cagey gardeners cultivated oleander knowing that animals would avoid them and thus spare the non-poisonous plants they grew to decorate the graves. If he decided that Digger was going to die, he would use oleander to do it. Since the poison affected the gastrointestinal, nervous and cardiac systems severely, Nut had to devise a way to make it look like a heart attack. And planning for the worst, if a curious coroner found Digger had been poisoned, have a simple explanation for his unfortunate exposure to the beautiful but deadly plant. Perhaps arranging a bouquet for the wake and accidently ingesting the sap? Nut shivered as he thought about this gruesome plan. He whispered quietly, "What am I doing?" And then he thought about

Digger eventually beating his mother to death after he left for the Green Berets. He soldiered on.

BISHOP O'HARE

Coach Gallagher was doing everything he could to keep us sharp. We were undefeated, were about to enter a Christmas tournament in Delaware that featured top teams from Maryland, Delaware and New Jersey. But we had to play league archrival Bishop O'Hare at their gym first, a tough place to win. Most of the players for O'Hare were kids we grew up playing against, saw all summer in town leagues. They had no size but their guards were skilled and pesky, like Scoot on our team. They made up for a lack of size with sheer tenacity. O'Hare had a losing record but we knew somehow they would make us sweat. So Coach Gallagher played a practice team of six guards against us, pressed us on every possession. He tried to simulate the mayhem we were about to encounter. As we ended our last practice he warned, "Don't let those little pissants outwork you."

The O'Hare gym was packed and rocking. As soon as we entered the floor for layup drills, we spotted the homage to Truck—their mascot dressed as an 18 wheeler with the head and back side of a pig. The costume was elaborately made from cardboard, with a likeness of Truck woven into the pig face. I chuckled but could tell that my large buddy was not amused—smoke was coming off his beet red face. As predicted, the little pissants hounded us relentlessly. They kept subbing fresh kamikazes in to wear us out. Although we had practiced all week against the heat, it didn't simulate the frenzy. For the first time all year, we were behind at half, 20-18. Truck was so wired he got 3 quick fouls, sat much of the half. Making things worse, both Fran Philips and I played lousy.

Coach Gallagher was surprisingly calm at half time. He looked at us stone-faced, "Okay, gentlemen, it's first half to the pissants, who's going to stop playing not to lose and play like they want to win?"

And then he walked away, left the room, went back to the court. Drum spoke first, "All we have to do is protect the ball and work it into Truck. If he's covered, he whips it to Fran or Dylan. If they miss, everybody crashes the boards. This isn't a basketball game, this is war. We have to block out and dominate the boards. No matter what they do to screw up Truck, let's out work them, get every missed shot."

I felt good about that till Truck said, "If I get a chance, I'm gonna smash those little fuckers."

We did a better job protecting the ball. Fran Philips was a superb dribbler, so I stayed away from him, got free for easy passes as they doubled him. When they tore after me, I'd whip it back to Fran. He made two perfect passes in a row to Truck, who scored easily. The 3rd quarter was close, but we stayed a few points ahead. But on the opening possession of the 4th quarter, Truck got hammered as he went for a hook. As he untangled from the defender, he swung a wicked elbow that knocked the smaller kid to the floor, dazed and nearly unconscious. The ref blew the whistle, gave Truck a flagrant foul. When Truck argued vehemently, he got another technical and was out of the game before we knew it. I saw the fire in his eyes, grabbed him, pulled him to the bench. I looked him in the eye, "If you say anything else, they will suspend you for the season, just shut up."

Truck slumped onto the bench, exhaled deeply. Coach Gallagher was still arguing the technical but lost the discussion. He never looked at Truck, gathered us around, looked in our eyes, said simply, "Crush them." Suddenly the shots started to drop. Scoot and Drum terrorized O'Hare on defense and got steal after steal for easy layups. I continued to shoot bricks but it didn't matter, we won by 15 points. And then it got crazy.

As we lined up to shake hands, the mammoth father of the kid Truck decked came flying out of the stands. "Big tough guy, let's see if you can fight someone your own size." And then the big lug pushed Truck. Just as Truck was about to deck the guy, Nut appeared suddenly, put the father in a Full Nelson and frog walked him out of the gym.

We looked at each other dumfounded. Finally, I asked, "Who was that masked man?"

But Catholic League rules said if a player got a second flagrant foul, he was done for the season and could not participate in the playoffs. Next day at practice, Coach Gallagher gathered us around to explain the situation. He looked at Truck intently, "Every team from now on will try to bait you. You have to stay composed, no matter what. Let Dylan do the fighting for you, he'll do it without getting a technical."

I looked at Coach, "Is that a compliment or are you saying I'm sneaky?"

He grinned, "Yes." And then we all cracked up. And then he added, "Better yet, let's get Nut to patrol the stands for troublemakers. I'll bet that big dad's shoulders still aches." None of us said anything, but we knew our season hung on the precarious ledge of Truck's temper.

♦

On the way home from practice, I suddenly remembered what haunted my subconscious about Truck's mom. And I knew Drum could help. Drum's father was the county postmaster and occasionally got us odd jobs delivering phone books or other random mailers. It was easy work but you got well paid. One of Drum's bizarre skills was memorizing all the zip codes in Philly. If you named Frankford, he'd spout "19124."

Usually, I commented, "So, who cares?" but it didn't deter him.

He'd sneer, "So test me, how about Port Richmond? Is it the same as Richmond? Oh, yea, it is, 19134." He would go on like that forever. But I recalled Truck showing me the envelope the mysterious letter came in. I remembered seeing a stamp in the corner. Maybe Drum would know it.

So I called Truck after dinner, told him my idea. "If we know where the letter came from, maybe we'd have a shot at finding out who sent it. A long shot, but at least a shot."

Truck was quiet. And then said, "Hold on, I'll get it and look." He was back in a few minutes, "Yea, it's got a stamp with markings on it. What's next?" I said I'd be over to pick it up right away.

Something came to me. "Drum asks a million questions, what do you want me to say?" And then I added, "I'll keep you out of it. Just say I got a few weird letters and want to know where they came from."

Truck was quiet. "I love Drum but I really don't want a lot of people knowing what we're doing, just you and Nut. That alright with you, Dylan?"

After getting the envelope, I called Drum, asked if I could drop by. Drum was super bright and never studied, so I wasn't surprised to hear him say, "I'm about to watch Star Trek, can you wait till it's over or stay quiet while it's on?" And then, "I know it's impossible for you to shut up, so just drop over around 9 pm. I know you're gonna bust my chops about my love for Spock, so I'll be prepared for you."

I got there at 9 sharp. Drum let me in, had hands on his hips. I smiled, "Live long and prosper, Drum. Hope you enjoyed the "Trouble with Tribbles" episode. I really think that shows James Tiberius Kirk's gentler side, don't you think?" Drum raised his middle finger in reply.

We went to his den, I showed him the envelope, explained that I was getting love letters from an anonymous source, was intrigued. Drum grinned, "If she saw how shitty you played against O'Hare, she'll probably stop writing anyway." He had me. I nodded, said nothing. He studied the envelope carefully, bringing it close. "This is a cinch; the letter came through the Reading central post office but was mailed in Shillington on November 15th. See that blotchy ink mark overlapping the stamp? If you look close, you can make out the name and date. Your stalker's got quite a hike to make the games."

I didn't quip back, asked about Shillington. "It's a suburb of Reading, small town, locals just say they're from Reading, not Shillington. My parents go there all the time to shop at the outlets. And they get meat there, too. The bacon is amazing, almost like a steak."

I nodded like I cared about shopping and bacon before asking if there was a way to trace the letter back to the mailer. I expected the answer to be "no" but Drum paused before responding. "If she mailed it at a mail box, you got no shot." And then he looked at the envelope again. "This is an odd size and the color's odd, almost pink. If it was mailed at the post office, the clerk might remember the person. Shillington's a really small town." He frowned, "Probably not, though."

I thanked him, walked to the door before adding, "May warp speed be always at your back." I dashed out before he smacked me.

MONSIGNOR CONNER DANCE

There was a mixer Friday night after our Cardinal Carroll home game. The gym was rapidly transformed with strobe lights and a makeshift space for the disc jockey. Twice a year the priests at Conner allowed us to fraternize with the fairer sex. But to spoil the fun, the priests circled through the crowd looking for drunks or lewd behavior. Since we were all horny, guilt-ridden teenagers, the patrol got plenty of action. Conner was a huge school, just under 4,000 boys. With that quantity, you were bound to have some real knuckleheads who got blind drunk and either blew lunch on the dance floor or groped girls with abandon and got nabbed by the vigilant priests. It was one of my favorite nights of the year. You got to witness up close the incredible stupidity of the Catholic male.

I kind of envied this carefree burst of recklessness. As a player, you were already under tight wraps and with the expectation of a Catholic League and City Championship, watched closely. So I remained a spectator to the bedlam. We thrashed Cardinal Carroll that night but my shooting woes continued. As we walked from the locker room, Drum whispered, "If your stalker hadn't lost interest after the O'Hare game, I'll bet she did tonight. You were shootings bricks, my man."

Drum was a terrible shooter, so I said; "Now I know how it feels to be you. At least mine's temporary, you have stone hands every day. Maybe think about being a brick layer instead of college. That must blow, kind of like getting leprosy, I mean incurable." While Drum pondered a comeback, we entered the freak show.

It didn't take a hound dog's nose to smell the acrid combination of beer, sweat and raging hormones. I saw "Bucket Head" waiting at the entrance to the gym floor. Father Gilligan was the Dean of Discipline at Conner. He was also the chaplain of the basketball team and ran a squeaky clean school. He was nicknamed "Bucket Head" because his squat, powerful body grew up through a meaty neck and ended in an equally bulbous head. Almost like a watermelon standing straight up. When you looked at Bucket Head you got the feeling he would love to kick your ass, was just waiting for an opening. With my personality, you might have guessed he took special interest in me. Our paths had crossed a few times.

As we neared him, Bucket Head pointed at me, "You, Frazier, are dead center on my radar tonight. If I see any shifty business, you'll be in the athletic office Monday morning to get a paddling." Bucket Head's favorite punishment was what he called "the Board of Education." The "Board" was a paddle-shaped piece of Hickory that he used to spank anyone who broke his rules. He made you bend over a chair while he wacked you twice. That might not seem too brutal but the Board left a 6 inch welt on your butt that took a week to settle back to normal. He caught me freshman year walking around the corridors when I was supposed to be at gym class. To be honest, I was disrupting class by making cross-eyed faces at giggling classmates in Biology.

After that punishment, I couldn't sit down without a pillow. At dinner that night, mom asked why I needed a pillow. "Sorry, mom, I'm constipated." She rolled her eyes.

So I looked at Bucket Head, gave him my sincerest smile, "I'll make you proud tonight, Father. My bet is you'll watch my behavior, say to yourself, 'There goes, Frazier, a true Christian Warrior.' "

Bucket Head didn't smile, he glared a few seconds, "And now I'll be watching even closer."

He walked away. Truck walked up beside me, "Sorry, Dylan, you're on your own. There's no way I want Bucket Head watching me. I'm going trolling for babes. See ya." I looked at Drum for support. He also walked away without saying anything. So that's why I waited till Scoot and Fran Philips came out, strolled around with them.

Every time I turned, Bucket Head was lurking. Scoot whispered, "Old Bucket Head's creeping me out. It's like he's following us. Maybe we ought to spread out and see if we can shake him." Since he hadn't witnessed his threat to tail me, I nodded agreeably. So Fran and Scoot scattered and I made a beeline for the Coke stand. I figured Bucket Head would ditch me if I stood in line, sipped my Coke, the vision of innocence. As I was walking there, the haunting tune, "Where or When" was playing. As I listened to my favorite slow song, I started humming along as Dion sang, momentarily lost track of time.

As with most Philly kids, I was consumed by the American Bandstand scene. Philly was the epicenter of music. Dick Clark lived in our neighborhood. I used to deliver newspapers to him when I was a kid–before he became a big star. His reputation was true; he was a nice guy. I even went to his show once, free tickets as a

Christmas tip for flawless newspaper service. He never expected anything special. There were lots of nasty people that stiffed me on tips or wanted particular places for the newspaper to be perched each morning. Naturally, I ignored the crazy requests. When the person complained, I'd contort my face as if in anguish. Appeared almost near tears, said, "Are you serious, how did that happen?" That mischievous memory flashed by as I spotted Bucket Head in the middle of the floor, head spinning side to side. He'd lost me. I ducked low, slinked off.

As I moved to the corner, I saw Fat Matt Kelley draped all over a poor girl, swaying to a popular slow song, "When I Fall in Love" by the Letterman. Although it was a cold night, Fat Matt was sweating like a moron at the SAT's. You could see the girl was struggling to keep as much space as possible from her dripping partner. Just then, Fat Matt spun and I saw Laura Hartley was the poor victim of the dancing water buffalo. I hadn't seen Laura since I delivered the statue of the Holy Mother to her house a couple years ago. St Tim had a tradition during Lent of saying a family rosary before the holy statue and then transferring it to another family. Over the last couple years, Laura had blossomed into an incredibly gorgeous girl, movie star beautiful. Never at a loss for words, this time I stared, mouth open. Her long dark hair hung to a slender waist, cascaded across her hourglass body as she fought valiantly to keep from getting drenched by the flop sweating Fat Matt.

Without thinking, I cut in, firmly pushed Fat Matt to the sidelines. Her beautiful face became more spectacular as she smiled at my quip. "Do you want me to get you a towel from the locker room? It looks like you got hit with a fire hose." I rubbed my jacket arm over her moist forehead to emphasize the offer.

Laura giggled, "Just get me as far away as you can. Matt's a friend of my brother, he feels sorry for him and guilt trips me into dancing with him. I love my brother but Matt can be scary."

I was busy staring at the radiant smile, said, "Tell your brother not to feel sorry for Matt, he's got the personality of a child molester." She giggled again, a nice laugh that made her face glow.

The dance ended, I stood awkwardly, not wanting to leave. To break the silence, "Did you see the game or just come to the mixer?"

She grinned, "I play basketball for Holy Child, our coach told us to come watch you guys play, that maybe we'll learn something." And then added, "I'm supposed to watch how you shoot. Coach says you have perfect form."

Thinking about my shooting woes recently, I shook my head. "Better not watch me anymore, I've shot like a blacksmith the past few weeks. Can't figure it out."

Laura shined her amazing face at me, "I think your right elbow is sticking out too far, Usually, you have it tucked in straighter, more in line with the basket."

I look at her dumfounded, not expecting that. She added quickly, "I've seen all your games and noticed that recently." And then Laura grinned, "Maybe I don't know what I'm talking about." Just then, Bucket Head rediscovered me, swooped in.

He looked at Laura, "I hope Frazier's behaving himself, Laura. I'm not sure your Dad would like you spending time with him, he's what the priests call a troubled soul."

Before I could defend myself, Laura said, "He's been a perfect gentleman, Father Gilligan. We were just talking about the perfect jump shot." And then she tucked her arm into Bucket Head's elbow, walked him off. As she left, she spun and winked at me.

As I stood with my mouth hanging, Drum came over, with Fran and Scoot, said they were about to leave to get cheesesteaks at The Deli. Drum added, "Truck already left with a bimbo, not much of a face but a rack on her that Bullwinkle the Moose would envy."

Fran laughed, "That sounds like one of Dylan's lines, I think he's wearing off on you."

I patted Drum on his head, "Don't worry, a flu shot will kill it." We headed toward the gym doors. I spotted Laura Hartley walking out with her brother. I wanted to thank her for helping out with Bucket Head so I sprinted after her. Actually, I just wanted to look at that face again.

As I got to the door, her father was waiting to escort her off. Her brother walked by me without saying hello, going back into the dance. We had some history, he thought I was an asshole. Probably a fair evaluation if I was forced to admit it. But I knew her dad pretty well, liked him a lot. He had been my Cub Scout master, was a local legend at our church. Trying to appear casual, I blurted out, "Hey, Mr. Hartley, I just wanted to thank Laura for the shooting tip."

He looked at me funny. I further explained, "I've been off lately, she said my elbow's been sticking out, kind of like a chicken wing."

He gave me a big smile, "Laura's like her mother, never hesitates to give advice. Most times she's right." He winked at me, "An irritating habit sometime."

And then he gave her a big hug. As they started to walk off, she looked at me, "Not like a chicken wing, more like a turkey." She and her father were chuckling as they walked down the steps. That line made me more intrigued.

Just then my buddies caught up. Scoot said, "Holy shit, is that Laura Hartley? Can you believe what a piece of tail she's turned into? It's hard to believe she's only a freshman." When I heard that you could have knocked me over with a feather. My dream girl was only 14.

Scoot must have read my mind, said, "She's jail bait, Dylan. Better leave her be."

To myself: Shit!!!! But out loud, "No problem with that. I'm not in any rush. Can you imagine how great she'll look in a few years?" Everyone just nodded. We switched gears toward what cheesesteak creation we'd go for. Me, I liked the classic—cheesesteak with fried onions, lots of ketchup, with a heated roll. A few minutes later I was living my dream, cheese and ketchup spilling down my shirt. But then Laura Hartley popped into my head: Shit, she's only fourteen.

THE CHASE

It was Sunday night; I was having trouble concentrating on homework. So I grabbed the newspaper, got a pencil. As usual, did crossword puzzles when I wanted to relax my mind. With an imagination like mine, my noodle got clogged sometime. My dad easily did the New York Times puzzle every Sunday. I started to "help" him at age 10 as a way to spend time. Kids in my class thought it odd that I knew what a three-toed sloth was. I remembered looking at another frowning 5th grader, "It's a basic to know what a slow moving arboreal mammal is, don't you think?" Thank God my teacher Sister John found it a charming, my obsession with words. I was figuring out the difference between a wildebeest and a hartebeest when I remembered we should go visit the funeral home where Truck's mom was buried. So I called Truck, made plans to shoot to Gideon's Funeral Home after school. By the way, a wildebeest is also called a gnu.

Gabriel's Funeral Home was a beautiful stone building on the edge of Garrett Hill, a small neighborhood near Drexel Heights. Spencer Victor Gabriel was the son of the owner; went to Upper Derby, was noteworthy because he always wore a bow tie to school. Most guys with this quirk would get the shit kicked out of them regularly, but not Spencer. He had the good luck to also be a terrific wrestler. Besides Nut, he was the best on the team. Being wrestlers and funeral home kids, Spencer and Nut had so much in common they became friends. When I first met Spencer I noticed instantly he was unusual. I soon learned he was devoid of a sense of humor. Naturally, this intrigued me, made me pick at it. When I'd discuss it with

Nut he shrugged, "He's just an earnest guy. He actually can't wait to get in the mortuary business. He believes he's easing the dead's way into the next life."

I looked at Nut, "Tell me again why you think he isn't deranged?" Nut rolled his eyes, chuckled.

Truck parked in the back of Gabriel's. We got out, ambled up the steps. Truck had been quiet on the ride there. I looked at him, "I'll do the talking, I know this must be tough for you." He just nodded. Spencer was there, told us Nut had asked him to help when we came. I introduced him to Truck, told Spencer we wanted to know some of the details of Truck's mom's burial. I explained that he was young when she died and he wanted to understand everything better. Spencer immediately got a somber look on his face. "People deal with grief in different ways. Some compartmentalize the pain; sort of put it away until a day when they can handle it. I see this all the time. Give me a few minutes and let me see what I can find." He walked off.

Truck looked at me, "Is he for real?"

I shrugged, "I'm pretty sure Nut body-slammed him one too many times, jarred his bean." Truck laughed, I was glad he was loosening up.

Spencer came back with a folder marked "Gerda Carr," handed it to Truck. And then added, "My maternal grandmother was German too. She had the same 1st name, but she spelled her name Gerde. It translates to "protected" in German. Don't you think that's interesting?"

I nodded sincerely like I thought he wasn't insane. He led us to a nearby office, left us to peruse the folder. Truck looked at me, "I didn't know my mom was German. My dad always called her Gert. I thought her name was Gertrude." And then he paused, lost in thought. He suddenly said, "I just had a flash of my mom's voice. She used to call me her 'good boy' all the time." I looked puzzled so he added, "But she pronounced 'good' like 'goot.'"

I watched my hulking buddy get a big grin on his face. That grin made me feel really good. This chase was paying off.

I looked at the copy of the birth certificate. "Says she was born in Halle, Germany, that her father's name was Bruno Heydrich. Maybe that's where you got the blue eyes, you know, Aryan blood." I could see him puzzling that information. And then I noted his mom was *Catholic, baptized in St Stephan Church in Halle.* I leafed through the rest of the file and found the death certificate that also said, *overdose* as a cause of death. I looked at Truck, "It doesn't say anything about suicide. It looks like it was an accident. The cause of death says *undetermined*. They probably do that when can't prove it one way or the other, probably just took too much medicine by accident. You know, like how you forget if you took a vitamin in the morning." Truck took a deep breath, exhaled. I could see the burden being lifted.

I scanned the documents, found the cemetery where Gerda Carr was buried. Oddly, it was Holy Cross Cemetery, many miles away on the edge of South Philly, not close to Truck's old neighborhood. I remembered riding past it many times as we took one of my father's famous short cuts to the Jersey Shore. My dad went out of his way to avoid traffic. My mom used to quip, "Your dad likes to go by way of Jerusalem to get to Cape May."

I said what we were both thinking. "Why didn't your dad bury her nearby? I mean Carlington Cemetery is so much closer." Truck didn't know. And so we decided to extend out journey, left Gabriel's to head to Holy Cross.

On the ride, Truck said, "I wonder what was wrong with my mom. I mean what was she taking medication for? It must have been strong stuff if it could kill you." Before we left Gabriel's, I had made a copy of the Birth and Death Certificates, looked at the section "Significant Conditions Leading to Death" and found it blank. When I told Truck that, he sat quietly. Finally, "Maybe I'll ask my dad again. I mean I'm old enough to handle this now." And then he turned, "Would you mind coming with me when I ask. Maybe he'll say more if you're there. For some reason he likes you." And then he grinned, "That doesn't say much for his taste." I let him have fun. He needed it.

◆

Holy Cross Cemetery was a desolate, forlorn place, overgrown and uninviting. The place screamed, "Everybody's dead here!" I wasn't a big fan of death anyway but this would be the last spot I'd want my bones. The graves were crowded together and many were in disrepair, kind of falling over each other. By contrast, Carlington Cemetery near our houses was immaculately landscaped and full of beautiful trees, almost like an arboretum. I silently made a vow to be buried in a cheerful place. I mean, you're dead, why rub it in? I kept this to myself. I didn't want Truck getting gloomy again.

I spotted a sign for "office," told Truck to make a right. We parked, made our way to the paint-chipped front door, entered. Inside was just as messy as the burial plots. We made our way to an austere looking woman. Her hair was peppery gray, was wound in the tightest bun humanly possible, like she was afraid her brain would leak out. The bun also pulled her eyebrows back, gave her a startled look. Like somebody snuck up on her, yelled, "Boo!" She never acknowledged us as we stood in front of her. Finally, I cleared my throat, "Excuse me, can I get some help."

Without looking up, "You'll have to wait your turn."

I looked around at the empty room. Not able to resist, "There's nobody else here, I guess that puts us in first place."

Again without lifting her eyes, "I'm on my break, I'm meditating." She exhaled deeply, like she was hoping it would blow me away.

I turned to Truck, "Why don't we meditate too. That way we won't be wasting time."

Truck belly laughed and then I started. We composed ourselves after a few minutes. The old crone finally looked at us, never seemed to notice our laughing like hyenas a second ago. "What can I do for you? Do you have an appointment?"

I figured I better get serious, "Sorry ma'am, we don't. This is our first time here; we don't know the ropes. My friend is trying to visit his mother's grave and we need some directions. She died when he was young, he never got to pay his respects. Sorry about not setting up an appointment."

This seemed to soften her some. "Give me the name, date of death and funeral home. I'll see what I can find."

After we gave the information, she got up, walked to a nearby file cabinet. We ambled over to nearby chairs and sat while she did the search. After a few minutes, she walked to her desk, read through the retrieved folder. We were only a few feet away. I watched her pull a thick piece of paper out, read it carefully. She had a frown on her face, seemed puzzled. She slowly put the paper back and continued to leaf through the information. Finally, "Here it is, Gerda Carr is buried in Section C, row 12, about midway in." She shut the folder, got up. "I'll get you a map. It's not that easy to find your way around."

And so we drove to section C, found row 12 and moseyed toward the middle. The head stones were very small. Most had partially sunk into the ground. But we never found a marker for Gerda Carr. I looked at Truck, "Maybe we ought to split up, start at opposite ends, go slowly. Must have missed it."

A few minutes later we met. Truck shook his head, "Nothing. Do you think the headstone sunk in so deep we can't find it?"

I agreed, "That must be it." And so we got on our

knees, slowly moved down the row, looking for a gap where the stone might be hidden. Found nothing. We did it again, this time together but still found zilch.

Truck said, "There isn't even an open space in this row. Maybe the lady screwed up. Let's go back."

When we walked in, told her there was no headstone for Gerda Carr, she seemed annoyed. She went through the folder again. "No mistake, you must have missed it." When I started to argue, she said firmly, "No mistake! Look again."

And then she went back to her other work, pretending we weren't there. I looked at Truck, "Let's try again." And we did with no luck. We hurried back, ready for an argument.

Truck barged in, fire in his eyes. Told her there was nothing there. Seeing his aggravation, Miss Unhelpful put up her hands, told us to wait and went into the adjoining room, started talking to an older man, maybe her boss. I snuck over to see if I could overhear. She was talking softly. I couldn't hear anything clearly. But I saw the guy got agitated as she talked. Then he pulled out a paper from the file, studied it, seemed to be thinking but went to his desk and made a telephone call. His back was to me, I couldn't hear squat. As he put the phone down, I shifted back to Truck. The secretary returned, "I found the answer. Your mother was cremated. There is no burial plot. Sorry about the mix-up."

Truck looked at me, blurted out, "Were Catholic. They don't allow cremation, do they?" He was right.

Catholics were not allowed to be cremated. I remembered that from religion class.

But the crabby lady seemed to regain her composure. "It happens all the time. Maybe your mother's family insisted on it. Families disagree about burial matters."

When I started to debate it, the woman looked at me, "We're done here. The office closes in a few minutes, I have to clean up. Please leave, next time make an appointment." She lowered her eyes, started flipping through papers, clearly irritated.

Truck looked like he wanted to pound her so I grabbed his shoulder, spun him to the door. We got outside and he said, "Let's look again." We did but still found nothing.

On the ride home Truck looked straight ahead, finally mumbled, "There's no way dad cremated my mom. He's as Catholic as you can be. He still goes to Confession all the time, asks for forgiveness for living with Aunt Sue when they're not married. I've heard him pestering her all the time that he'll go to hell if she doesn't make him an honest man."

It didn't make any sense to me either; Mr. Carr was a fixture at mass every morning, just like my mom. Saying what we both were both thinking, "That's another question for your dad." I could see Truck squirming. I said, "Whether he likes it or not, he owes you some answers." I didn't say anything but wasn't looking forward to our talk with Mr. Carr.

◆

I couldn't get to sleep that night, so I listened to WIBG, silently lip-syncing the hit song "Running Scared." I always listened to the radio before bed since my father turned off the TV at 9 pm every night. We had to read or listen to the radio in our room. My friends found that odd. "Doesn't your old man ever watch the Tonight Show or anything?"

When I told my dad what my friends thought of his dislike for TV, he smiled, "Tell your buddies it's good practice for when they're in prison. Nobody entertains you in the slammer." How do you argue with that? My dad had a way of ending discussions quickly. Anyway, when the song was over I listened to Hy Lit mindlessly delivering a commercial for The Sally Starr Show. During his babble, I replayed the earlier scene at the cemetery. The unfriendly lady was clearly anxious about something she read in Mrs. Carr's file. It was almost like she was hiding something, kind of like what Roy Orbison just sang about: Running scared. And later her boss got nervous, made a call. And then she came in and told us the cremation story. Maybe they had cremated her by accident, were worried about being sued? That tumbled through my mind as I dozed off to a fitful sleep.

A DAY AT CONNER HIGH

It had gotten much colder so my morning walk to Conner High School was done in a semi-sprint. One of my duties at school was hall monitor, so I had to be there early. Select seniors got the dubious honor of policing behavior in the corridors as students walked to class. Most of the monitors were bigger kids. One of the rites of passage for freshman was getting pushed around as you hustled to your next class. You had to maneuver through hordes of students, make it on time or risk detention. Some of the monitors enjoyed picking on the smaller boys. I never did that and would intervene if I saw one of my comrades getting too abusive. I never liked bullies, Nut and I had that in common. But I could only control a small section so lots of little twerps took a licking.

As I went to my assigned spot, I watched the tiny freshman pour in, remembered how my little buddy Scoot always got his ass kicked years ago. After a few weeks of thrashing at the beginning of freshman year, Scoot asked if he could walk in with me so he wouldn't get picked on. He didn't ask because of my charming personality. I was 5' 10" as a freshman, always wore a menacing smirk, never got hassled. So Scoot thought he could slip by without getting noticed if he walked with me, a big guy who looked mildly crazy. We agreed to meet next morning by the front entrance.

Picturing Scoot that day years ago still made me laugh. I walked up, found Scoot standing alone, shifting back and forth, clearly nervous. Not only was Scoot really small, the funny part was his hair stood straight up in the air, like he'd been electrocuted. "What's with the hairdo, Scoot? Did you stick your finger in an electric socket?"

He stared at me. "What are you talkin' about?" I told him to look in the glass window of the front door.

He turned back. "Jesus" was all he could say.

I started smudging his hair down. "You might as well put a flashing neon sign on your head: I'm a dork, please beat me." It turned out Scoot's mom put his jacket in the dryer every morning right before he left for school. Being a nice mom, she was trying to keep him warm. The static electricity wired him up. She was trying to keep her little boy cozy but ended up electrifying him. We solved his freshman hazing.

Those pleasant reveries poured through my mind as I directed underclassmen safely through the corridors. But simultaneously my mind wandered, I worried about my best friends. Nut was thinking of killing his father and Truck was chasing memories that his father wanted forgotten. I thought: How did I get so lucky? Couldn't I have normal friends that chased girls and just wanted to play basketball? But I was always drawn to unusual people. And then I had this insatiable curiosity that got me in trouble. That's when I remembered that Nut wanted to visit the funeral home again and snoop through his dad's records. He wanted me along to help him figure it out. As I ended hall duty and walked to Trig class, I found myself absorbed by both problems. Maybe I could help? Not understanding why, I felt good about that.

◆

I walked into the gym that afternoon for practice, saw Truck dribbling full court, going all out. Most days Truck shot foul shots and bullshitted with me. I didn't give it more thought until we started doing drills. One of the second team players, Barney Branch, was a huge kid without much talent but who made the team because of his aggressiveness. He was a terrific football player, an All Catholic tight end, going to Penn State on a full scholarship. Barney usually played the star big man for our opposing team in practice. His job was to make Truck work hard. Barney didn't have any skill but made up for it with toughness. He and Truck were friendly but Truck forgot friendship once the ball was tossed up. They had some real battles but always did it cleanly.

But I could tell today was different. Truck really went at him in rebounding drills. Barney outweighed him by 25lbs but couldn't compete with Truck's footwork and ferocity. Barney kept landing on the ground, time after time. Truck got every rebound and swung his elbows like weapons, snapping Barney's head back time after time. Coach Gallagher liked the effort but looked at Truck, "Ease up, big guy. Save it for the game tomorrow."

Truck stared at him, "I play hard, if Barney doesn't like it he can go play dolls."

Barney fired back, "Screw you, Carr. I'll show you who plays with dolls."

Gallagher glared at both, "Settle down, I mean it." I could see our wise coach knew something was bothering his star, so he stopped the drills, started the simulated game. He would talk to Truck after practice.

But things didn't settle down for long. Barney was still pissed so he banged on Truck harder than ever. Every missed shot was like a gladiator fight for the loose ball. Finally, Truck snared an offensive rebound, went right back up, slamming his right elbow into Barney's chest as he shot with his left hand. You could hear the thud and Barney's gasp for air. Truck just turned and ran down court to play defense. He acted like nothing happened. Finally, Barney regained his breath, looked down court and charged Truck. Knowing what Truck would do to him, I went for Barney and tackled him to the ground. By then, Coach Gallagher was blowing his whistle, getting control. I got to my feet, walked over to Truck and looked into his enraged eyes. He slowly shifted his focus to me, murmured, "There's no way mom was cremated."

MR. CARR

Truck's dad, Bob Carr, was working late. The holidays were a busy time at the butcher shop. Sue left early to make dinner for Truck. He smiled as he thought: Even I call him Truck. And then he smiled again as he thought how well his son was getting along with Sue. It had been a difficult period for his son, losing his mom at such a young age and then having another woman move into his home. He probably thought she was stealing his dad, trying to make him forget about his first mother. But something had changed lately; they were getting along. Not affectionate yet, but comfortable together. He was satisfied with that. As Bob reminisced, the telephone rang. He picked it up, expecting another last minute order. People went all out, liked to eat well at Christmas. That was okay with him, the more they ate the more money he made. But the call was like a shot to the gut. He listened wordlessly as the caller filled him in on Truck's recent trip to the cemetery and unsuccessful effort to locate the grave. Bob was stunned but mumbled, "Yes, I understand, I'll take care of it." He hung up, paused for a second, slumped into a nearby chair, closed his eyes.

He hadn't thought about Gerda for months. But then Truck had started to ask questions recently and all that bad history flooded back. His time in the Army seemed like a million years ago. He had been lucky, first getting in the MP's and then being assigned to England as they prepared to invade Europe from Omaha Beach. He spent a hectic year in the dreary English countryside as the massive invasion force was assembled. His job was directing the relentless flow of traffic, monstrously large vehicles moving parts from one place to another. Not a glamorous job, but at least he was spared the hell of combat. And then when the war ended, he was assigned to Nuremburg, Germany to guard VIP's as the military trials began. When he asked the sergeant why he got picked for this duty, he was told, "Take a guess, Carr." When he gave no answer, the sergeant finished, "You look like a prize fighter with those thick shoulders and meat-hook hands. People won't fuck with ya."

After heavy Allied debate, Nuremburg was chosen for the war trials because it was considered the birthplace of the Nazi Party and thus a fitting place to host its destruction. And the massive Palace of Justice was unharmed by Allied bombs, considered as ideal for the trials because of enormous office space and also because it had a prison as part of the complex. He was lucky again. He didn't have prisoner duty. That would have been rough. He wasn't sure he could have resisted beating those heartless killers. He hadn't seen a concentration camp, but word spread and then pictures surfaced. It made him sick. His job was to guard the witnesses and officials involved with the military trials. The Allies were trying the most important political and military leaders of the Third Reich. But they also tried lesser monsters. All told there were hundreds of criminals who committed atrocities. So, the place was hectic, there was a malignant energy that hummed through the complex.

And that was where he met the beautiful Gerda Heydrich. She was hard to miss, tall, blonde, blue-eyed and fluent in English. They hit it off immediately. The other MP's teased him, "We get to guard gnarled-up old men,

Carr gets a German movie star. It just ain't right." He couldn't argue, how did he keep getting so lucky? He would escort her to and from the trials for almost three months. After the first month, he was smitten. It took him awhile to gain her trust but after a relentless pursuit, he began to spend time with her after his shift. That Bavarian part of Germany near Nuremburg was beautiful. He let her show him the wonderful local sights when they had a rare day off together.

Their trip to Neuschwanstein Castle was the most magical weekend of his life. It literally looked like a Grimm Fairy tale setting. And so in a burst of pure joy, he asked Gerda to marry him. He remembered how she stared at him for a long time without answering. She seemed to be working something out. But on the ride home she finally said "no." But he was relentless, wore her down after a few weeks of unbridled love and attention. And that began the best and worst time of his life. All this forgotten history ran through Bob Carr's mind after he got off the disturbing telephone call. He stood there quietly, finally let out a deep breath. In his empty office, he said aloud, "How can I make this all go away?"

CHRISTMAS TOURNEY

Our Christmas tournament was starting tonight. Since teams came from Maryland, New Jersey, Philadelphia and Delaware, they picked Wilmington as a site most convenient for everyone. Slezium Academy was an elite private school in suburban Wilmington and was hosting the event. My father travelled to Delaware all the time, I asked him for directions and what he knew about the school. Dad shrugged, "The Du Pont family owns the whole state but I doubt they have anything to do with the school." I asked him why. He looked at me seriously, "If you were a smart, incredibly wealthy family that ran the whole state, would you name a school Slezium?" You had to love my dad.

We were playing Lower Marion High School from the affluent Main Line of Philadelphia. One of their best players was Frankie Merlano. I played against him for the past two summers in the Narberth Basketball League. Since I wasn't a gifted player like Truck or Fran Philips, I played in every league I could. If I worked harder than everyone, I hoped to overcome their edge in skill. At least that was my plan. Frankie Merlano was the same type as me, some talent, ferocious and made up for deficiencies with sweat. But I was a much better shooter and had gotten the best of him most times. He was a funny looking guy—tall but blocky, hairy like a lowland gorilla, with a droopy lower lip; like someone hung a dumbbell off it when he was a kid.

To go with that questionable appearance, Frankie was a non-stop chatterbox. He started yapping the minute you lined up for the opening jump ball and didn't take a breath till the final whistle. Part of the noise was his natural personality; part of it was his trying to mess with your concentration. Since I employed the same tactic, it didn't work too well against me and that frustrated Frankie. The first time he guarded me he said, "Hey, Frazier, pretty boys like you belong in the Sears catalogue not on the basketball court."

As soon as the ball got tossed, I answered, "Merlano, the Philadelphia Zoo called, they said the Orangutans miss you. Want to know when you're coming home." And thus began our competitions over the past summers.

Lower Marion was a mostly rich area but it had pockets of blacks and immigrant Italians. Most of the basketball team was drawn from these two sections of town. Their teams were always tough, a perennial power in the suburban public school league. Because of the reputation for diversity, Lower Marion was also the home to many black pro ballplayers from the Phillies and 76ers. Occasionally, the pros had sons who turned into pretty good players. This was one of the times—Kenny Durand's dad had been a star player and Kenny Jr. was first team all-state last year. At 6'8' and 230lbs, Kenny was a formidable opponent. Add Merlano to the mix and we knew we were in for a game.

A week ago, Coach Gallagher had taken us to a Lower Marion game to scout, knowing we'd match up with them at this tournament. Drum sat next to Coach and made note of whatever weaknesses he saw. He looked at Truck, "Durand always catches the entry pass then fakes left but ends up right; every time. Stand on that side and you'll get some charges, frustrate the shit out of him."

Coach said, "Watch the language, Drum."

Drum nodded, "Sorry. Truck, frustrate the feces out of him." Coach just shook his head. And then Drum added, "Merlano is a lefty but he dribbles well with either hand. But when he goes to shoot, the ball's coming back to the left hand. But remember, he swings the ball away from his belly button, away from his hip, not straight up, when he brings the ball up to shoot"

I nodded, "I played against him all summer; tell me something I don't already know."

Drum thought for a while. "He has terrible breath." Even Coach chuckled.

And so the game began at Slezium Academy. Merlano lined up beside me, "Tonight's my night, Frazier. I'm gonna be glued to you like stink on a skunk." Truck won the tap and Merlano got up close to me as Fran Philips brought the ball down court.

I said to Merlano, "Drum's right, Frankie, you could really use a breath mint." And then I cut to the hoop and as Fran threw me a perfect back-door pass, I made an easy layup. But that was the only time we led in the half. Durand went wild, had 20 points, mostly from outside shots. He hadn't gone into the post as expected and Truck let him take the longer shots uncontested. We were down 34-26 and had to scramble just to keep it close.

We expected Coach to change strategies at half. We were surprised when he said, "I know you think our strategy isn't working but we're going to stay with it. Durand won't shoot that well the second half and I'm betting his legs are getting tired. He's a leg shooter and will start missing. Truck, let him go outside, sucker him into the long shot, then clean up the boards when he misses. And then he looked at Fran Philips, "They're keying on you and Truck, get Dylan the ball on the wing, he's wide open. Once he makes three or four in a row, they'll have to guard him." He pointed at Truck, "When you get the ball, go right at Durand, he's tired and will start getting sloppy on defense. Let's see if we can foul him out." And then he said to me, "Shut Merlano down. No points." And then Coach turned and walked out to the bench.

Things didn't go exactly as Coach had predicted in his half-time speech. Durand got the ball the first two times and drilled perfect jumps shot to give Lower Marion a 12 point lead. And I missed both wide-open shots from the corner. And then while guarding Merlano on the next possession, I remembered Laura Hartley's advice about my flaring right elbow. I made a conscious effort to keep it straight and the next shot swished to cut the lead to 10. Next time down, Truck dared Durand to take another long one, it clanged off the front of the rim. Following Coach's plan, Fran kept feeding me and I hit the next 5 shots in a row. The game was tied. Lower Marion called time.

It wasn't easy the rest of the way but it went as Coach had outlined. Durand started missing his outside shot and then started to bang underneath. Truck held his ground; suddenly Durand had four fouls and had to play tentatively. They started covering me again and that freed up Fran to isolate against his defender and glide past them for seemingly effortless shots. Truck played his usual great game, ate up any loose rebound, ended with 25 points and 20 rebounds. Fran Philips poured in 22 points, mostly in the second half. Fran made the game look easy. I didn't score another point after my barrage but I did hold Merlano scoreless the second half. We won by 10 points and afterwards, Merlano told me, "You were lucky."

I grinned at him, "That's what happens when you have nice breath."

That turned out to be our toughest game at the tournament. Every team thereafter tried the Lower Marion defense, left me open. My shot had returned and I hardly missed an open shot. The defense couldn't overplay Fran or Truck without paying a price. And Scoot and Drum played great. We pressed full court and Scoot stripped the opponent's best ball handler so many time they had the center bring the ball down, knowing Truck wouldn't waste energy hawking the ball. And Drum always found a way to get a loose ball or errant rebound that Truck missed. When I asked Drum about his uncanny ability to find the ball, he grinned, "Geometry. The ball goes where it's supposed to. The angles don't lie." And he wasn't kidding.

My parents never came to our games. "It makes me too nervous," mom said. And then added, "You're not big enough to play sports." Since I was 6'2" and almost 200 lbs, I realized she judged every athlete on Truck and Nut. Compared to them, I did look puny. And my dad was a fair weathered fan, always turned off the TV if his beloved

Phillies fell behind. "They're going to lose," was his favorite prognosis. If the Phillies rallied and won the game anyway, he'd opine, "They would have lost if I kept watching." But my parents took great pride and interest in my athletic ability, asked for total replays of the game when I came home. I was a fluke in our brainy family tree but they liked it.

So when I walked in with the championship trophy, they gushed with pride. My dad said, "Maybe that's why you got a call from the coach at St John's. He seemed to know you won and had played a good game." I didn't get much college interest since all eyes were on Truck and Fran Philips. Jack Hanley was a legendary coach, someone I idolized since age ten. I couldn't believe the Seahawks were interested in me.

My mom snapped me out of my prideful reverie, "You're too small to play in college."

Even my dad laughed at that, said, "Kate, if he gets in for free, let's risk it. What's a broken bone or two?" My dad was a thrifty guy. Free tuition was big.

I headed to my room, starting to feel pretty good about myself when it hit me—are they using me to lure Truck to go there? Coach Hanley had the full court recruiting press on Truck since last season and hadn't made much headway. Truck was leaning toward North Carolina or Kentucky, the big time. They probably knew Truck and I were best buddies. They'd have a shot if they gave me a free ride. Get a stallion if you buy the plow horse too? I flipped on Hy Lit, listened to the radio blare

"Kathy's Clown" by the Everly Brothers. Was that a sign? Was I being played for a clown? If I was honest with myself, there was no way I deserved a scholarship to a good basketball program. With that bolt of truth, I picked up The Bulletin, looked for the crossword puzzle. I stared at the 1st clue. What was the reclusive cousin of the ring-tailed lemur?

♦

Truck sat in his room savoring the tournament championship. He was glad Dylan got over his shooting slump. He laughed thinking about Dylan's comment: "I was worried a shot-putter had invaded my body." But then more somber thoughts came up. Ever since he heard his mother was German, he kept having flashbacks. Certain words popped into his memory. Like the way she said "vy" for "why" and how she scolded him if he said it like her. "Robbie, you vill talk like a proper American boy, you vill zank me for zat one day" floated through his memory banks. And her golden blonde hair and sky blue eyes, just like him. Dad has dark hair and brown eyes. There was no mistaking who he took after. It wasn't until Spencer Gabriel at the funeral home mentioned the German name that her voice came back. He couldn't stop thinking about her. Memories collided, unsettling him.

But then he got frustrated at the cemetery and his hope faded. He left Gabriel thinking he'd finally be able to visit his mom's grave. He knew it was stupid, but he regretted he was never able to say goodbye. He breathed heavily, thought: Even if she's dead and buried, I can visit her and try to say the things I never had the chance to say.

He had gotten great comfort from that idea but then the nasty bitch at the cemetery said she was cremated. That had to be bullshit. But then he wondered: Maybe dad wanted to erase all memories. Maybe it was just too painful. And then he thought about how pissed off he'd gotten, had taken it out on Barney in practice. He breathed deeply again, said aloud, "What's wrong with me? I have to get control of myself." He leaned back in his chair, promised himself: I'm going to find mom's grave and make some big changes. I'm tired of being angry.

As he sat in that comfortable chair, he thought about his dad being an MP during WWII, how he served in Germany. He wondered if they met there. And then he thought: Why didn't dad ever talk about that? It was eating at him. If Sue hadn't been with dad when they road back from the Christmas championship game, he would have brought it up, risked the cold shoulder treatment for bringing up mom. But he knew it would be too awkward with Sue there. And then he smiled, realized how much he had grown to like Sue. He had to admit, she makes dad happy. It was weird how these random events made him understand that maybe his dad was waiting for him to get comfortable with Sue before they got married. And then it hit him: Maybe Sue is the one waiting for him to soften. Does she want my blessing? He got up from his desk, turned on the radio. Listening to Jerry Blavat on the radio, he plotted his discussion. He would rehearse it with Dylan. His pal always had the right words.

♦

Bob Carr decided to stay late at the shop, told Sue he

had to catch up on the paperwork. He smiled at her, "You know how I always put that off. It finally caught up with me. The accountant's yelling."

Sue came over, hugged him, "Don't be too late, I'm having those veal chops you cut this morning. I snuck a few away when you weren't looking." She had a contented look on her pretty face as she added, "Truck loves them. I'll enjoy spending time with just the two of us. He seems to have finally gotten comfortable with me." Sue smiled, "It's nice. I can now see he has a lot of you in him. Tough on the outside but a teddy bear inside." She grabbed her woolen car coat and headed out into the cold winter night.

Without wanting to, Bob's mind wandered back to the troubling call about the cemetery. Truck was getting progressively interested in Gerda's past. He wondered aloud, "How do I handle this? I can't tell him the truth. It's too complicated. Too risky." Bob Carr knew his son wouldn't stop. He had to find a way to mix in some truth, but just enough to satisfy his curiosity, put an end to the questions. Bob grabbed a dozen whole chickens, began cutting them into parts. He was the first butcher in town to sell chickens already cut and ready to cook without the messy home butchering. People loved the simplicity and he made twice the profit from a single bird. He got into his routine, realized he'd never get to the overdue paperwork. But as he labored at the mindless cutting, a plan came to him. He relaxed for the first time since getting that alarming call. He sighed, shook his head: Maybe this will work out okay.

EXPERIMENTAL FRENCH

I spotted Truck walking to his hall monitor post next morning, asked him, "Any chance in hell you'll go to St John's?"

He looked like he was waiting for the joke. I sat still. He shook his head, "No way, I'm getting outta Philly. I'm definitely heading south."

And then he asked why. So I filled him in. "Got a call from the Seahawk's Assistant Coach, he talked to my dad so I still don't know exactly what he wanted. Dad said it was about playing ball there." Truck didn't say anything, so I added, "He wants to get you hooked, thinking you might be interested if I go." Truck looked uncomfortable. He was trying to figure how to tell me that wouldn't make any difference. To get him off the hook, "Don't worry, Truck, I'm going to tell him I've had enough of you. You're overrated and a ball hog. It's time for me to shine in my own spotlight." We laughed as we headed toward class.

I was in an advanced French class. It wasn't that I was gifted in language. It was that my grade school, St Tim's, was in an experimental French program and started all its pupils in the 5th grade. Even the knuckleheads like me picked up a lot and thrived when they got to Monsignor Conner's 1st year French. In fact, the freshman course with Father Marcus was a total repeat of what I already knew so I got perfect scores on all the tests. But when I got my 1st report card I only got an 80. When I went after school to protest, Father Marcus listened to my plea, finally explained, "You got 100% on every test, but you can't seem to pronounce the sentences well in class, you had to be cheating, you just aren't an A student." When I told him I'd taken French since 5th grade, he raised his eyebrows. "Wow, well that explains it." He never corrected the grade, explaining, "If you are that good, you should have participated much more in class." When I objected to that, he added, "Consider it character building."

As proof that life isn't always fair, I had Father Marcus again for my final year of French. My pronunciation had improved but I was still self-conscious when I had to say long sentences. Drum and Scoot were in the class, both could speak fluently. In fact, Scoot was so talkative that he dominated the class, keeping the pressure off me. And Drum read classic books like "Les Miserables" in French, just for mental gymnastics. When I teased him about showing off, he'd counter, "I consider myself the Jean Valjean of Conner." To my puzzled look at the reference, "Carrying moron friends like you and Truck is a sore burden, like dodging Inspector Javert."

I had read the book that summer so I was able to retort, "You remind me more of the perverted "Master of the House" innkeeper."

Just then Father Marcus walked in, called roll. When your name was said, you had to raise your hand to prove you were present. Having some fun, I raised my hand, said, "C'est moi, mon pere, monsieur Frazier."

Father Marcus paused, but then smiled. "C'est bon, monsieur Frazier." Drum rolled his eyes. But Scoot got all excited waiting for his turn. When his name came, he belted out, "Salut, pere Marcus, Je m'appelle Scoot, enchante'."

This time Father Marcus wasn't amused. "You won't be so enchanted when you come here after school and scrape bubble gum off all these desks."

Later that day, I had to explain to Coach Gallagher why Scoot was late for practice. "You know how much Scoot talks; he was showing off again in French class. Thinks he's Pepe Le Peu."

Coach shook his head. As he walked away, "Somehow I think you're involved in this, Dylan."

NUT

Nut had given a lot of thought about Digger stealing his customer's jewelry. His father was super-precise. He must have kept records. Whenever he had opportunity, he scoured Digger's bedroom for files or some documentation. He wasn't sure what he'd do with the information; it was just something he wanted to prove. Digger made a big deal about his generosity to the parish. St Tim published a monthly pamphlet on what each person put in the collection box. Mom said they were trying to "shame people into giving" but Digger loved it. "The cheap bastards ought to be singled out. People should know who pulls their weight." Digger did his best to get top billing, to be the biggest donor. Nut wouldn't be surprised if he stole the money to be able to be the biggest benefactor and have bragging rights. Digger volunteered to manage every fundraiser for the parish. And he wormed his way into managing the ushers who helped direct traffic and take up the collection at church each Sunday. Digger liked control. The big-shot.

Most parishioners thought Digger was the most generous man around, always giving his time for St Tim. Part of his scheme was being so visible that he'd be the first choice for burials if someone died. Nut smiled as he thought about marching into Monsignor's Pugh's office and laying out how Digger had filched parishioner's valuables. He would love to humiliate Digger publicly. He wondered what Monsignor Pugh would do. Would he take the information to the police or keep it hushed up? Nut could see the Monsignor might tell Digger to repay the money, trying to keep the Church out of the newspapers.

Nut wanted Digger to be shamed. He'd have to think about how to proceed if he found enough evidence. But so far, Nut found nothing.

♦

Nut had a major wrestling tournament Saturday afternoon; I was looking forward to seeing him in action. Nut always liked wrestling, even before he went to Upper Derby and did it seriously. As a kid, he came to my house Saturdays to watch Haystack Calhoun and the other crazy matches, then practiced on me. The weird part was how observant he was. Nut could immediately duplicate what the professionals did. It was all a blur to me but I learned as Nut explained the way to use leverage and render your opponent helpless by twisting their body like a corkscrew. He never hurt me but my body went in directions it wasn't supposed to go. Through that torture, I learned to appreciate the skill and dedication it took to do the moves.

This past summer, I helped Nut perfect the "Camel Clutch." We practiced to the point of exhaustion—at least for me. Nut always wanted to do it again. "One more time, Dylan, I've got to shave another second off it."

I'd throw up my hands, "How about no more times. Every time I see a Camel cigarette commercial, my butt tightens up." But he'd sulk and we'd go at it again. The Camel Clutch was basically getting behind your opponent as you pull them to the ground, trapping his arms with your arms and then wrapping your hands under his chin and sitting backwards. If you did it right, the match was over. Nut had never used it in a match, wanted to unveil it at this meet. I wanted to be there to watch someone else become a soft pretzel.

My teammate Fran Philips came with me to Upper Derby. He had never seen Nut wrestle and was excited to see our friend who had become a sensation. Fran was my earliest buddy at St Tim's. He was always a happy, mellow kid and loved sports. Since he lived across from the courts and I was there every day, we became close at age ten. And oddly our coordination kicked in at the same time and we became a championship backcourt by 8th grade. But Fran got really good and ironically seemed to care less about that gift as he grew older. And then he started smoking and drifted as a student. But the natural skill was so great that he just kept excelling on the court. But he seemed to have lost his drive; I wanted to probe that on our walk to wrestling.

I asked about college, he was being heavily recruited. "I'll probably end up at some school in the South, maybe the Midwest; they're easier to get into. My marks are shitty, but the boards are okay. That might save me." He didn't seem concerned. We hadn't had any serious talks for years, kind of drifted apart as Nut and Truck became my best friends.

But we had this early bond. It bugged me that Fran didn't seem to care. Being incapable of not butting into people's business, I went at him. "Fran why don't you work a little harder on the marks, you could go anywhere you wanted. Why settle for some shit-hook school?"

He laughed, "That's what my parents ask after each report card." He shrugged, "I guess the truth is I'm bored with the subjects and get distracted easy doing homework. Then pretty soon I light up a Camel and start reading a novel. And before I know it, the Tonight Show is on and I'm hooked on the Carnac monologue. If they tested me on Best Sellers or Carson trivia, I'd ace my marks." I always marveled that Fran was allowed to smoke, even in his bedroom.

I once asked my dad if I could smoke, he nodded, "Sure, but only after you sprout wings and fly to the moon and back."

From an early age, Fran and I always had books in common. We loved to read. Since grade school, we'd swap books back and forth, trade theories on the plot. But I did my homework and got by. Not letting it go, "I mean, can't you stay after school for extra help or maybe go to the study hall and do enough to get better grades. I mean, you're smart. I'll stay with you if you need company. We could kill time before practice and get all the work done."

He chuckled, "Same old Dylan, trying to solve everybody's problems. You were always that way." And then he said something that shocked me, "You might not believe this but I'm going to quit basketball after college and travel the world. I think I have something to offer, I just need to find what it is." And then the kicker, "I've even thought about bagging college and heading to Europe or Asia." My eyes got wide. I didn't know what to say, our arrival at Upper Derby halted the conversation.

We moved into the gym, grabbed spots near the mats. During our walk, it occurred to me that Fran was a great listener. He got you to say what was on your mind without pushing. It struck me odd that he was such a bad student. Usually people that listened carefully were the best students. For instance, I was an average student because I was always looking for a funny twist, a way to make a quip. Not a trait for a scholar. That ran through my mind as we settled in the stands. And then Fran asked what I was reading now. "The Fixer," by Malamud, it's about a Jewish handyman in Russia that gets falsely arrested for murder."

Fran nodded, "I read it last summer, it's great. Can you believe how Yakov Bok refused to quit?" We traded ideas about what we'd do if imprisoned for something we didn't do, how we'd survive. Fran smiled, "When I was reading it, I kept thinking of you, always trying to fix broken things." When he saw I didn't know how to take that, he added, "That's a good thing." And then, "Makes up for the ball-busting." I laughed.

The meet started and we watched Upper Derby plow through the competition. Nut was being saved for last. While there weren't many fans in the stands, there were some obvious scouts there to watch Nut. I pointed at the one guy I recognized, "He's from Iowa. He also coached the Olympic team. He's putting the full-court press on Nut to be a Jayhawk. Pretty much promised him a spot on the next Olympic team." Since I knew Nut was headed for the Green Berets but hadn't told anyone but me, I let that information hang. I watched our buddy Hank Greenberg chatting with Nut, getting him loosened up before the match. Hank had a nice, self-deprecating manner. I could see Nut grinning at something Hank said.

And then I spotted a group of girls from Conner's

sister school, Archbishop Kender. I had a number of memorable run-ins with these girls in the past. Sue Rossini had a crush on me in freshman year, never got the message that my only interest was her amazing body. Plus she buttered my ego like I was Errol Flynn. And since I had a classic case of Catholic guilt, every time I got horny and caved in, I'd instantly regret it and head to confession. The priest's advice was clear, "Avoid the near occasions of sin." Sue Rossini's body was about as perfect an example of sin as God ever made. Over freshman and sophomore year I lost a lot of battles with "near occasions." Finally in junior year I got other girlfriends and definitely broke it off. Sue wasn't happy, tormented every new girl I went out with. And that's when I learned how mean she really was. It wasn't jealousy; it was her need to have her way. I remember her screaming at me, "No one breaks up with me!" Her two posse members, Pat Rudella and Diana Rafanelli were with her today, had been part of the gang who harassed my recent girlfriends. I wondered why they were there.

Fran interrupted my thoughts, "What are you staring at?" I told him. Fran laughed out loud, instantly recalling Sue and her crew coming to the courts a couple years ago, taunting me while we played. Sue was pissed because I just backed out of a date the night before. My Catholic guilt overwhelmed me when I started thinking about mortal sin; how I didn't want to roast in hell with pus-dripping maggots on my balls. Naturally, I came up with a lame excuse about an important practice but Sue wasn't buying it. She gathered her friends, came to the courts, disrupted the game until I agreed to sit down and tell her the truth. The last thing in the world I wanted to do was face Sue and her thugs. The older guys had to literally lift me off my feet, hauled me down so they could continue the game. It became one of the legendary court stories. I told Sue that night I was obsessed with basketball, didn't want a girlfriend to distract me. I needed to focus on a college scholarship. Sue scoffed at that, hated me ever since. Her parting comments were, "You'll regret this."

With that sour past, I wasn't excited about seeing her again. But Fran seemed to read my mind, "They're here to see Nut, I saw them hanging on him at the O'Hare game. Every time I see those girls I think about you getting carried into that throng two summers ago. It still makes me laugh." I started to chuckle. It was a really weird story, one of those bizarre things that happened to me more often than it should.

The mean girls, Sue, Pat and Diana made their way to the bleachers, spotted me pretending to be invisible. Sue smiled at me, then gave me the finger. I said, "Is that the new peace sign or your I.Q.?" All three gave me the wagging double bird.

Fran leaned in, "You probably better shut up." Reluctantly, I obeyed.

Finally, Nut was announced. "Two-time defending state champion, John O'Hanlon will be matched against undefeated Lonny Reppert from Chester Valley High School. Gentlemen, take your neutral positions." Unlike most of the opponents who fought Nut, Reppert didn't seem intimidated. Maybe the fact that he outweighed Nut and was a hulk of muscle helped. Anyway, Reppert had a strategy. He kept circling on the edge of the mat, trying to give Nut less room to work with. He seemed to be trying to get penalty points by suckering Nut to force him off the mat. Or maybe he was just trying to tire him out. Finally Nut retreated to the center, said to the referee, "Can you ask him to wrestle? He seems stuck to the edge." The referee nodded, told Reppert he'd get a penalty for stalling if he didn't start to wrestle.

Reppert looked at the ref, started to argue but suddenly charged Nut, trying to catch him off-guard. But Nut pivoted, caught his opponent's burly arm and threw him to the mat. As he had done to me countless times last summer, Nut scrambled behind him and put a classic Camel Clutch on Reppert, stunning him. Having totally disoriented Reppert, Nut reversed himself and pinned his shoulders to the mat. Match over. The big lug lay limp on the mat, like a bus hit him. The thing so amazing about Nut was how easy he made it look. If you looked at Reppert walking down the street, you'd move to the other side, he was physically scary. But Nut tossed him like a Tinker Toy. I turned to Fran Philips, "Aren't you glad Nut likes us?" He chuckled.

We sat in the stands for a while, waiting for my former girlfriend to leave so I could avoid another full bird salute. I had told Nut we'd meet him in the lobby after he got dressed. Hank Greenberg wandered in, sat with us. I smiled, "Another tough match for Nut, huh?"

Hank shook his head, "The funny thing is, that guy Reppert hasn't lost a point in any other match but today he looked like a sap. I mean, Nut just toys with them." As I was about to agree, there was a loud scream from the lobby. We hopped down the stands, went to see what the commotion was about. As I swung around the corner, I spotted the mean girls surrounding Nut's girlfriend Reneé. They circled her, taunting. And then I saw Sue Rossini slap the bewildered Reneé on the side of the head.

Hank, Fran and I got between them and pulled Reneé behind us. I looked at Sue, "I see you're up to you old tricks again. You have an interesting way of making friends. Tell what your style is again, the Marquis de Sade's Rules of Etiquette, right?"

And then Fran jumped in, "Come on girls, you're better than this. Let's take it outside and try to work this out. Come on, let's settle down. I can see this went a different path than you wanted." I waited for them to smack Fran but oddly they seemed to quiet down, followed him out the door.

Reneé started going too but Hank grabbed her gently. "Let Fran handle them, he's got that soothing voice. You better stay here till they leave." Reneé was still upset, so we moved into the gym to give her time to get composed. I asked how it got started and wasn't surprised to hear they warned her about seeing Nut.

I gave her the background on my dealings with Sue and was surprised to hear her reply. "You Catholic boys are sure a challenge to date."

I recalled our tempestuous past, said simply, "You've got a point."

Reneé made us promise to say nothing to Nut. She

would take care of that herself on their walk home. Just then, Nut peaked around the door, ambled toward us. "Hey, Nut, maybe I should start wrestling. I give you a better tussle than those weenies you've been fighting. I mean, it took you at least ten seconds more to throw the Camel Clutch on me and I didn't wet my pants like that mope." Reneé walked up to him, gently put her arm around him. She looked so tiny, like a little bird next to a bull. And yet somehow they looked perfect together. I had never seen Nut so relaxed as when they were together. And then I thought about him heading off to become a Green Beret, going to Nam and entering that world of violence. I wordlessly thought it was hard to believe we were only 18 years old.

My day with Fran Philips reminded me why we were such great childhood friends. I recalled Hank's comment about Fran's soothing voice. Hank was right; you almost got hypnotized when you chatted with Fran, you felt relaxed being around him. He played basketball the same way, like a peaceful walk in the park. And yet he always stayed cool, no matter how hard you fought to rattle him. I shook my head, thought: It's a gift; he just has it. When I left the gym, Fran was standing by himself, deep in thought. I walked over, "Pretty nice work, how did you tame those crazed savages ?" Fran shrugged, like it was nothing. I added, "I could have used you last summer to prevent me from getting dragged like a dead tree down to face that angry gang of hornets. I really don't like being the only guy in courts history to be held for ransom." Fran laughed. We began our walk home. Before we split off on our own ways, "You ought to think about doing that for a living. Like a hostage negotiator or something. That was impressive."

He got an odd look on his face, "You know what Dylan; I was just thinking the same thing."

TRASH CAN LESSONS

Monsignor Conner was an interesting place to go to school, hysterically funny stuff happened all the time. And you never had to wait long; an oddball occurrence was always lurking like a snake in the grass. With nearly four-thousand boys, Conner was a cauldron of male energy. Consequently, the priests had a strict code of justice. The toughest priests taught the religion classes to the seniors. I had Father Von Vorstad, who was more than up to the challenge. He was about 6'2" and wiry strong. His snow-white hair and steel blue eyes made him look even more intense. I tried my funny religious questions routine as a freshman and promptly got assigned to kneel in the corner while balancing books on both arms. Try that for a few minutes and you'll understand why I walked the straight and narrow thereafter.

But my classmate Tommy Scala was a slow learner. Tommy's dad worked in the post office for Drum's dad, was famous for getting done his route by 11 am and then goofing off at home till check-out time at 4 pm. The Scala's had the nicest lawn in the neighborhood; the result of Mr. Scala spending his working hours manicuring his grass rather than doing shit jobs back at the post office. Drum's dad knew Scala was a screw-off but looked the other way rather than cause a stir in our parish by canning the lazy bum. Consequently, with his old man around so much and a fawning mother, Tommy Scala was spoiled, a world-class mama's boy.

And that's where he ran afoul of Father Van Vorstad. Every night we were assigned chapters from the Bible, had to write our own interpretation of what it meant. Some of the stories were obvious but some took a lot of thought, particularly the Old Testament. For instance, there is lots of confusing, conflicting and perverted information in Leviticus, so Father Van Vorstad skipped the racy sections about having sex with your mother, sister, brother-in-law's wife, other males, animals, etc. He didn't want to discuss them in class, knowing the silliness of teenage boys. But you had to read them overnight and explain what was said. It became obvious that Father never looked at the homework, so Tommy Scala took a shortcut and just wrote nonsense answers, skipped the reading entirely. Not a good move unless you are flawless in execution.

One day, Tommy Scala passed in his assignment. He stupidly wrote a re-cap of the St Joe/Temple basketball game the previous night and Van Vorstad spotted the point guard Jimmy Linahan's name in the 1st paragraph. Father stopped mid-track, started reading the entire assignment. When he was done, he glared at Scala, "Funny boys don't do well in my class. See me at detention after school. The bathroom needs cleaning in the priest's quarters. I'll have a special toothbrush for you." Tommy Scala didn't get home till 7 pm that night and his mother was freaked out with worry for her baby boy. Tommy gave his mom a slanted explanation of his sin. She was hopping mad that her little angel was the victim of such cruelty.

The next day, Mama Scala came to Father Van Vorstad's class, knocked on the door, demanding to speak to him. I sat next to Tommy, asked what this was about. With a smug look on his face, "My mom's gonna chew him out for keeping me so late, tell him he has to call her before he keeps me after school and makes me miss the bus. My mom is gonna put him in his place."

I looked at him, smiled my smuggest smile, "This should be fun." The whole class strained to hear what was going on outside. You could hear Mrs. Scala screaming and Father yelling back. Pretty soon they marched off towards the Head of Discipline's office and everybody sat back in their seats.

Tommy Scala smirked at me, "Told ya."

I smirked back, "We'll see."

About 15 minutes later, Father Van Vorstad ambled back, shut the door softly and turned to face the class. He started talking about the ponderous mysteries of Leviticus and after a couple minutes, stopped mid-sentence. "I almost forgot, Mr. Scala, come to the front of the class." Tommy reluctantly marched to the front. Father gestured at the trash can in the corner. "Fetch that can and put it on my desk." After Tommy did that he looked very wary. Father grinned, "Now kneel on my chair and place your head in the trash can. Make sure you don't tip the can over and make a mess." Tommy Scala stood frozen, trying to absorb what he was supposed to do. Van Vorstad moved quickly, gently grabbed the paralyzed Scala and helped him get into the precarious kneeling position. We watched as Scala knelt on the chair, which was moved close enough to the desk so that Tommy could fit his head inside the trash can without tipping it. Without another word, Father grabbed a wooden pointer, continued his talk on the perversions mentioned in Leviticus and whenever a key fact was made, slammed his pointer into the tin trash can for emphasis. You could see Scala shudder at the resounding noise.

And so the class continued. Father Van Vorstad went into great detail about the seeming inconsistencies found in the Old Testament versus the New Testament. He explained that the Old Testament set the basis for modern day Judeo-Christian faith and foretold the coming of the Messiah. I had a million questions but didn't think he wanted to be interrupted. Parts of the Old Testament were so poetic and beautifully written, but other sections seemed so cruel. How could you reconcile the two? The Old Testament God seemed angry and unforgiving compared to the New Testament's kindness of Jesus. I sat silently, thinking I'd ask Monsignor Pugh at the next CCD section. And then I realized that Father Van Vorstad was just like how I imagined a priest in the Old Testament—stern and punishing. But then you had Monsignor Pugh, who was kind, understanding—a priest that the New Testament described. Was there place for both styles? Before I could think that through, Father stopped lecturing and asked if we had learned anything new today.

I was tired of so many deep, gloomy thoughts so I raised my hand. "What is it Frazier?"

With my straightest face, "Father, I learned if my mother wants me to master how to kneel perfectly balanced with my head in a trash can, she should come by and interrupt your class." The whole class roared, even Father Van Bredakoff smiled.

JUDO AT JIMMERS

We didn't have basketball practice, so I met Truck and Nut after school. Nut told us he was headed to Jimmer's house for a judo lesson. I remembered witnessing Nut stunning the punk on the subway with a palm slap a few weeks ago and wanted to see if I could pick up that move. The legendary court commissioner Jimmer Keilmann lived across the street from me and was like an irritating but protective big brother since I moved to Drexel Heights. We knocked on the door, Mrs. Keilmann answered. She was a dour lady, not one to smile much. However, she had known me for years, for some reason found me funny. "Hey, Mrs. Keilmann, is Jimmer home? I heard he was giving judo lessons and wanted to get some tips. My mom's been pushing me around a lot lately. I thought maybe she needed to be taught a lesson. You know, a couple well executed shoulder tosses might back her off some."

Since my sweet mom was under five feet and weighed 98lbs, that was quite a vision. Truck started laughing and pretty soon Mrs. Keilmann smiled. Shaking her head, "He's in the basement boys, just like he always is. I wish he weren't so physical. Why can't he play the piano or something artistic?" I thought to myself: Because he's violent and mildly off center? But I passed silently, headed down the steps.

We were still giggling as we moved into Jimmer's lair. He stared at us, "What's so funny, did my mom frisk you at the front door?"

Nut filled him in, "Dylan told your mom he was going to smack his mother around with some of your judo moves. You know what a big, tough lady she is."

Jimmer didn't miss a beat, "Sometimes the little ones surprise you. You can never be too prepared." With that as a starting point, Jimmer went to the record player, put on a Bob Dylan album. Since I was nicknamed after the scrawny singer, I wondered what song Jimmer had chosen. He turned to us, like an orchestra leader directing his musicians, "Listen, young lads and pay attention, for indeed these are solemn days." Just then, "The Times They Are A-Changin'" cranked on. Dylan began, "Come gather round people, wherever you roam, and admit the waters around you have grown and accept it that soon you'll be drenched to the bone, if your time to you is worth savin', then you better start swimmin' or you'll sink like a stone, for the times they are a changin'." And so the gloomy, foreboding song went.

We listened intently, knowing Jimmer would quiz us afterwards. Different thoughts swirled. Was the song about racial unrest or Vietnam? Or was it both? The late 60's were weird times, people were wound up. They wanted action. My world revolved around basketball, so the cultural angst didn't hit me much. It wasn't that I didn't care; it was just something that didn't affect me directly. I was trying to win a city championship and help my two buddies get their lives on course. That drove me hard enough. In fact, it obsessed me. But Jimmer was different, he felt passionately that the world was screwed up and he was going to do something about it. As a History and Philosophy major at La Salle College, Jimmer was notorious on campus for challenging the professors. He was a born debater, loved twisting words to make the teachers look silly. Legend had it that one scrawny professor took a swing at Jimmer when he told him in front of the class, "You don't know Francis Bacon from a BLT sandwich." I watched Jimmer for years and never saw anyone best him verbally. I listened carefully to Dylan's song, formulated what I hoped was a sensible response.

The song ended. I watched Jimmer breath in, as if absorbing the wisdom. He began, "Okay, gentlemen, what have you learned? We don't begin the lessons until I'm sure you aren't morons. I mean, it isn't smart to teach monkeys to fight." None of us raised our hands. Jimmer smirked, "I've got all day, no say, no play."

Nut started, "I think it's about the Vietnam War. That Bob Dylan thinks it's stupid, that we shouldn't be fighting." He paused, added, "Personally, I think Bob Dylan's a pussy."

I seized the moment before Jimmer erupted, "I think Nut means that as a compliment. That Dylan supports the Feminist viewpoint. That he's a seer, almost a visionary that's in touch with the female sensibility." I looked at the grinning Nut, "That is what you meant, right?"

Truck jumped in, "No, no, what Nut really meant was that Bob Dylan is a pussy. But in a good way."

Jimmer cocked his head to the side, sneered a little; looked us over slowly, "I think maybe the Three Stooges got some competition. Let's begin."

Jimmer's basement wasn't like my moldy cellar, it was fully finished, had been transformed into a combination martial arts and weight lifting room. Posters of body builders Charles Atlas and Joe Weider adorned the walls. There were life-size shots of muscle men, all greased up and rippling. These men were Jimmer's physical role models. A speed bag and heavy bag hung from the ceiling. Jimmer dabbled with boxing for years but recently switched to Judo. His goal was to be a Sensei, the highest honor in his opinion. Judo appealed to his sense of the underdog fighting against a bigger, stronger opponent. Truck wasn't interested in judo, so he wandered over to the speed bag, pounded away. I watched as Jimmer began working with Nut, trying to give him tips on using more of judo's balance and leverage in his wrestling moves. Jimmer was very stiff on the basketball court, so I was amazed to see how fluid and efficient he moved on the mats. I decided to keep that to myself; knew he'd bury me with a retort if I gave a half-assed compliment.

I wandered over to Truck, said quietly, "Did you get to talk with your dad about the cemetery?"

He looked to see if Jimmer was paying attention. He and Nut were deep in discussion. "Not yet, I was going to the other day but didn't want to ruin the mood. Sue was in the car, my mom has to be a sticky point for her." He looked at me, "How about we hit the store tomorrow after practice. Sue's been leaving early to get dinner ready." I still wasn't sure it was smart to have me there, said so. "I might chicken-out if you aren't there. You know, you can give me moral support. Plus my dad usually shuts me off when I bring it up. Maybe you can get him to talk. You have that way of saying bad stuff without pissing people off." And then he grinned, "I told dad about religion class the other day when Scala got his head in the trash can. He was laughing about that all night." I nodded, wondering what I would say.

Just then I heard Jimmer drop Nut to the mat with a thud. "Jimmer looked at him with expectation, "Did you feel how that jarred your kidney? Kinds of sends a chill through your spine, right?"

Nut sat on the mat, thinking. And then, "That's amazing, just by angling the fall you can add a new dimension to the shock." He nodded his head in admiration, "Perfect, Jimmer, perfect."

I wandered over, "Jimmer, can you show me that ear smack you taught Nut? He really rang the guy's bell on the subway the other day. That schmuck looked like he had a cherry bomb go off in his head."

Jimmer took me over to the heavy bag and went through the mechanics of the slap. "The trick is getting the palm flat enough to create air pressure into the ear; kind of like an implosion forcing all the pressure inward. Just punching his ear with the fist doesn't work. It will hurt the guy, but not disable him immediately." And then he looked at us with maniacal glee, "Watching his eyes spin back is much more fun."

Nut and Truck nodded approvingly. I looked at them. "Maybe I need to hang around with higher caliber friends. Seems I'm surrounded by Neanderthals." Jimmer nodded, "That's why you fit in."

I practiced the swat and Jimmer kept refining my hit. He showed me how flat he got his palm as he struck. He was right; his strike had a different sound, almost like a pop. Mine had a thud sound. I did it until my hand hurt but never quite got it right. Jimmer nodded, "It takes practice. You're hand is too tense. Once you learn to relax it, the strike will improve. Like everything, it takes practice. Stop over the next few days and we'll work on it."

Nut walked over and smacked the bag, getting the perfect pop noise. Nut turned to me, "It took me a week, doing it for an hour a day. Once you get it, it's like riding a bike, you just do it automatically."

And then Truck walked over and hit the bag with his fist, producing a tremendous crunch. He looked at us, "The other way is smacking the piss out of the guy."

Jimmer smirked, "My Neanderthal comrade has a point, there are other ways to skin the cat."

♦

On the way home from Jimmer's, I asked Nut if he had any luck with Digger's hidden records. He shook his head, "They must be at the Funeral Home. I've looked everywhere else."

Truck asked, "Do you really believe he's ripping dead people off? I mean; that is really psycho." As close as they were, Nut never told Truck about his abusive father. I'd been pushing him to bring Truck into the secret. My thinking was it might help both of them to discuss their problems. Truck had finally opened up to Nut about his mother, about his dad lying to him; it seemed to soften him somehow. But today without warning Nut started talking. He put his arm around Truck's massive shoulder, began, "Let me tell you how really sick Digger is."

As we stood on that quiet corner of Shady Lane, Nut poured out his heart. Truck stood with his eyes wide open, didn't even seem to be breathing he stood so still. At the end he hugged Nut, and then looked at him, "That fuckin' bastard. I'll kick his ass."

And so it began. My closest friends were now voicing their dark secrets. When Nut talked about killing Digger, Truck never flinched. Instead, fury in his eyes; "Let me know when you need help." That instant response got me thinking. These two were like brothers in torment but I had nothing in common with the misery that had torn them for years. But I did feel that I was helping by just listening, pushing them to say what they were thinking, not keeping it bottled up. I mean, I didn't know what the hell to do, but I did know it was better to go through it with someone. Now I understood better why Truck had become such an angry fighter, so ferocious. Now I knew why Nut worked so hard to literally wrestle his demons. I looked at these giant boys, resolved to help them find some peace. Normally I found something funny to say to break the tension. Today we parted silently but I could see both Truck and Nut walked a little easier.

MORAL SUPPORT

Truck and I talked about how to approach his dad as we walked out of practice next day. I warned mom I'd be a little later than normal. "Have to go to Mr. Carr's shop after practice, he needs me to help him clean up at the shop." She never questioned me helping Truck. She had a soft spot for my sad friend.

On the drive there, Truck looked at me sheepishly, "I'll start out with dad but if I start to go off track or blather too much, take over, okay?"

I could tell he was jumpy. To break the tension, "How can I tell when you're blathering? I mean, most of the stuff coming out of your mouth is either profanity or something to do with a girl's body." His head spun around as I added, "What I'm saying is that blathering is a step up from your normal perverted ramblings. Why should I slow up your maturity progress?" He started to roll his eyes as I added, "Relax, I'll help out if you need it. It will all be over pretty soon." What I didn't say was my apprehension or the likelihood for making any progress. Why would Mr. Carr suddenly open up?

We parked behind the shop, spotted his dad's car. Truck exhaled, "Good, Sue's car's gone. She's been leaving earlier to make sure I had a nice dinner after practice. Usually, dad is about 45 minutes behind her and we eat together." He added, "It's pretty nice. I can see she makes dad really happy."

Truck didn't normally add personal comments so I

pushed him, "Do you think they'll ever get married?" I could see him struggling with an answer. I quickly said, "I mean otherwise your dad will go to hell and get boiled alive with worms and snakes for living in sin."

Truck frowned but recovered quickly, "You really are an asshole." But then, "But since you mentioned it, I've been thinking about telling Sue I think they should get married. I think they waited long enough. My dad needs to be happy."

Truck got a sad look on his face. I patted his thick shoulder, "That would probably make all of you happy."

We entered the shop, watched Mr. Carr waiting on a customer. They were haggling over the price of rib-eye steak. The customer said, "In my day, Bob, prime rib-eye used to cost 25 cents a pound. Where you get off charging a buck? What is it some sacred cow from India?"

Bob Carr looked patiently at the wizened old man, "In your day Mr. Lorenz, the cows were outside the store and you just shot what you needed, no middleman to worry about. Times have changed." The old bird just shook his head, ambled off. And then Mr. Carr noticed us, got a big grin on his face. "That old coot drives a Caddie and lives in Forest Park next to the rich beer families. He could eat steak breakfast, lunch and dinner and never put a dent in his wallet. Just one of those guys who likes to bitch."

I looked at Mr. Carr, "Do you want me to egg his house on the way home."

Mr. Carr chuckled, "Tempting, very tempting."

And with me loosening Mr. Carr up, I looked at Truck, raised my eyebrows for him to begin. "Er, ah, Dad. I've been meaning to, er, ask about how Mom, er, ah, died." Truck looked at me to take over but I shook my head, signaled him to continue. He stammered, "I want to talk about mom. Was she sick or something? Why was she taking medicine? Dylan and I got a copy of her death certificate, it said she died from an overdose. What was wrong with her?"

Mr. Carr didn't reply, looked at Truck, "Why is Dylan here. This is a family matter."

I said the only thing I could, "Moral support. Even though Truck is a big, tough lummox, he has a hard time when it gets to his mom. I just want to help him." Mr. Carr usually laughed at my quips. This time he stared through me. He was angry but didn't seem surprised by Truck's questions about his mother. That struck me as odd. But I stayed quiet, watched Mr. Carr while he talked.

Mr. Carr shifted his gaze to Truck, his anger boiled up again. "This is between you and I. Dylan should leave."

Suddenly I saw that burn in Truck's eyes, like he got before pummeling someone. He spits back at his father, "He stays. I'm sick of you dodging the questions. Tell me about mom. I deserve to know."

I jumped in, "It's okay, Truck, I'll leave if your dad wants me to."

He spun toward me, pointed his meaty finger, "Stay!"
I stayed.

Mr. Carr seemed to have regained his cool. "Okay
son, let's go into the office and sit. This is a long story."
We moseyed into what he called an office, just a desk and
a few chairs surrounded by butcher-block tables smeared
with dried blood. I thought silently about the bloody
setting. An omen?

Mr. Carr began a tale of his fortunate assignment to
England and eventual duty at the Nuremburg Trials. He
talked about guarding Truck's mom, falling in love with
her, asking her to marry him and their return to the States.
He looked fondly at Truck, "Your mom was like a
beautiful fairytale princess." I kept my eyes forward,
worried I might start to cry if I saw Truck starting to lose
it. Mr. Carr continued, "But your mom had a hard time
adjusting to life in Philly. She missed her family and
friends. Pretty soon she started having nervous problems.
We got pills to calm her down." During the monologue, I
watched Mr. Carr closely, was surprised how smoothly he
went through the story. He didn't get emotional. I knew I
was. Maybe it was so long ago he just buried those
feelings? I decided to dismiss my thoughts but was puzzled
by his composure. I had always watched people's body
language, found it interesting. There was usually a story
beyond the words. But this was Mr. Carr, who I liked a lot.
Maybe I was way off, misreading composure for
something he had to reconcile long ago. Something he had
finally faced and put to rest.

Anyway, Mr. Carr explained that eventually the

depression got too great and apparently she took too many pills by accident, died from an overdose. He looked at Truck, "I think she just lost track. I didn't want to tell you about all this because I didn't want you to have bad feelings and memories of your mom. Maybe I made a mistake hiding it from you." I again noticed Mr. Carr looked strangely still. He said all the right words but he seemed too mechanical. Again I swallowed my jaded impressions, listened to the finale. "Your mom was a strict Lutheran and made it clear she wanted to be cremated. That's why we never visited her grave. She wanted her ashes returned to Germany and scattered in her home village." That last sentence shocked me. I looked at Truck to see if he reacted the same way. My huge friend was slumped in his chair, emotionally sapped. But alarms were exploding in my head.

But I kept my mouth shut, waited outside the shop for Truck and his dad to have time together. I shifted from one foot to the other, nervous about what I was going to say. Finally Truck came out, we walked to his car. I looked at him, "Let me drive. I have to tell you something that might distract your driving."

He looked at me oddly, "What?"

I pushed him to the shotgun seat, "Just get in and listen." And then I added, "Don't overreact, maybe I'm wacked out." He listened wordlessly as I told him my worries. "Your mom's death certificate said she was Catholic—not Lutheran. Plus your dad told that story like he was reading something from a book. Almost like he wrote it out." Truck still hadn't said anything. "And I wonder if he got a call from the cemetery people that we were snooping around. That's why he threw in that story about sending her ashes to Germany."

Truck's eyes kept blinking. He started breathing fast. And then he turned to me and howled, "Fuuuuuuuuck!"

I pulled the car over about a block from my house. I'd given this a lot of thought since our cemetery fiasco. And Mr. Carr's performance made me more certain. I told Truck my plan. "Maybe I'm way off base. But I think if we poke around your old neighborhood, maybe visit the church there, we can find out if she was buried or cremated. I mean some neighbor must remember something. Right?" He nodded, still quieter than I liked. I grabbed his arm. "Stay cool with your dad till we figure this out. If he is bullshitting you there must be a damn good reason. Your dad worships the ground you walk on. There must be some reason he's doing this. Can you stay cool?"

Truck exhaled, got a serious look on his face, "I know my dad loves me but I think you're right. He's lying for some reason. I just can't understand why." And then he got a determined look on that strong face. "I've got to find out what really happened to my mom. It's tearing me up."

Since spouting my earlier theory, I had a troubling thought. That his mom committed suicide and his dad was trying to spare him anguish. That had to be it. But Truck needed to know the truth, no matter how painful. But then I wondered silently if maybe Mr. Carr wasn't right. Maybe he was trying to prevent Truck from worrying he might have inherited the same mental problems. What had I done. How can I back out of this?

WESTBROOK ACADEMY

Our next game was against Westbrook Academy. It sat on the western fringe of Philly, within a world-class loogie spit from the tony Main Line, light years away in wealth. Westbrook was a private school that traditionally got many of the best players from the public school system. Parents sent their kids there to avoid the harsh realities of the inner city system, to give them a jump-start to a better life. Many of those athletes couldn't afford the tuition but scholarships were made available if the kid was a great player. They always had a powerhouse team, many alums played in college and some made the NBA. This was a non-conference game to get us ready for the post season. As a private school, Westbrook would not be in the city title competition. We would face no team this good on our march to the elusive city title.

As usual, the brainy Drum scouted Westbrook in advance, came back with a rare approach. "I told Coach that I evaluated their strengths, matched them against ours and then devised a way I would attack us if I were them."

Truck looked at Drum, said what we all were thinking, "What the fuck are you talking about?"

Coach Gallagher shushed him immediately, "Truck, watch your mouth, let him explain."

Drum smiled back at us, "Let me break it down to simpler terms for the numb-nuts like Truck." Coach Gallagher started to scold him but shook his head and waved him on. "What I mean is rather than the normal way of studying them and devising a defense, I devised how they would probably defend us and built an offensive scheme to beat it." He paused as he saw the lights go on in our faces. "So, we will do the opposite of what they expect. If we frustrate them enough by being unpredictable, I think it will also screw up their offense and get us an edge."

We sat there, silently absorbing the plan. And Drum added, "Their best guy is Sal Palducci. After Scoot hounds the shit outta him, Dylan gets him at half court and stays on him like shit on a pig."

Gallagher jumps in, "Clean it up Drum."

He nodded, "Sorry Coach, like excrement on a porcine beast is what I meant to say." I howled, then the whole team erupts. When we quieted, "As I was saying, Sal has a weird quirk. He likes to draw contact when he drives. He keeps his left arm out, feels for contact then pushes off. I don't know how but the refs never call him for an offensive foul." He looked at me, "Dylan, using your best charm, ask the ref to watch for it. Maybe we'll catch a ref that doesn't have his head in his a…" He looked at Coach, "Er, his rectum."

And that's how we prepared. We always pressed at the start, played full-court man-to-man, occasionally mixing in some 2-3 zone. On offense, Drum said Westbrook always played zone defense and would expect us to work the ball into Truck. He'd try to score low and if covered, he'd flip it Fran Philips cutting into the lane. Everybody expected that but could rarely stop them. But this game we brought Truck to the high post to draw the wing defenders to him. And then he was to feed Fran or me for open wing shots. Scoot was a safety valve for Truck if he couldn't get the ball to us. Drum would watch who was getting the shot and move to the opposite side for the possible rebound. (Drum advised that 70% of our misses were long and went to the opposite side from the shooter. We just nodded at him like we already knew that.) Truck would fill in Drum's vacant spot in case the rebound didn't go to Drum. Naturally, Fran and I were expected to make our easy looks.

Defensively, we played zone and mixed in half-court traps after scores or free throws. Except that Scoot would guard whoever brought the ball down court, pestering them like an angry bee. The rest of us stayed back in a 2-2 zone until Scoot got over half-court and stopped his kamikaze routine. It took us a couple days to time the new system but we finally got it down. Westbrook was undefeated, slaughtering most of their opponents. They were like playing against an all-star team, much bigger than us, with tall, quick guards. But they never had someone like Scoot on their tail. From years of him tormenting me, I knew they had a shock waiting for them—no matter how good and quick they were.

That night against Westbrook, I felt confident as we went into lay-up drills. But then I noticed the look on Truck's face. He was always determined as he stepped on the court. But tonight he was mumbling to himself, not talking to anyone. When I looked at his eyes I knew Westbrook was in trouble. He had been much calmer since we started digging into his mother's death, almost at peace. But the rage seemed to return after our bullshit session with his father. I let Fran and Drum pass me in the drills so I could get beside Truck. I wandered up as he waited for his turn. "Hey, Truck, you look awful, are you constipated or something? I told you to lay off the bananas, they bind you up."

No smile. He looked at me, "Those private school faggots are gonna pay." He darted for his final layup as the ref blew his whistle.

Drum's plan was a masterpiece. Westbrook looked confused as Truck made shot after shot from the high post. If he missed, Drum grabbed the rebound, scored easily or fed Fran or me for wide-open shots. Scoot stripped their guards twice for quick hoops. It got to the point that no one wanted to bring the ball up—Scoot scared the shit out of them. Our defense confused them. They were clearly ready to play against our man-to-man and started lofting long shots in frustration. My worries about Truck proved wrong. He played hard but scored so easily he didn't have to use his normal ferocious inside game. We were up by 20 points at half. As we walked into the locker room, Drum rejoiced, "Am I the fucking Einstein of hoops or what?"

Coach Gallagher yelled, "Watch the language Drum."

He grinned, "Sorry, Coach, but ya gotta admit, my shit is rosy." Coach rolled his eyes.

Westbrook adjusted in the second half. We couldn't hit a shot and their big guys started gobbling up every miss, laying them in. I could see Truck getting agitated, like he was about to take over the game. But even my talented friend couldn't stop the Westbrook assault. By the end of the third quarter, our lead was down to four points. Coach Gallagher looked at us, eyes never wavering, "Okay, guys, back to our normal defense and offense. The surprise is over. They adjusted and now it's time to get back to what we do best. Let's get back our momentum. Back to man-to man defense. Dylan, you got Palducci, remember what Drum told you."

Till that point, Palducci spent his energy getting the ball past Scoot and then finding his big guys for easy buckets. But suddenly, Sal Palducci started getting clear lanes to the hoop and as scouted, seemed to wait for me, then jammed his forearm into my chest and got two quick fouls on me. When Sal went to the foul line, I walked over, "Your parents must be poetic." He scrunched his eyebrows in puzzlement. "I mean, Sal and Palducci rhyme. Kind of has a friendly ring to it. Just think if they named you Heathcliff or Hector. I mean that would have made you sound like a total dick. Your whole life would be altered." I could see him frowning as I walked away.

I walked over to the one refs I knew since grade school. "Hey, Smitty, Sal has that great move where he slams his left arm into my chest as he goes for a layup. I always thought that was a foul but I guess the rules changed, huh?" I smiled and walked away before he answered.

Smitty hung out at the local sports bar in Drexel Heights, drank like a fish but never seemed affected. My dad went to the same bar, told me, "Smitty's liver will be in the Smithsonian when he dies. That is one miracle organ."

But he was a respected college ref. He only did important high school games. I was hoping I planted a seed without seeming to be a whiner.

We maintained our four point lead, only had a 2 minutes left when all hell broke loose. Westbrook's star big man was Ronnie Musburger. He already had a full ride to Michigan. He and Truck had been waging war under the boards, with no clear winner up till now. It was a battle of the beasts. But Sal broke by me down the lane and funnels a perfect pass to Musburger. Just as he's about to lay it in, Truck thunders from nowhere, drives his forearm into his chest and takes him hard out of bounds. Smitty blew his whistle, gives Truck a flagrant technical for unnecessary force. When he starts to argue, Smitty T'd him again and tosses him out of the game. I could see Truck was about to blow. I grabbed him, pulled him toward the bench. As I got him seated, I looked at his enraged face, had never seen him this out of control. He mumbled, "My mom, I gotta find out about my mom." Without believing it, I looked in his eyes. "I promise I'll take care of it."

If this had been a league game, Truck would have been disqualified for the season. Since it was an exhibition between two non-league powerhouses, Truck could still play in the Catholic League. We ended up winning the game by four points as Fran Philips made a slithery drive and hit a pair of free throws as time expired. I didn't score much but got Sal Palducci to foul out with three quick offensive fouls after my chat with Smitty. I'd have to remind my dad to buy him a beer. But my joy was short-lived. I was really worried about Truck as we road home on the team bus. What should have been a fun celebration was somber because of Truck's violence. Coach Gallagher wouldn't even look at him, afraid of what he'd say. And Truck was worse. He wouldn't say a word, no matter how I goaded him. Finally, I just sat quietly beside him, letting him wrestle his demons. But on that quiet ride home I fought my own battle: How do we find the truth about his mom without devastating him? And then thought about Nut. Would he really kill Digger?

THE HUNT BEGINS

Truck was back to his version of normal the next day. He seemed to have forgotten his act of violence. Walking to class that morning, I poked him about it. "Dylan, the guy's a punk. He was asking for it. He talked non-stop about kicking my white ass. I just had enough. Forget about it." I decided to let it pass, not mention how he'd screw the team if he got disqualified. My surly friend had enough on his mind. I had been thinking non-stop about tying the loose pieces together on his mom's death, came up with two ideas. First, make a run to far off Shillington, poke around the post office to see if we could find something about the phantom letters. But that would take us most of a day. We'd need to do it on an off day from school and practice.

I had another idea that we could do right away, ran it by Truck as we walked to our locker after our last class. "Why don't we head to your old neighborhood, see if anyone remembers your mom. Maybe some of your old neighbors are still around." Even though I was now convinced his dad was just protecting him about his mom's suicide, it might soften the blow if he met some people who knew her before she got depressed.

Truck's eyes lit up, "I kinda remember a lady across the street, I think she watched me sometime. I think I can find the right house." We had the day off practice after our grueling win over Westbrook. We headed off to Sharon Heights to do some detective work. Truck's old neighborhood was careworn. Once a thriving mill town, Sharon Heights was now losing the battle to neglect. Like

Truck's family, anyone who could afford to moved away. There were still nice pockets of homes but many were beat up, ramshackle.

As we entered the tattered area, I looked at Truck, "Lucky you moved, if you had stayed you'd be more disturbed than you already are. I mean, with your temper, you'd be beating up dogs and cats when you ran out of other kids to pound." As a reply, he slammed his meaty fist into my shoulder, grinned. I feigned injury, "Better watch it Truck, Coach Gallagher needs me healthy to score after you get thrown out of the league."

Truck grinned wider, "The way you've been shooting lately, he better find another solution." He had me there.

We pulled into Truck's old street, parked in front of his former house. It was a nice Victorian, complete with elaborate moldings but desperately in need of a paint job. The original burgundy, white and gray colors were chipped and faded to a neutral hue. Truck looked at it, "Sad, looks like an old battleship. I kinda remember it being so big and cool. There were lots of little rooms and hiding places. Now look at it."

I gave him a pat, "Let's walk up and knock on a few doors." I was a step or so behind Truck, realized how big he was, like a side of beef. I was used to seeing him but I wondered how scary he might look to some old man or lady opening the door and seeing this hulking stranger.

"Hey, Truck, let me go first. Stay behind me so you don't scare them. I mean you aren't the prettiest face in the beauty pageant." He chuckled. Maybe he was snapping out of his funk. I was trying to act nonchalant but last night still had me spooked. I'd never seen him so desperate. The first house was a bust.

An old lady came to the door, looked at us skeptically. "I ain't need no new vacuum cleaner. The old one still works good." She added, "Wish it had more power, though. Enough to swallow up that old man a mine. Now there's one useless piece of nothin'." She got a contented look on her face, pleased with that thought. Turned to us, "Beat it!" and slammed the door shut.

I looked at Truck, "I guess she didn't think I was the Avon Lady." We ambled back to the sidewalk before she called the police.

Truck stood still, started looking at the houses across the street. He nodded, "I think that old brick one might be the lady I was remembering. I'm pretty sure mom used to take me there once in awhile." And then he thought some more, "Might be Mrs. Donlan or, er, something Irish, I think."

We knocked on the door, waited. Nothing. We hit the doorbell a few times but didn't hear anything. "Might be broken," I surmised brilliantly.

Truck then hit the door hard enough to register on the Richter Scale. He grinned, "If she doesn't hear that, then she won't hear anything."

I nodded, "Or you'll scare the shit out of her and she'll call the fuzz." We were halfway down the sidewalk when the door started to open. A nice looking, red-haired lady stared at us. She was wearing an old dress, but it was neat and clean, like she couldn't afford much but still had good taste. She seemed hesitant to open the screen door to strangers, particularly a couple of big teenagers. Breaking the ice, "Sorry to bother you ma'am, my buddy Bobby Carr used to live across the street and is trying to find some information about his mom."

I watched happily as this handsome lady stared at Truck, got the biggest, prettiest smile on her face and pushed the door open. "My dear God, Robbie Carr, you're the spitting image of your dad but you have Gert's eyes and blonde hair."

She threw open the screen, rushed up to him, gave him a crushing hug. She kept staring at him. "What a sight for sore eyes. Come on in. Let's get you boys something to eat." Wished I could have filmed the look on Truck's face—pure joy. Hadn't seen him so happy for years. And then I remembered she called him "Robbie," just as he remembered his mom called him and also the mysterious letter writer. As we walked through the tired looking house, I noticed it was spotlessly clean. Not much money, but a ton of dignity.

We made our way to the kitchen and watched Mrs. Delaney, her name, as we learned, rummaging for snacks. I said, "Bobby isn't real fussy about what he eats. If you have some possum and grits or bag of toe nails, that'll do him fine."

Truck looked at Mrs. Delaney, "Ignore him, he's my best friend but he has a few screws loose." She chuckled pleasantly, enjoying having company.

She put some chocolate chip cookies and a glass of milk in front of us, sat and watched us devour her snacks. "Now what can I do for you."

Per our plan, I was the mouthpiece. "Truck, er I mean Robbie is trying to find more information about his mom. Mr. Carr has been reluctant to talk about her." I lifted my shoulders as emphasis, "Must be too painful for him. Anyway, Robbie wants to hear more about her, maybe visit her grave and just try to learn more about her, that sort of thing."

Mrs. Delaney beamed, "Gert was my best friend, you've come to the right place." She sat back in her chair, getting more comfortable. "I can believe your dad doesn't want to talk about it. He was really broken up. He shut off all the neighbors after Gert passed. Didn't say a word to anybody. And then he ups and moves. I haven't heard a word from him since." And then, "It will be good for him to talk it out some, I never felt right about how it ended. He was acting almost like Gert never existed."

Mrs. Delaney went on to tell us some interesting facts. "Gert was my best friend. After we got Robbie off to school, we'd walk to 9 o'clock mass, have tea and cookies after church. We used to gab away about everything. She'd tell me about growing up in Germany, how simple life was in her village. Er.., before the Nazi's took over, that is." She paused, seeming lost in a pleasant memory.

I jumped in, "So, Mrs. Carr was Catholic? We weren't sure about that."

She nodded her head, "Gert was a devout Catholic. She knew the mass forward and backward in Latin. Sang the hymns out loud, she had a beautiful voice. I enjoyed going to mass with her. Her devotion was contagious." Mrs. Delaney got a nice look on her face, "Gert had a real gift with languages. She spoke French and English like she was a native." And then she grinned, "Well she did have a slight accent but her grammar was perfect, she could have been an English teacher if she wanted to. Gert was one smart lady." Again she paused before adding, "But she was even better in math. She did the books for your Dad's shop. I think she was an accountant in Germany." I sat quietly, trying to sift through facts, trying to form a picture of Gert Carr. She sounded impressive. But I was shocked by the devout Catholic information. Why had Mr. Carr lied? Thought about her cremation; it didn't add up.

Truck had been silent, but suddenly asked, "Do you remember anything about my mom's funeral. Or where she was buried." His voiced tailed off; I thought he was about to tear up.

I jumped in, "Robbie wants to visit the grave and can't seem to get anywhere with the cemetery."

Mrs. Delaney got a puzzled look on her face. "That day is still a blur. I watched Robbie during the church service. Your dad wanted a closed casket and private ceremony at St Cyril. None of the neighbors were invited."

I interrupted, "So, St Cyril might have a record about the burial?" Not looking at Truck, I added, "There seems some idea that Mrs. Carr wanted to be cremated. That make any sense to you?"

Mrs. Delaney shook her head vehemently, "That's ridiculous. Gert Carr was the holiest person I ever met. She thanked God daily for sparing her from the Nazi's and loved this country even more for letting her live in peace. Gert Carr felt this was her home. She would have wanted to be buried here. She was ashamed of Germany."

I decided to switch gears. "Do you know if Mrs. Carr was sick? She seems to have died from taking some medication incorrectly."

Mrs. Delaney stared incredulously, "Gert was healthy as a horse. We were with each other every day for years. I never knew her to be sick. In fact, I can't even remember her getting a cold." And then, "I'm the one who was sick all the time. Gert used to make me herb teas to help my congestion. I don't know what was in them but they sure cleared me up."

And then I hit the punch line, "So, do you know what Mrs. Carr died from? I mean; she was pretty young."

Mrs. Delaney looked at me thoughtfully. "I heard it was heart problems, like a stroke or something. But it was so shocking because she was so robust, the picture of health. And then all of a sudden, she was gone." She became silent, gulping deeply, composing herself. "Her passing left a big hole in my life. I had never married, had no family around anymore. She was like a sister to me."

We parted company, with Truck giving her a big hug and promising to drop by soon. I looked at my hulking friend; smothering this sweet lady with the affection he was never able to give his own mom. Then I started to gulp, trying to hold it together. I turned toward the street and exhaled. Phew. Truck got in the car, looked at me fiercely. "My dad's been bullshitting me. Every thing he said the other night was a lie. What's going on?"

He was getting fired-up when I stopped him. "There has to be some reason why your dad kept this from you. Your dad is crazy about you. Thinks you're the second coming. That you walk on water." To lighten the moment, "I told your dad you better carry a life preserver 'cause your fat ass is gonna sink any day now. But he won't listen, still thinks you're some kind of prize."

Truck's expression went from near rage to reluctant puzzlement. "You really are an asshole, Dylan." But soon added, "But you're right, there must be some reason we just can't see. What could it be?" He said quietly for a few seconds. As he started the car, "Thanks for helping. I couldn't do this alone."

We rode to St Cyril to see what we could find out about the burial service. We knocked at the rectory. A portly woman answered the door. Her hair was in a high, tight bun, so tight that it looked painful. Reminded me of the surly lady at the cemetery. I couldn't help myself. "My mom wears her hair in a bun but can't seem to get it tight enough. Has hairs flying out the side. Kind of like they're trying to escape from prison. Got any tips I can share with her. She'd appreciate it."

At first she looked annoyed but relented. "The trick is getting enough pomade on first. Plaster it down firm, then don't let go of the ponytail till all the hairs are gathered. Then you pin up the bun. Don't spare the bobby pins."

She nodded proudly, "Takes effort. People now days like to slough off. A good hair bun and slackers don't make good bed fellows."

I gave her a sincere nod. "Great tips, thanks."

But that was the only fun we had. A retired priest, Father Gallimore showed us the records, let us look at what they had. There wasn't much but we learned Gerda Carr's funeral service was held at St Cyril. The casket was closed and a mass was said. The records showed she was buried at Holy Cross Cemetery. No mention of cremation. Just to be sure, I asked, "Anyway Mrs. Carr could have been cremated and then buried?"

The old priest looked at me quietly, "Not unless somehow the monkeys start running the zoo. Cremation is forbidden in the Roman Catholic faith."

I chuckled, "So you can't get through the pearly gates unless you are properly buried. That's what I thought. Thanks, Father."

We ambled back to Truck's car, compared notes. Truck summed it up. "My dad is covering this up for some reason. But why?" I had been thinking the same thing.

Had Truck's mom killed herself and Mr. Carr covered it up? Was he just sparing Truck this heartache? Didn't want him to think he might inherit the coo-coo genes. But to Truck, "We'll figure it out. We just need to keep looking. There's an obvious answer we're missing." He shook his head, put the old car in gear. We drove home in silence.

♦

When I got back from Truck's old neighborhood, my mom was busy making dinner—it was pork shank that melted off the bone, mashed potatoes and carrots cooked with the pork drippings. I wandered over to my tiny mother, gave her a bear hug. She turned, "What's that for?"

I hugged her again. "I don't care what dad says, you are the best cook in the world."

She smiled, "What does your father know, he grew up in that dour German home eating sauerbraten and dumplings. It spoiled him for life. Lucky for him I saved him." I looked at the feast we were about to have, wondered how it must be for Truck to never have a mother who took care of him. I settled in beside my mom, helped her finish the preparations. Time with her had become far more precious. And then my thoughts turned to Nut as I mashed the potatoes, making certain there were no lumps, just the way mom liked. This mindless task gave me time to think.

PARTIAL INDULGENCES

I met Nut on the way to CCD that night. In the dim light it was easy to spot my muscular friend. "Hey, knucklehead, you get more ape-like each day. Pretty soon National Geographic's going to send someone to study you, you're definitely missing link material."

As usual, he shook his head. "What am I going to do for aggravation when I go in the Green Berets, Dylan?"

I had decided to go at him again about his plan to kill Digger but was waiting for the right opening. "Count your blessings while you have them, Nut." And then, "Been thinking a lot about your crazy plan for Digger. Do you have any idea how insane that is? Sane people just don't knock off their old man." I pointed at him. "There has to be some other way. I've thought it over. There is no way you get away with that. You'll end up in the slammer. And then what will your mom do?"

Nut had a serious expression on his granite strong face, as he said with no emotion, "I have a special talent. It's what makes me a natural for the Green Berets. I can compartmentalize my emotions from my actions. I can do the things people want done but don't have the stomach for." He looked at me blankly. "Do you think killing Hitler would have been wrong? He was a monster who killed millions of Jews with no remorse. How much different is he from Digger? He's going to kill my mother one day." I didn't answer. "Sometime you just have to judge the greater good. The world will be well rid of Digger. He's one of those cowardly bastards that hurts people his whole life and gets away with it." He shook his head. "I won't lose an ounce of sleep when I kill him. I'll send him to hell where he belongs." The iciness in his voice chilled me. We finished our walk to church without another word. I kept thinking about what he said. I couldn't argue, the world would be better off.

♦

Monsignor Pugh was in a good mood. He really enjoyed having Hank Greenberg in the class. Hank was enthusiastic about everything. It was one of his best traits, you liked being around him. After my outing with Truck and heart-to-heart with Nut, I needed something uplifting. Reneé had stopped coming to class. I asked Nut about that. "She's evaluating the differences between what she's hearing at CCD and what she hears in Synagogue." Nut frowned. "She says they're mostly the same." And then he grinned, "But the Jews are much more intense about it."

Hank overheard that, jumped in, "That's why my parents stopped going, said they came home bound up after getting reamed-out by the rabbi each Saturday."

I looked at Hank, "If they got reamed-out, wouldn't they shit like a goose?"

Monsignor Pugh looked at us as we laughed, said, "Okay, if the Three Stooges are done their routine, let's talk about mortal sin."

And so it began. One of the things I liked about the Catholic Church was they didn't pussyfoot around about sin. If you committed a mortal sin, didn't repent and ask for forgiveness, you went to hell. No exceptions. But the tricky part was your intention. If you didn't intend to do grievous harm, then you could avoid slipping into mortal sin territory and got a venial sin designation. Venial sins were much less a problem. For them, you only had to do some time in purgatory before getting admitted to heaven. Hank raised his hand. "Monsignor, I was reading about plenary and partial indulgences for this lesson. It said that by reciting certain prayers, you got partial indulgences and could reduce the time you spend in purgatory. But with plenary indulgences, all your sins were forgiven. What's the difference? Can you explain that to me?"

Monsignor Pugh shook his head. "Partial indulgences are prayers of repentance that help the sinner receive a remission of temporal punishment. They are intended to help sinners think about the evil they did, to pray for forgiveness and also to receive God's strength to resist temptation when it arises. Saying the prayers of indulgence helps the sinner reflect. But plenary indulgences are far more rare and difficult to achieve. For instance, getting a papal blessing is one requirement. So, for today's lesson, let's focus on the partial indulgences since they are most likely to apply to the average person." Hank nodded, indicating he understood.

And now, my fun started. Partial indulgences had always been one of my stumbling blocks. I spent countless hours at age ten pouring through prayer missals looking for the partial indulgence prayers that took the most time off your purgatory sentence. In one old missal it had underlined after the famous prayer "The Magnificat" —one hundred years indulgence. And I started praying "The

Magnificat" one-hundred times, thinking that would get me out of ten-thousand years in Purgatory. My reasoning was: Was I really so bad that I'd have to spend more than ten thousand years in the slammer before heaven? Not likely. I mean, I was a tad sarcastic and had some odd character flaws but that's a long sentence for being a wise-ass. I was only a kid and really didn't have the imagination at that point to do anything really horrible. And so I phrased my question to Monsignor Pugh, explaining my past research, my Magnificat theory, and asking whether he thought I was in the clear. I already knew this was ridiculous but wanted to lighten the topic and frankly couldn't help myself.

The whole class laughed out loud. Monsignor Pugh spread his arms in disbelief. "Dylan, where do you come up with these questions? Do you spend the whole week trying to twist God's word into a pretzel?"

He usually chuckled at my stuff but I sensed he was irritated so I switched gears. "I know I phrased that badly but I really can't fathom that God spends any time adding up who said the most indulgence prayers. What's the point of putting the number of years off your purgatory sentence after the prayers?"

Monsignor Pugh exhaled slowly. "The church is made up of men and women who interpret Catholic doctrine in ways that people can understand. That practice of naming "years off" is a symbolic designation. The intent of indulgences is as I explained it to Hank; indulgences are prayers of contrition to help you avoid falling repeatedly into the same pitfalls of life. Indulgences are prayers of contemplation for those who sinned. It helps people to find peace, to find a way to forgive themselves and live a good, holy life." I decided to stay quiet the rest of the lecture on indulgences. I sensed Monsignor Pugh wasn't up for my witless observations.

♦

But I did listen intently to the next dialogue on mortal sin and raised my hand again. Monsignor Pugh looked skeptically, "A sensible question this time?"

I nodded, "I'll do my best. But remember, Monsignor, I am a sinner and you're a priest so you have to forgive me when I fail, right?"

This time he smiled, "Now I know why your mother goes to church every day."

I pointed at him, "Bingo. But I do have a serious question. What if someone was so evil that he was beyond help? I'm talking about a man who beat his family for years and will probably end up killing them all. But a neighbor notices this is going on and tries to help but soon realizes he can't stop it. And finally, out of a pure desire to save this abused family, he kills the man. Would that neighbor who sincerely believed he was saving the family be committing a mortal sin and lose his eternal reward?"

I could see Nut's eyes getting big, so I avoided looking at him. But Monsignor Pugh was listening intently. He sighed. "A sad tale for sure. But as the Catholic Church teaches, two wrongs never make a right. The neighbor took the law into his hands when he should have involved the police. The neighbor was right to help but was misguided in his actions. There is never a justification for murder except self-defense."

Nut almost came out of his chair, "But what if the police didn't do anything about it and just considered it a family matter. What if the neighbor did everything he could and after trying everything else, he finally killed the bum because he knew the whole family would soon be dead."

There was smoke coming out of Nut's ears, so I barged in. "Monsignor, my real question is, is that action a mortal sin because the neighbor had no intent of evil? He truly believed it was a life or death situation."

One of the things I liked most about Monsignor Pugh was he didn't preach platitudes. He tried to apply Catholic doctrine in sensible terms. I watched him thinking the whole matter through, struggling to give a practical answer to a horrible problem. "The horrendous situation you described isn't black and white. I think the neighbor would be brought to court and would likely be convicted of a lesser crime than murder." But then he hesitated, seeming unsure how to phrase the next part. "But, if the neighbor truly acted for the best interest of the family, I do not think he committed a mortal sin and could be forgiven in God's eyes."

Without being obvious, I looked at Nut. He seemed to literally shrink back in his seat. He seemed to get calmer. I looked back at Monsignor Pugh. "Thanks. I just read about Josef Stalin and all the Russians he murdered. The idea of monsters living in this world seemed so real.

People like Stalin deserve to die. And I couldn't believe his killer would toast."

Monsignor Pugh started to say something, but then threw up his hands, said nothing. He looked at the class. "A lively discussion tonight. Thank you for your participation, it's important to understand your faith." And then he smiled, "Go out and make the world a better place."

◆

I dropped by Jimmer's house on the way back from CCD. Wanted to perfect that ear smack and needed his dummy to practice on. Plus, Jimmer wouldn't hesitate to tell me if I did it wrong. He cocked his head to the side as he watched. "You hit like your smacking a bug off your ass. Pop the son-of-a-bitch!" Without thinking, I banged the dummy and heard a different noise—more pop than thud. Jimmer exclaimed, "Perfect. The son-of-a-bitch will drop like Nixon's popularity ratings." And then he grinned, "Might even shit his pants."

I laughed, "In that case, maybe I better stick to doing it wrong. Don't want my delicate senses assaulted." Jimmer smirked, "Maybe Nut's right, you might have been adopted from the Korean Baby's Fund. Too weird to be from the Frazier bloodline. Everyone else in your house is squared away." And so my practice continued, mixing in some inane chatter with Jimmer. Time flew by. Somehow, when we yapped mindlessly, it relaxed me. And that made some sense. Compared to Jimmer, I didn't look too bad.

◆

Nut came back from CCD, found his mother cleaning up the kitchen. He gave her a gentle squeeze, was always worried about her. "Mom, why don't you sit down and read the paper or watch Ozzie and Harriet. I can finish up for you." As usual, his mother looked exhausted, almost shrunken. Without being obvious, he was checking to see if she had new bruises. Digger had been in a good mood lately, business was booming. It seemed fitting that he was happiest when death was involved. His mom looked okay but he asked, "Dad been okay lately? You know you promised to tell me if he hit you again."

He looked closely, seeing if she hesitated. Without looking at him, "Your father has been fine. He's had a hard life. You should have known him before he went in the Army. I really do think the war changed him. Made him harder." Her eyes shifted to him. She touched his cheek, "As long as I have you, all is well."

After a little more encouragement, his mom went to watch TV. Nut finished sweeping the kitchen floor. He thought about his mother's words, "As long as I have you." And that made him think about his plan for Digger. Even if there was a respite in the beatings, he was sure they would continue when he went off to Green Beret training. He shook his head, thinking about Dylan's question to Monsignor Pugh. Would killing Digger be a mortal sin? Would he go to hell? He thought to himself: Even if I would, I would do it anyway. As Dylan put it: Monsters deserve to die. He smiled thinking about his zany friend. Dylan makes everyone laugh but he zeroes in on any problem, can't seem to let go. Nut knew that Dylan worried about him. He exhaled deeply, clearing his mind.

Kept returning to his decision. It's either mom or Digger who's going to die. He gritted his jaw, determined.

♦

That night, Truck was doing Algebra homework and listening to Hy Lit on the radio. But as he listened to "Where or When" by Dion and the Belmonts, he started thinking about his dad. It was hard acting normal with him. His father raised him mostly by himself. They were incredibly close. That's why his aloofness and lying about Truck's mom didn't make sense. His dad was a tough guy but was always there for him. He thought back to grade school. His dad left the shop early to make certain he got back from school okay. Most times he brought him to the shop to do his homework or to help him prepare dinner orders. Truck could butcher a chicken like a pro before he was 10. As he got older, his dad would drive him to football and basketball practice, picked him up after. He never felt weird not having a mother, his dad was always there. But when he started asking about his mom, his dad wouldn't talk. He could see him get edgy and switch the topic or tell him they'd talk about it later. The years went by and Truck stopped asking. But those recent letters brought it back. He wondered how his mom died.

Dylan told him he had to stay cool, not pester his dad. That there was a reason he wouldn't talk and they'd have to find it without his help. Truck kept thinking she might have had mental problems, that his dad didn't want him to know she wasn't right in the head. And that ugly thought kept coming back: Maybe she killed herself. And then he thought about Mrs. Delaney. She was mom's best friend. She didn't think mom had any illnesses. She said she was healthy as a horse. Truck scratched his head. He hadn't made any progress but he felt better. And then he thought: Maybe I should call Mrs. Delaney and see if she wants to come to my next game. I could drive over and pick her up. Try to get some more information.

Knowing Mrs. Delaney was his mom's best friend made him feel closer to his mother. That pleasant thought settled him. He went back to the Algebra but the sour thought crept back. Did mom commit suicide? He exhaled deeply, fought back the dread.

NEW MASCOT

We played North Cathedral next. They were the top team in the Northern Division of the Catholic League. You only played the other Division teams once, rotated home and away each year. This year we played away. They had a small, boxy gym that they used for basketball and bingo. The ceilings were so low that I couldn't shoot my high arcing shot from the wings without it clanging on the support beam. Since that was where I usually shot from, Coach Gallagher had designed new screenplays for the top of the circle. Coach looked at me seriously, "Don't think about the low roof. It'll mess up your mind."

I shrugged, "I think somebody beat them to the punch. Don't ya think?."

He grinned, "I mean worse than it already is. Just shoot like normal when you're out front."

North Cathedral always was another short, scrappy teams. It was like playing a team of Scoots. They'd press the whole game and never quit–no matter the score. Drum had given us his scouting report but summed it up this way. "They run around like they got hornets in their jock."

Coach Gallagher shook his head at the description but added, "That's about right. Nothing fancy about this team. They design every play to attack the basket. They only shoot outside as a last resort. Any questions?"

I raised my hand. Coach nodded for me to speak. "Can we stay after the game to play bingo?" With everybody chuckling about that, we headed off to practice against the second team. Coach Gallagher added an extra man on defense. We went about trying to stay calm in a testicular hornet's nest.

Truck had asked permission to drive to the game separately. When he explained he wanted to bring Mrs. Delaney and about her background, Coach nodded. "I like that. Maybe her presence will keep you from getting too intense and getting another flagrant technical. It might be just what you need. She can be your good luck charm. Forget about driving separately, ask her if she wants to ride on the bus with us. She can sit up front with me on the way to the game. And if you play well, you can sit with her on the return. Deal?" And that's how Mrs. Delaney became our mascot. Coach Gallagher was a smart man. He saw immediately how Truck responded to her, hoped that would keep Truck in line the rest of the season.

When Truck told me about his plan for Mrs. Delaney being at our games, I reminded him his father might not appreciate the move. I explained, "Kind of like rubbing dog shit in his face. I know you might like that right now but I doubt your dad will. Plus you don't want to tip him off we've been snooping again. Didn't buy his horseshit tale. Might piss him off."

Truck shook his head, "You really are a J-bag." And the nodded, "But you're right. I'll tell her to lay low, sit in the opponent's section. She'll get it. I told her about dad clamming-up whenever I bring up mom." And he added, "She even said she understood. That my dad was completely nuts about mom and he probably can't stand to be reminded of her."

I never argued but didn't buy it. Mr. Carr was lying. That degree of lying wasn't something you did out of grief. There was another cause. Maybe it was the damage her suicide might cause Truck. Or that he might have inherited her problems. We just didn't know what it was yet.

We kicked North Cathedral's butt that night. Fran Philips was sensational. Scored 30 points and didn't have to breathe hard. Truck had a good game but nothing like his normal dominance. He seemed to be less manic, doing the same moves but without the intensity. I wondered about it but kept it to myself. Every time he scored he glanced to the visitor's section and nodded to Mrs. Delaney. Mr. Carr didn't seem to notice. Before the game I told Coach that Mr. Carr wouldn't like Mrs. Delaney being there because it might upset Sue and that we were keeping it low-key for now. He looked at me funny. "You two up to some monkey business? I thought this was to keep Truck calm?"

I gave him a big smile, "Blessed are the peacemakers and pure of heart."

He shook his head, "Now I know I'm being snowed."

Truck sat with Mrs. Delaney on the ride home, talked non-stop. He asked question after question about his mom. I watched him sitting motionless as he listened intently. I now understood the term "drinking in information."

I didn't want to snoop on their conversation, so I sat with Drum, asked what he thought of the game. "I thought it would be much tougher. Especially with Truck

playing like a zombie. Never saw the big dude so passive."
He shook his head, "But Fran was on fire. The bad part of
pressing us is that Scoot can almost break a press by
himself, that leaves Fran one-on-one. Nobody stops him if
he gets the ball in the open court. The cat just glides." He
looked at me. "And I don't think you've missed an open
shoot for the past two games. Keep drilling the J's and
we're hard to guard." But then he grimaced, "Unless Truck
keeps playing like he's got rocks up his ass." I didn't say
anything, but that was exactly what I was wondering.

♦

We got back to Conner High. I drove home with
Scoot, Drum and Fran. Drum's parents gave him a cool
'58 Chevy as incentive to do well at school. He was a
brilliant guy but never did well in any subject but Math and
Science. He had gotten perfect 800's in both SAT's so his
parents knew he wasn't making any effort in the liberal arts
courses. When he first got the car he drove to my house to
show off his new wheels. It was light blue with lots of
chrome and spiffy hubcaps. I told him I loved the car. He
looked at me impishly, "My parents think they can buy my
attention to grades." He winked as he looked at the
shinning car, "They might be on to something. I can be
bought for the right price."

Drum's car had a great radio. As we pulled out of the
Conner High lot, Jerry Vale blasted "Love is a Many
Splendored Thing" and Drum jammed the channel button
to get some rock and roll music on WIP. I grew up in a
house where my dad dominated the music selection. He
liked opera and classical music. Consequently, I was

brainwashed from a young age about what crappy music was now being played by the American public. The coolest thing my dad allowed was ballads by people like Jerry Vale and Sergio Franchi. If dad wanted to be exotic, he'd let us listen to Engelbert Humperdinck or Pat Boone. Oddly, I became a fan of their voices, took endless shit from my buddies about "homo music." And so when I protested that night when Jerry Vale was silenced, Drum looked at me deadpanned, "Hey, Dylan, did ya hear Jerry Vale has a greatest hits album out?" I shook my head, knowing something was coming. Drum finished, "Ya, I picked it up the other day." He paused for effect. "One sides blank." Everybody howled as we drove off to get a burger and fries at a new place called Scotties.

MARY

Nut's mother had a rare night at home by herself.
Nut had a date with Reneé and Digger had a wake that
would run late. Since Jimmy had joined him at work,
Digger had been in a good mood. Jimmy had the same
aptitude for the funeral business, seemed to always know
the right thing to say. But Mary knew that Jimmy meant it,
that Digger just played a game. Mary exhaled deeply and
whispered aloud, "Anything for some peace and calm."
Digger hadn't hit her in a couple weeks. She knew he was
wary of Nut and that seemed to be working. That and
Jimmy taking some pressure off him at work seemed to
calm her brutal husband. To the outside world, Digger
seemed successful and self-assured, a natural leader in St
Tim's parish. She shook her weary head: If they only knew
the truth.

Mary decided to comb her long hair out, get in her
robe and watch *Father Knows Best*. Robert Young was
always relaxed despite the mayhem from Bud, Princess or
Kitten. She had a rare smile as she thought about their
loving, peaceful TV family. Mary pulled the Bobbie pins
from her brown hair and let it cascade down her shoulder.
Although flecked with gray, it was still beautiful, her
crowning feature. She grabbed the old brush, combed it
out easily, hardly a knot to unravel. Digger never let her
wear her hair down, said it made her look like a floozy. She
shuddered thinking of the violence she endured since their
marriage 26 years ago. Digger had been a dashing,
confident young man when he courted her. His good looks
and determination swept her off her feet. He was so kind
and considerate. They were soon married, then the war

started and Digger was sent overseas. She exhaled deeply: When he returned, everything changed.

Mary looked in the mirror, admired her beautiful locks. She shook her hair from side to side, watching how the hair moved in waves. And then she spotted Digger looming in the doorway. She gulped for air and started moving away from the mirror. Digger was on her in seconds. "So, this is what you do when I'm out slaving for a living. Sitting in front of the mirror, sashaying around like a whore." He grabbed her lovely mane, pulled her violently backward, threw her to the ground. And then he tore off her robe and pajamas. He glared at her, nostrils flaring in rage. He growled, "Get on your hands and knees like a dog. I'll show you what I do to harlots." He started pulling down his pants. Mary closed her eyes, dropped her head down and did what she always did when Digger tortured her. She prayed.

DETECTIVE WORK

Nut had called Sunday night. "Digger's got a funeral tomorrow. Are you free to do a little reconnoitering? Truck says he can drive."

Without hesitation, "I'm in." And then I added, "Tell Truck to eat some chili before we go, that way he'll be able to fart on command, one of his usual howitzers, warn us if Digger shows."

Nut waited a few seconds before adding, "But we have to drive there with him. It might not be worth the risk."

I chuckled, "Might prepare you for that gas chamber test in basic training. Truck is like a walking sulfur cloud when he's percolating. You'll be ready for anything Charlie throws at you." I listened to my friend's warm laugh as I hung up. And then I got the image of Nut standing in a rice paddy, surrounded by enemy fighters. They pointed rifles at this big American warrior. I shook my head to scatter the vision. My close buddy would be out of high school in a few months with an express pass to Nam. It was hard to believe.

◆

Truck picked me up first, I asked about his dinner that night. "Nut told me about the chili. I hate to disappoint you but Sue made lasagna with meat sauce tonight." He grinned at me. "But she loaded up the garlic bread so I think I'm all set. I can feel the bubbles forming."

I laughed, "Hold it for another 30 minutes or so. My stomach's a little queasy. Don't want to blow lunch in your car." Changing topics, "You seem to be getting along with Sue. Like you might even kinda like her. Am I right?"

Truck swiveled his head, wagged it up and down. "We get along great now." And then he looked away. "It finally sunk in. My dad loves her and wants to get married. I think she's held off to get my approval. I've been such a prick that I never figured that out." I already knew that, decided not to make a comment. My tough pal was starting to mellow. First he befriends Mrs. Delaney, now Sue. We rode quietly as I pondered the changes in my formidable friend.

My wordless questioning was interrupted as we came up Nut's driveway and he loped from the house. I had been thinking about where Digger might hide his records when Nut said his house was clean. But I hadn't been to the funeral parlor enough to have a good guess. I said to Nut as we drove, "The best hiding places are out in the open, where everybody can see it but it blends in. Like it's so obvious it's invisible." I looked at Nut, "Like Drum's ability to analyze opponents. I mean. You look at Drum and your first thought is borderline mental patient, lock up the women and children. Who would know he's so intuitive?"

Truck giggled, "I never thought about Drum that way but now that you mentioned it, he is a little loco looking."

I continued my other ideas of where to look. "Next place is where no one wants to touch, like a toilet, I mean, who wants to poke at someone's shitter?" Nut rolled his eyes. I persisted, "Last place is where it's so hard to get to that you don't want the hassle. Your laziness takes over. Like hiding it down a sewer that makes you crawl through a long pipe with scum on the walls, rats and roaches jumping around. That kind of place."

Nut grinned, "I'm glad you're on my team. Your imagination is like a science project gone wrong."

Truck looked over, "I feel like I'm riding with The Hardy Boys."

We got to Digger's funeral parlor. Nut went inside to see if the coast was clear. To keep Truck occupied, "I did read all the *Hardy Boy* books as a kid. Fancied myself Joe Hardy when I was ten but soon figured I was more like Frank, kind of sensitive and mature, a natural leader that attracts people like bees to honey. Don't you think?"

Truck grinned, "You remind me more of Maxwell Smart, except your feet stink so bad the shoe phone is probably outta order." And then he belly-laughed. And that made me laugh.

Just then Nut showed up, looked in the window. "What's so funny?"

I shrugged, "Truck just said he thinks you and I are acting like Agents 86 and 99, except you're too ugly to pull off the Barbara Feldon role. I was arguing that if you lost some weight and shaved your pins you might look kind of slinky in a black dress."

Nut shook his head, "I should never leave you two

alone."

We went inside, leaving Truck on sentry duty. The distinctive smells struck you when you went in the embalming workroom. "How do you stand that stink, Nut? I think of Lon Chaney when I walk in here."

He looked at me without expression, "What smell?"

I shook my head, "Never mind. Remind me not to give you cologne for Christmas."

Nut said we had about an hour before Digger would wander back. I looked in his desk first. "Probably nothing here, too obvious. But let's rule it out." We lifted out everything and inspected it carefully. Nothing. "How about secret compartments? I'll look underneath." I crawled where the chair slid under and looked for anything odd. Nothing. "Clean under here."

Nut agreed, "This isn't the place."

Following my "no one wants to touch" thinking, we went to the embalming area next. I mean, this is where they drain the body of blood and all the other disgusting stuff. Who wants to poke around here? I looked at Nut, "I keep waiting for Bela Lugosi to pop out of the closet."

Nut didn't laugh, "Digger is a bigger ghoul than him, only he's real. He's sucked the life out of our family, 'specially my mom."

I could see the controlled rage simmering. I patted his massive shoulder, "We'll get him. I promise."

Nut didn't respond for a few seconds. Added, "One way or the other."

That revived my worries but I said nothing.

I looked at the odd equipment beside the worktable. "Although I'm not sure I want to know, what is all that shit?"

Nut pointed, "That's the aspirator, centrifugal pump and trocar. Without being too gory, you use them to drain the blood and other fluids. Then you pump the embalming fluids in the carotid artery to stop decay. Most funeral homes use an outside embalmer, then they just groom the body to make it look good." Nut got another look of fury, "Not Digger, he does it all himself. Makes more money that way. He learned how to do it in the war, got lots of practice after we invaded Normandy. He got so good at it they made him the full-time mortician." Nut shook his head, "Only thing Digger's good for; fixing up dead people."

I was adjusting to the smell of formaldehyde but my nose still burned. Scrunching my nose to manage the odor, I rummaged around the table. There were no obvious places to hide a book or ledger, so I moved to a group of large ornate wooden half doors near the wall. "Nut, what's that?"

He said matter-of-factly, "It's where you put the new corpses before they are worked on."

I counted eight separate compartments. "Why so many?"

He sighed, "For when a whole lot of people die at the same time. Mostly when families get in bad car wrecks, that kind of thing."

I asked the obvious question, "Anyone in there now?"

Nut walked over, "Only one way to find out." He pulled open each door and peered inside. Looking back at me, "You're lucky, no customers on deck."

I wandered over, peered inside. I looked in each one and started to close the doors when something came to me. "Are those drains in the middle of each compartment?"

Nut nodded, "They're for any leakage. You know, before they get embalmed. Helps minimize the mess."

I got close to the nearest one, inspected the drain. Hating every second of it, I stretched deeper and messed with the drain. I pulled up; it popped off easily. And then I crawled closer, looked to see how it worked. I was looking to see if there was anything hidden. Or if there was some place to stash a ledger. Disappointed, I saw the drain fed in a small pipe, no place to hide anything. Being anal, I went through each one and came to the last compartment. I reached inside, pulled the drain and glanced quickly. Nothing. As I put the drain back, I noticed a different color to the wood on the drain wall. I lifted the drain again, poked the wall and it opened like a swinging door. I reached in, pulled out a leather book and slide back out. I grinned at Nut, "Bingo!"

We went to Digger's desk and opened the book. Nut looked at the first page, noted, "This starts in 1950. There's a column for date, $'s and then a series of numbers and letters." The first entry read, 410267-B-1397-1#. And the next one was 302149-W-0890-9#. He flipped to the last page. "Look at this entry, that's the same code we saw on Mrs. O'Callaghan's topaz." He looked at my puzzlement, "I memorized it."

And then I glanced at the page; "There's two more entries after Mrs. O'Callaghan's burial. Digger's been a busy boy." We then flipped through each page, found exactly the same coding format, six numbers, a capital letter, and then four numbers, a dash and another number. The only letters used were C, T, B and W. I asked the obvious, "What do they mean?"

Before he could answer, we heard furious beeping. I looked at Nut, "That's Truck's signal. Digger's back." Nut grabbed the book, ran to the compartment, hurriedly put the ledger back, jammed back the drain and shut the door. Per our plan in case he showed up early, we ran toward the rear entrance to avoid getting caught. As we blew through the door, I almost tripped over the startled Digger. Apparently he decided on the rear entrance. So much for my brilliant plan.

Digger recovered quickly, "What are you two doing here?"

Nut didn't answer, was too shocked about getting caught. I jumped in, "On our way back from my practice at the Palestra. Nut came along. I've been bugging Nut about seeing where he worked. Thought we could drop in.

I see how well you've done and was thinking about maybe majoring in Mortuary Sciences in college."

Digger looked at me stone-faced, "You're too much of a smart-ass to be in this profession. People want stability at a time of loss." He paused, "You, Frazier are a screw-up."

Nut was still silent. I looked at Digger, "So, I guess I can't use you as a reference for college?"

On the way home Nut didn't say anything for the first 5 minutes. I filled Truck in on finding the ledger and our narrow escape. Suddenly, Nut burst out laughing, almost hyperventilating, murmured, "I guess I can't use you as a reference for college." He explained to Truck what I'd said and we all howled.

After calming down, I said, "We have to get that ledger and more importantly, we have to figure out what the code means." I turned to Nut. "If he's been ripping people off since 1950, we can get him put in jail."

Nut shook his head, "Not unless we can prove he stole that stuff. I've given it a lot of thought, it's our word against his if we can't prove it."

I'd also been thinking about that. Even if we exhumed the bodies and found the jewelry missing, Digger could say grave robbers did it. No proof he did it. Plus, would people really let us dig up the bodies based on our crazy theory? I looked Nut right in the eyes. "Let's crack the code first, get the ledger and then we'll figure it out. There must be a way." I could tell by Nut's expression he didn't share my optimism.

FERDINAND

Our next game was with Bishop Renwood. They had a so-so team but their star player was the league-leading scorer. He had a memorable name, Ferdinand Da Gama. Drum did his normal scouting report, Coach Gallagher asked for his comments. Drum looked at me, "Dylan should cover him. He can shut him down. The guys not that good, he just shoots his ass off every game."

Coach jumped in, "Watch the language, this is a Catholic School. Okay?"

Drum continued, "Sorry, Coach. As I was saying, he shoots so much it taxes his Gluteus Maximus to the maximum." He looked at Coach, "More acceptable phrasing?"

Gallagher doesn't bite. "Continue, Drum, and easy on the theatrics."

Drum focused on what Ferdinand did best and what his preferences were. "He's all right handed, Dylan, never shoots with his left. Even if he dribbles left it's only for a few steps then it gets back to his right hand. Plus he shoots kinda on a line drive, easy to snuff. I think you can eat him up." Coach asked if we had questions about our game plan. I was going to comment on Ferdinand's name but let it go.

This was an away game. Renwood was out in the sticks of Lancaster County, almost to Amish country. We hated playing there because the bus ride was so long. Mrs. Delaney sat with Truck. I sat with Fran Philips, watched the interaction between this gentle, lovely lady and our big star. As Truck laughed at something she said, Fran leaned in, "She definitely has a calming effect on him, doesn't she? He's like a different person."

I nodded, "It reminds of the horse whisperers I've read about. They can just rub the crazy horse, pat them on the head and suddenly they get still. She's got that affect on him."

Drum was sitting behind us, listening to the conversation. He added, "She's more like a snake charmer. But wait till the game starts and Truck gets elbowed going for a board. You'll see how long the spell lasts. Eventually the cobra's going to strike."

I looked at Drum, "You're full optimism, aren't you?"

He looked at me deadpan, "I know my vipers."

On the ride there, I spent time thinking about Digger's thefts, letting the numbering code run through my mind. What did the combination of letters and numbers mean? I was tempted to see if Drum could make sense of them but knew I'd need to run that by Truck. As that was sifting through my mind, I thought about Truck's mystery writer. We weren't too far from Shillington, where the letters were postmarked. I told Truck we'd shoot there when we had a day off from practice but still wasn't sure what we could accomplish. What were the odds someone would remember sending a letter to Truck? I mean, he was a big star but Shillington was on the edge of Reading, almost 60 miles away. But it would make Truck happy just to try; maybe an idea would hit me. Worth a shot.

As we were warming up before the game, I watched Ferdinand running his drills. He was smaller than me and didn't look too good shooting the ball, kind of line-drived the ball at the basket. His shot seem hard, nothing like Fran Philip's soft touch. Fran's ball floated out of his hand; hardly made a noise if it hit the rim. Ferdinand's ball clanged as it hit the rim. Just then Drum, came by, saw me watching. He said, "You'll eat him up. Don't worry."

I shook my head, "That's not what worries me, did you ever meet anyone normal with a name like Ferdinand. His parents must really be wacky. Maybe he'll kick me in the goobers. Kind of scares me a little." Drum rolled his eyes, used to my nonsense. I started to prepare for the game about to start.

As we lined up and shook hands, I asked Ferdinand, "Your parents must really love the Portuguese explorers, huh?" He grimaced in response. I clarified, "I mean to name you after Ferdinand Magellan and Vasco Di Gama takes some real imagination." Just then the ref blew the whistle and Truck tapped me the ball. I flew by the befuddled Ferdinand for an easy lay-up. But I soon learned why Ferdinand was the leading scorer. He wasn't afraid to take any shot, no matter how difficult or seemingly impossible. Plus if he missed, he went after the rebound and fired it up again. It was uncanny how many loose balls he got and then turned them into layups. He seemed to have unlimited energy. By halftime the score was tied and Ferdinand had 20 points. And I was exhausted.

As I stumbled into the locker room, Drum came beside me, whispered, "Nice defense, you held him to 20 points. I think Ray Charles could have done a better job on him."

I just shook my head; decided I deserved the razzing. Coach was a little gentler, "Stay after him, Dylan, the guy's got to run out of energy. I mean, he's already taken 25 shots. His legs have to be tired. Push him from the jump ball at half and he'll fade by 4th quarter." I shook my head, wandered to the water fountain. Coach yelled, "Don't drink too much, you'll get stomach cramps." I nodded, took a few sips and listened to the rest of the half-time speech. And then I heard Coach say something I hadn't noticed, "Truck, wake up, you look like you're sleep-walking out there. Where's the hustle? Where's your normal fire?" I had been so busy guarding Ferdinand that I hadn't realized Truck hadn't scored a basket. And then I thought about our discussion on the earlier bus ride. Was Mrs. Delaney having some weird affect on him?

Things didn't get much better in the 3rd quarter. Ferdinand continued his relentless play. We couldn't get much of a lead. In the huddle at the break, I pulled Truck aside, looked him dead in the face, "You can start to play whenever you feel like it." When he started to get pissed, I pointed at him, "Get your head out of your ass and start banging. I'm busting my hump guarding Speedy Gonzalez and you're acting like a librarian." Before he could react, I moved away, hoping I woke him up. Luckily, Fran Philips and Scoot were playing great since I was too tired hounding Ferdinand to do much on offense. I hadn't scored a point or even taken a shot. We needed to get some offense and I needed to slow down this relentless scorer.

As we lined up to jump the ball for the last quarter, I stood next to Ferdinand, said, "I hope you're having fun. I wasn't guarding you close before so you'd feel good about yourself. That's how nice a guy I am. From now on, I'll be on you like toilet paper in a shit storm."

He grinned at me, "I'm just getting warmed up." He wasn't kidding. He whirled past me on the first possession, scored easily. The next time down court he stood dribbling at the top of the key, dared me to steal the ball. When I took the bait, he dropped to his knees and put on a Harlem Globetrotter dribbling exhibition to humiliate me. Try as I might, I couldn't get the ball. Suddenly, he sprung to his feet and hit a driving bank shot.

But he made a mistake when he taunted me on the way down the court. Truck was beside me, said to Ferdinand, "Don't come down the lane anymore, wise-ass or you'll pay." It wasn't an idle threat. Ferdinand did his normal series of fakes, slipped by me but Truck was waiting, fouled him hard but not flagrantly. Truck helped Ferdinand up, whispered, "That was just a patty cake hit. Next time I'll nail you; you'll wanna cry."

From that point, Truck took over the game. He scored at will and dominated the backboards. Ferdinand started taking longer shots and Truck gobbled up the misses. I started to overplay him outside, trying to get him to drive, knowing that Truck still had 4 fouls left and he wouldn't waste them with sissy plays. Ferdinand took the bait, sailed down the lane for a layup but Truck snuffed him so hard he never got off the ground. The ref called a jump ball. On the way up for the tip, Truck slammed his forearm into Ferdinand, knocking him to the ground. The ref blew a whistle on this one. Ferdinand missed both foul shots and Truck rebounded, tossed the ball to me and I hit a nice jumper for a six point lead. Ferdinand was timid the rest of the game and we went on to a ten point victory. Truck scored 18 points in the fourth quarter, Fran Philips ended with 30 and Scoot a career high 15.

I scored a whopping two points. Coach patted me on the head when he saw how bad I felt. "Tough game, Dylan, sometimes the other guy wins."

Drum overheard the pep talk and jumped in, "You did hold Ferdinand to 44, though." He looked at me deadpan, "I think that's his season high." And then he added, "Maybe we can get Little Stevie Wonder to guard him next game, maybe hold him below 40." Even Coach Gallagher laughed; pretty soon I did too. A bad day for me but at least we won. And finally Truck snapped out of his funk. But on the ride home, I saw how he relaxed when chatting with Mrs. Delaney, thought to myself: Has my warrior friend lost his edge? And after a few seconds: Would that be all bad?

SHILLINGTON POST OFFICE

We had vacation on Monday. It was a "teacher's day" and we had no practice. Truck and I planned the trip to Shillington to see if we could snoop around the post office to get a lead on the phantom mailer. Normally Nut would come with us but he had school, Upper Derby didn't have the same holiday schedule as Conner High. I still wasn't sure what we were trying to accomplish but I knew that it seemed to make Truck feel better. He looked at me as I voiced my uncertainty, "At least we're trying something."

And then he looked ahead, "I don't know why but those letters shake me up."

For something to say, I asked, "Did your mom have any relatives here in Philly? Maybe it's coming from one of them that you just don't remember."

He shook his head, "She was from Germany. As far as I know they're still over there." And then, "I asked Mrs. Delaney about that and she said the same thing—my mom was all alone except for us. Truck drove on quietly but after a few minutes, "I can still her calling me 'her goot little boy.'" He had a rare calm look on his rugged face. I spent the rest of the drive thinking about looking for this needle in a haystack.

Shillington was a suburb of Reading, which was only 65 miles from Philadelphia, but was like going to another planet. Reading was the 5th largest city in Pennsylvania, once a thriving railroad and iron market. My parents frequently drove to the Reading farmer's markets for exotic foods and scoured unusual antique shops in this hub of Pennsylvania Dutch country. Until old enough to protest, I had to go along and was subjected to endless treks through meat stands offering the best bacon in the world and other beefy boasts of greatness. Actually, they did have the best bacon I ever had—we used to have thick slabs for dinner sometime. My buddies thought that odd but I never gripped about having breakfast meat for dinner. My thrifty dad knew his way around a deal. He'd stock up on rare meats and put them on ice to protect them during our daylong forays.

My parents both had German blood so dad regaled us with history about this once predominantly German settlement. I can hear him saying, "Reading, not only a name on the Monopoly board for a railroad, Reading is also called the 'Pretzel City.' Nobody makes pretzels like the Germans." And then he'd spout, "It was settled originally by the Lenni Lenape Indians before William Penn pushed them out and sold the land to emigrants from Germany. The Lenape got a raw deal, didn't know what hit them when those industrious Germans piled in." And as my eyes rolled back in my head, Dad continued, "And then the Amish moved in, took that pristine farm land and pushed it to new heights. There's nothing like the rich soil of Pennsylvania." I remember dad singling me out years ago, "You have the gift of gab, Dylan, it wouldn't hurt you to learn Pennsylvania Dutch."

Fortunately mom came to my aid, "Frank, you want our son to learn an archaic, western German dialect when he lives in America?" That only shut dad up for a while; his enthusiasm wasn't easily curbed.

Those meandering childhood journeys ran through my memory as we entered bucolic Berks County. I had studied a map beforehand and veered Truck toward Shillington, on the edge of downtown Reading. "Once we get nearby, I'll ask one of the locals where the post office is." I looked at Truck, "You don't happen to speak Pennsylvania Dutch, do you? It might come in handy if we get one of the Amish or Mennonites by accident."

Truck chuckled, "Yea, right. I have enough trouble with English, don't you remember?"

I patted his shoulder, "That's just one of the many things you have trouble with. No sweat, I'll start talking about bacon if they get snippy."

Truck frowned, "What?"

I nodded, "Long story, it might get lost in translation. Keep driving where I tell you."

Sure enough, we rolled into the edge of Shillington, pulled over beside an old coot walking down the street. I wound the window down, put on my nicest smile, "Excuse me sir, can you tell us how to find the post office?"

The old guy looked wary, "You ain't from these parts are ya?" I shrugged, "Actually my relatives were from here, big pretzel people before the Bachman's came in and pushed them out. My granddad says his pretzels were so crunchy they would crack your false teeth." I threw up my hands, "At least that's how I remember it." The guy scratched his head, not knowing what to say. I jumped in, "So, how can I find the post office?"

The old fella recovered, "Just down the road a piece, ya can't miss it." Actually we could miss it. Twenty minutes and more directions later we wheeled up to a large brick building.

I had Truck bring the last letter and envelope with him so we could have something to start the conversation with. As we ambled up the steps, I looked at Truck, "Try not to grunt or scratch your nuts while I'm talking to the clerks. You look menacing enough without any weird actions. Don't want to scare people off thinking you might be an escaped lunatic." Truck chuckled, pushed me up the final steps. The inside of the post office was also brick with ancient hard wood floors that badly needed a buff. There was a short line so we got in place.

A nice old lady was in front of us, scarf on her head and loaded down with letters. She smiled at me. I asked, "Don't trust the mail box, huh?" She nodded knowingly, "Can't be too careful is how I see it. Government is screwed up enough when you bring the letters here personal. Who knows where it'll go if you jam it in that metal box."

I shook my head. "My feelings exactly." I leaned in, nodded at Truck, whispered to her, "I'm teaching my buddy the ropes of mailing letters. He got dropped on his head a few years ago, hasn't been right since."

She patted my arm, "What a nice friend you are."

Just then a couple mail clerk stations opened up. We marched up to a grizzled guy who looked like he had the cares of the world on his shoulders. He sighed, said with no interest, "What can I do for you?" So I pulled out the letter Truck had given me and unloaded the story of the phantom letters. I could see his eyes gloss over, puzzling how to tell me he wasn't interested in this wild goose chase and maybe we should just buy some nice commemorative stamps and go away.

Reading this reaction, I plowed on, "We think this is a relative of Robbie's who's reaching out to get in touch. Any clues you can give us would be great."

I handed the envelope over. He looked at it briefly, said, "Could be from anyone." Anticipating this, I asked if we could speak to the postmaster. The clerk was befuddled but he said nothing, headed toward the rear office.

Since his dad was a postmaster, I talked with Drum a few weeks ago, looking for advice on how to maneuver inside the Shillington Post Office. He was a perceptive guy so I continued the story about anonymous love letters from a fan. His first comment was, "It makes more sense since you're out of the shooting slump. But I'll bet they'll stop if she saw how Ferdinand ate your lunch last game." But he finally said if you got no cooperation from a clerk, to insist on talking to the postmaster. "They are the problem solvers in the place. Most of the others clerks are numb-nuts just collecting a paycheck. Insist on the postmaster, most of them are pretty sharp. Try to make it interesting for them, give them a challenge to liven-up their day." I remembered that comment as I stood waiting.

The line behind us had built up. People were starting to moan. I looked at the codger behind me, said loudly, "I think the clerk had diarrhea, he kind of took off in a hurry, like he didn't want to squirt it on the floor, maybe have to shut down the building." Truck put his head down, started to giggle. Pretty soon the whole line was laughing.

The clerk returned, looked at the gaggle of laughter, asked, "What did I miss?"

I leaned in, "One of the old men in line broke wind out loud." He looked horrified but told us to proceed to the side door, wait outside the postmaster's office. He'd be out to see us shortly.

Vernon Herbein was a distinguished looking man, maybe 60, full head of silver hair, pencil straight posture. We sat in the chairs in front of his desk as he watched us intently. Quiet for a few seconds as he sized us up. "Now tell me how I can help you young men. I hear you have a secret admirer or something." And then he added, "I hope you're not here to have a little fun at our expense."

I liked the look of this man, decided to tell it straight. I told him the whole story of Truck's mother dying when he was young, that she was the only one ever called him Robbie, that there might be some relative afraid to get in touch because they knew his dad didn't want to be reminded of the sad past. And finished with, "It's important to my friend. Everyone deserves to know about their mother."

Vernon Herbein looked dead in my eyes, "That's quite a tale." And then he added, "And I can tell you're being honest by the look on your friend's face."

I glanced at Truck. My huge buddy's eyes had welled-up. Emotion covered his strong face. And that choked me up. I looked at Herbein, "We're dead serious. Anything you can do will be appreciated."

I handed the letter and envelope over. He perused it intently, read and re-read the last letter. And then he looked up, a question on his amiable face, "Are you Truck Carr the basketball player? I love basketball, especially high school ball. We get all the Philly scores in the local papers."

Now I knew we had a chance getting some help. This guy was a fan. And so I answered for Truck since he was still overwrought. "In person."

After a few seconds, Truck spoke up, "At first I thought it was a crank letter but the reference to Robbie threw me. Nobody called me that but my mom."

Herbein nodded, thought awhile, "The letter definitely came from here but that's about all I can tell you." And then added, "We get thousands of letters each day, not much here to go on."

I saw the dejection in Truck's face. Not to be discouraged, I asked, "Can we put up a sign or something in the lobby? Maybe have a picture of Truck saying he's looking for lost relatives. Something like that?"

Herbein weighed his answer carefully. "That's against government regulation. The only thing we can post is postal changes and of course the 'Most Wanted' criminal pictures." Before I could protest, he said, "But if someone snuck a sign up that I didn't approve, who would be the wiser?"

I grinned, "If someone was that irreverent, how long do you think the sign might last before some do-gooder took it down?"

Herbein shrugged, "I'll bet it could last at least a month under those circumstances. We don't have many rebels in Berks County so we aren't usually that attentive."

Who says the milk of human kindness has dried up? We spent a few more minutes yapping about basketball. Herbein's son coached Lansdale Cathedral. He was well aware of our team record and the expectation for our team. We got up to leave and something popped into my head. "You don't happen to remember one of your customers that spoke German, do you? Truck's mom is from Germany, maybe the relative is German."

Herbein scrunched his eyebrows, thinking. He shook his head "no" but suddenly his eyes brightened. "There is a lady around here that teaches Pennsylvania Dutch to the locals who are interested. She comes in here once in awhile to mail things, a tall blonde lady. I remember Lester, one of the clerks, saying he was thinking about enrolling in her group, wanted to stay connected with his German roots. Of course, the Amish speak Pennsylvania Dutch but they never use the post office. "

Unfortunately, he didn't know the lady's name and the clerk Lester was off his shift. Herbein took our telephone number, said he would call if he got any information. He also let us make a picture of Truck with their camera and I typed out a brief note saying he was looking for information about relatives living in the Reading area. We left my telephone number since we didn't want Truck's dad to know we were snooping. I posted the note below his picture and Scotch taped it to the wall thoroughly, so it wouldn't blow off. Herbein watched us from his office door. He mouthed the old Sergeant Schultz line, "I see nothing, nothing."

Truck and I walked over, thanked him again. I looked at Truck, "You kind of fit in with the 'Most Wanted' posters anyway, another big lug. No one will notice anything strange." Herbein chuckled as we walked off.

Truck was really happy on the ride home. He turned to me, "I really think it could be one of my mom's relatives sending me the letters. Or maybe a close friend like Mrs. Delaney who moved up here. Got to be." He turned to me, "Dad doesn't want to have anything to do with the past. It's just too painful, that's what I think." He wasn't looking for my agreement; he already made up his mind, liked the way it felt.

As we drove home through the rolling farmland, I noticed a barn had "GOD IS LISTENING" in large block letters on the side facing the highway. And that made me think of my recent bouts with religious doubt. I glanced at the contented look on Truck's face, wondered if God had intervened to let him find peace. But then I thought of Nut's demonic father who abused him and his family relentlessly. I peered out the window; let my mind drift. Was God listening to what Nut had in store for Digger?

LAURA SIGHTING

I had a fitful night's sleep. The nightmares wouldn't stop. Nut had been sent to Vietnam, was on a secret assignment to Khe Sahn. His mission was to scout the Ho Chi Minh trail prior to the South Vietnamese Army invasion. No one had heard from him for a couple weeks. His captain had called to let me know he was missing. He said he was either dead or just in deep cover, unable to communicate. The captain was asking me to come to Nam to head up the search. In the dream I said, "But I'm not even in the Army." But then the dream switched to Digger. Nut asked me to watch over his mother while he was gone. He had never acted on his plan to kill Digger. I knocked on her door before going to school, after a long wait, opened the door on my own and saw her lying unconscious on the kitchen floor. And that's when I started awake. Disturbed, I couldn't nod off.

Rather than fight sleeplessness, I decided to go to 6 am mass to see if God was really listening. My angelic mom always went to the 9 am mass, her routine after getting us off to school. When I rolled downstairs early, mom and dad were starting breakfast. Not used to seeing me that early, dad said, "Are we having an earthquake I don't know about?"

I shrugged, "Getting an early jump on the devil, trying to keep him off balance. I'm heading to mass to see if God will root for our team to win the city title."

Mom shook her head; "He's got bigger fish to fry, like teaching you not to give Monsignor Pugh a hard time at CCD." When I looked surprised, "He told me about your probing questions on indulgences." As I started to protest, she raised her hand, "Don't worry, he was laughing as he told me."

We were only four blocks from church, the brisk walk and cold weather helped wake me up. I always sat on the left side since that was the closest side as you entered the church from my home. Most people followed the same practice, not taking any extra steps. Weird but true. That made me think: Next time I'll be crazy and go to the right side, cause the gossipers to go amok. I used to serve mass in grade school, was notorious for pranks while assisting the priest during communion. One favorite was crossing my eyes, dangling my tongue as friends received the sacred host. Most started chuckling, choked as they tried to swallow the blessed wafer. Got glares of disapproval from the priest. I never got caught by the priest for being the instigator. Not once. It was only after entering High School that Monsignor Pugh put two and two together. By then it was too late, I was someone else's problem.

Shortly before mass started, I saw Laura Hartley and her dad enter the other end of my pew. I hadn't seen her since getting the shooting tip. As she settled in, she shook the beautiful head of hair and pulled it back with her hands. It was before the roosters were up but Laura looked like a movie star. How can anyone look that good in the morning? Her face was flushed from the cold, her dark coat set off her brown and auburn hair. I always dated pretty girls but I had to admit, Laura Hartley was in her own league. What a face. She still hadn't noticed me. I tried not to stare too much. Didn't want her to think I was a stalker or anything. I listened to her sing the hymns with gusto. She had a nice voice. That didn't surprise me. She was about perfect. Both she and her dad were intent on the service so I found myself concentrating harder, caught by the rhythm of the prayers. Without forethought, I prayed for Truck and Nut.

Before I knew it, the mass had moved on and we were heading for the communion rail to receive the Blessed Sacrament. I thought about my boyhood pranks, figured I'd do some burn time in Purgatory for my silliness. But I had already practiced my defense as I went before St Peter for the final reckoning. I'd look at him sincerely, innocence dripping from my eyes, "But you made me this way!" That plan ran through my mind as I left the pew. I waited until Laura and her dad got out, hoping my manners would win points. When Laura saw me waiting, she got a huge smile, the gorgeous face lit up even brighter. As she scooted past me, she said, "What a gentleman." Her dad also smiled at me, mouthed a thank you. I followed them to the priest and altar boy, took Holy Communion without any nonsense. When I returned to the pew, Laura had her head down, praying for some special intention. I dropped my head, said to myself, "Help my friends, that's all I ask."

Mass ended, too soon for me since I just liked being in the same row with Laura Hartley. As she exited the aisle after her dad, she turned to me and winked. And then she was off. Her dad's car was parked right near the church steps. They sped away before I could get another look. Walking home, I tried to convince myself that fourteen years old wasn't that young. I was a good salesman but even I knew that was iffy territory. As I started to get upset, I had a comforting thought. What's the rush, I'll just wait till she's older. The weird thing was I was pretty sure that Laura Hartley was already more mature than me. But then I thought: Who isn't? That made me chuckle as I walked into the house. Mom saw my smile, "What are you so happy about?"

I pointed at her, grinned, "I'm pretty sure I got proof that angels are real."

SPIDERS

Nut walked into Sellers Library to do research. He had hatched what he thought was a foolproof plan. At the right moment, he'd run it by Dylan to see if there were any holes. As he thought that, he got a concerned look on his sculpted face. He knew Dylan thought the whole idea was crazy, mostly because he thought Nut would get caught. Dylan's worry was what caused him to reevaluate. Not about killing Digger; but just how to do it in a way that left no suspicions. The other day when he was wrestling, he recalled his survival training at Parris Island. More specifically, he remembered the instructor cautioning him about Brown Recluse Spiders. This deadly spider had migrated beyond its normal borders, was now making a home on the island. "One bite will put you in a world of hurt," was the Drill Sergeant's dire warning. And the light went off in his head: Who could ever blame him if his father got accidently bitten?

He went to the Arachnid section, which was on the second floor of Seller's Library. He pulled a book called "Arachnids—the perfect killing machines." Nut got a smile on his face, liking the sound of that. This writer loved spiders, describing them as perfectly engineered for hunting, but he ended the article by calling them "the stuff of nightmares." Nut discovered that tarantulas were also arachnids and that the Chinese Bird Spider bite can be lethal. He scratched his head, thought: Where would I get that exotic spider without a trip to Asia? As he read about this deadly spider, he ruled it out. They could be 8 inches long, much too large to be inconspicuous. Plus their bite was very painful, not the more subtle approach he was planning. And then he read of the legendary Black Widow Spider. When he saw that severe muscle spasms and paralysis were symptoms, he got intrigued. Should he use this more common spider for the job? He stopped when he saw the Brazilian Wandering Spider; read it was the most venomous spider on earth; but it also large and not easily explained being found in Philadelphia. He'd have to think about that. If he got one, was it too much a stretch that it was mixed in a shipment of South American flowers sent for a viewing at Digger's Funeral Home?

Nut settled back in his chair; let his mind wander over his strategy. Digger always wore a waterproof suit when he did the embalming. He always stripped to his underwear, slipped the suit on. It had feet built into it for full coverage, small air holes to provide ventilation. The sleeves had rubber gloves built into the arms. The only thing not covered was his face, which he protected with goggles and mask. Digger was methodical. He cleaned the suit thoroughly, air dried it and folded it neatly for the next occasion. Nut would place the spider in the suit, refold it the precise way Digger always did and wait patiently. Per his research, the bites of the Black Widow and Brown Recluse were painless. The victim felt nothing. And both spiders didn't bite unless trapped and pushed hard–like if someone was getting a wetsuit on and slammed their body into your lair. Nut wanted to use more than one spider to make certain of multiple bites. He wanted nothing left to chance. He had settled on the Black Widow, common in this country. Now, where to get these perfect killing machines without leaving a trail?

CIPHER

I had written the codes from Digger's ledger in my school notebook. Nut made copies a few days ago when Digger was attending to a burial at Carlington Cemetery and passed them along. We agreed to work on them separately; hoping one of us had a revelation. As I did with hard puzzles, sometimes the meaning came when you were doing something completely different. I would flip open the book periodically during school, breaking the drone of the priest. But this magic formula had gone nowhere. I had doodled mindlessly with them for a couple days, gotten jack shit. So I went to the library to read about codes. Nut said Digger was highly organized so the numbers had to be some code that was clear to him but would make no sense to someone who stumbled on it. To get another set of eyes, I asked Drum to come with me. He was the smartest guy I ever met and since he never did homework, I knew he'd be available. Drum knew I was a puzzle addict so it wasn't too odd for me to be poking around for obscure facts. He picked me up in his new car; we drove to Seller's Library.

Drum was in a great mood. He whistled as he drove, looked at me, "Pretty sad shit that Drexel Heights doesn't have its own library. I mean, Seller's is in Upper Derby, which as we all know, isn't exactly in the same league as our fair town. Ever wonder about what we pay our taxes for? Doesn't it honk you off?"

I raised my eyebrows, "You don't pay any taxes; you're just a young, angry shithead that likes to complain."

He grinned, "But I will one day soon and I'm keeping track of the stuff that pisses me off. Nothing better than being prepared."

After a minute or so, I asked, "Are you getting this tax complaint from your father or is this just your own rant?"

Drum shook his head, smirked, "My old man doesn't have a clue what's going on. He couldn't find his own asshole without a map." I laughed for the rest of the ride.

As we mounted the steps toward the front entrance, who should come bounding out but Nut. He looked surprised to see us. When I asked what he was studying, he paused, "Er, just tying up some loose ends on a Biology project. Keeping a step ahead of the teacher."

I nodded my head, "Not buying that. Bet you were looking at nudie pictures in National Geographic. I heard this month has some exotic Watusi dancers." He didn't react, not wanting to hear what else I might add. So we bid farewell, started for the library door.

As Nut walked off, he said to Drum, "Try to be quiet in there, I know that's hard for Dylan."

Drum grinned, "Now there's a hopeless task." We went in, headed to Bibliography, looked up "Code Breaking." Surprisingly, there were loads of books. Drum read my troubled look. "Let's go to that section, thumb through the books; pick out a few that make sense. If they don't help, we'll grab more till we find one that's useful."

I grabbed one called, "Enemy Codes—How to Break Them." The first few pages weren't too obscure so I trotted to a nearby desk. True to form, Drum grabbed one in Japanese, said to me, "Now this could be fun." I chuckled, went back to my own reading. I learned that "code" was a secret language used to conceal the true meaning of a message. Since I already had figured that out, I plowed on. It seemed that the more complex codes used numbers. The trick was to use numbers that had no predictable relationship to the actual meaning. I sat back in my chair; let that sink in. Was Digger that smart? Would he go through that effort to disguise his tracking system? I decided it was best to assume he was canny enough since he went to the effort to hide the way he tracked each theft. I read on but decided to try another book

As I walked over to the racks, I saw Drum engrossed in his reading. Was my brilliant pal reading Japanese? That made me chuckle. I guess I was too loud since I got the skunk eye from the librarian who was stacking books. I raised my hands in the "sorry" signal. Scanning the books, I spotted "The Cipher—Unlocking the Puzzle." Just the title drew me in—I loved puzzles. I grabbed the tome, returned to my desk. Ciphering concealed a plain message by scrambling the letters. There were two types of ciphers: the substitution cipher and the transposition cipher. A good example of the substitution cipher was using the real alphabet and then creating a cipher-text alphabet that corresponded to the real letter of the alphabet. For example, in the cipher ABCD, it would spell HELP if you knew that A=H, B=E, C=L and D=P. All you needed was the cipher-text alphabet to decode a seeming bunch of gibberish. That got me thinking.

I decided that Digger's code was probably some form of transposition cipher. He used some real letters and numbers to keep account of his robberies. But he did it in such a way that if it were found, it would seem like nonsense—without a meaning. Just as I was about to put the book back, I saw a chapter on simple transposition ciphers. These simple examples used birthdays, telephone numbers, street addresses, towns, names and other basic pieces of information to give meaning only to the person who wrote them. That got me back to the question: Was Digger brilliant? Or did he use some other simple twist on codes or ciphers to hide an obvious answer? I exhaled, my head was hurting. I got up, put the book in the stack.

I moseyed over to Drum who was deep in thought. He finally looked up when he saw me staring. He scrunched his eyebrows, "Give me another few hours and I could read this sucker. Once you see the patterns, Japanese isn't that tough, know what I mean?"

I nodded, "I know exactly what you mean. I picked up Chinese over Thanksgiving break." I paused, "The Mandarin dialect, of course."

Drum stared at me, shook his head, "Shithead." And then added, "I think I got the gist of the Japanese code breaking philosophy."

I took the bait, "What is it?" He went on, "It's simple, catch the guy who wrote the code, strap him down, run an electric wire around his nuts and push the switch till he spits out the message." We got another stink eye from the librarian as we left laughing.

But I got enough information to mull over at the library. Drum was quiet for a change, so I sat thinking as we drove. Digger definitely used a consistent system. But whether it was a simple code or a cipher was the question. My gut said cipher so I had to figure what patterns were used. Drum leaned over, "Want to get a hoagie before we go home? I'm starved." So was I, we headed to The Deli. Our buddy Scoot worked there a couple nights a week, greeted us when we entered. He grinned, "Look what the mangy cat dragged in."

Drum was undeterred, "A couple of your finest Italians, Scoot. And don't use the day old rolls. Remember, we're your pals. And don't hesitate to pile on some extra meat. Be generous."

Scoot feigned disappointment, "Aw, shit, the only rolls left are the ones I dropped near the toilet." And then smiled, "But they are moist."

Scoot was a hard working kid, he always had multiple jobs, had a car that he bought with his own money on his 16th birthday. And he was way more mature than any of us except Nut. But despite the grueling work schedule, taking advanced courses in school and playing basketball, he was always upbeat. He was a guy you could count on, always went full tilt at whatever he did. We might have been best friends but he was always working, never around to hang out. He whistled loudly as he made our hoagies. I yelled, "Stop the serenade, Scoot, you'll scare off the customers that aren't paid to be your friends."

He grinned, "Do you want the hoagie that fell all the way in the toilet or just on the floor?"

Drum answered quickly, "I'm the only one who throws you the ball, choose wisely." But Scoot made us a fabulous hoagie, joined us since the place was empty. We spent the next hour solving the world's problems, like which was the best Tastykake?

ARCHANGEL TESTS

I hadn't been to CCD class with Nut and Hank Greenberg for a couple weeks. But my experience with "GOD IS LISTENING," renewed my interest. Plus my mother mentioned Monsignor Pugh had ratted me out. I wanted to stir things up again. Hank had become Monsignor Pugh's favorite. He believed Hank would be a convert to Catholicism. That was an overpowering draw for a priest. I was happy for Hank. His new friends were all Catholic and, according to him, "There must be something about being Catholic. I love all you guys. Nobody else ever treated me like you do." Hank had moved from a tough neighborhood in West Philly, must have had some bad experiences living there. I planned to ask about what he had gone through but kept forgetting. And that great gang of friends comment made me think about Nut. Why would he leave us to fight in Nam? I shook my head, trying to rid that thought.

Monsignor Pugh started the lesson. He explained the "The Annunciation of the Virgin Mary" was a key tenet of the Catholic faith. Mary was visited by the angel Gabriel; told she would conceive a baby and become the mother of God but remain a virgin. She was to stay silent about the miraculous conception and name the child Jesus, who was the Son of God. Only she and her husband Joseph were entrusted with the astounding news. I had heard this story my whole life, believed it implicitly. But I could see Hank thinking. This was tough for an older kid to absorb for the first time. He asked a lot of questions, mainly about the need for the human birth process. "Why not just have Jesus appear out of nowhere and have that be the miracle?" Monsignor Pugh explained the need for Jesus to have experienced the human condition and to make the ultimate sacrifice—to give his own life that all of us could enter heaven after death. Hank sat silently, taking it in.

I raised my hand. "How come Gabriel was chosen to deliver the message? Was he the top angel?"

Monsignor Pugh looked wary, deciding if I was about to lower the boom. He decided to plow on, "Gabriel was an archangel, recognized as one of God's highest angels. There is no Biblical explanation why he was chosen over Michael, Raphael or the other archangels."

I was getting warmed up. "Was there some special tests they had to pass to make archangel? Like being able to fly faster or being super strong?" I shrugged, "I've always been fuzzy on how you got into the archangel team. I mean it's like getting voted into the Baseball Hall of Fame. Like Willie Mays being the greatest centerfielder of all time. Making basket catches, that kind of impossible thing. What I'm saying is you had to be a superstar. But I thought all angels had super powers. How did a regular angel make the jump in rank?"

Monsignor Pugh grimaced, shook his head, "I'm pretty sure they had an angel Olympics each four years. The winner made archangel. Any other sensible questions?" The whole class laughed. Monsignor Pugh topped me. I shut up.

I walked home with Hank and Nut. Hank said, "Just the way Monsignor Pugh deals with Dylan really impresses me. If I pulled that stuff in synagogue class, they'd ban me for a month. The rabbi's have no sense of humor about religion."

Nut added, "Monsignor Pugh knows Dylan's going to hell. He feels sorry for him."

I didn't say anything, enjoyed hearing Nut having fun. Hank continued, "I asked him to help me with the conversion steps. He agreed to tutor me. H said it would be an honor."

I looked shocked, "I thought you wanted me to be your sponsor?"

Hank shook his head, "Monsignor Pugh said to avoid you, that you were a near occasion of sin. That it would hurt my chances of getting in."

Nut laughed, "That's an understatement."

We finished the walk talking about whom was the better basketball player, Wilt Chamberlain or Bill Russell. I ended my comments with, "Do you think Wilt will make archangel?"

OUT OF SYNC

Our final game of the season was a week away. We were playing St Joseph's, a tough center city team that won their football conference in the Catholic League this year. They had only won four basketball games, but all the games had been close. They were not really basketball players, just good athletes who competed fiercely. Coach Gallagher made it clear; "Their season will be a success if they beat us. They couldn't care less about their lousy record. Get ready for a war."

Coach asked Drum to give his scouting report. He looked at us, paused, "It's just as Coach said. They're a bunch of knuckle-draggers but they flat go at it. Wear your steel cups, is what I suggest. Those bastards like to kick some gonads."

Coach shook his head, "As usual, Drum gives us a colorful description, but he's essentially right, these boys won't have an A skill level, but they will have A plus effort. A very tough group."

Similar to preparing for Bishop O'Hare's team, Coach had us play 6 players who pressed the whole time. Our second team was better than some teams in our league, so we had to bust our butt. The first couple days of practice we were lousy, turned the ball over or rushed passes. By the end of the 2nd day of watching us screw up, Coach blew his whistle, threw up his hands, told us to get out of the gym. He walked off the court, turned when he got to the doors, "If you practice like that tomorrow, I start the second team, at least they're playing with some heart." He walked through the doors.

We watched, thinking he might come back. He had never walked out on us in the four years we had played for him. I turned to Drum, "I guess he's really pissed off."

Scoot answered, "He's right, we have to calm down." No one said much as we went to the lockers, showered, then went home.

I wish I could say we practiced great the next day, but we didn't. Coach could see that the effort was there. We were just out of sync. He blew his whistle in frustration. "Boys, where's the fire? What's the big hurry? Think out there. Take a deep breath and slow down." Trying to loosen us up, he tried something different. He had Drum throw the ball in to Truck against the press, instead of Scoot or Fran Philips. I took Truck's place as the safety valve pass down court. Although a moose, Truck was terrific at controlling the ball. Despite three guys pestering him, he protected the ball, found the open man. Slowly, we started to gel, getting the ball over half court and running our plays. Although we were much better, we still clanged our shots on the rim and struggled to score. When we finally ran a smooth play, Coach blew the whistle, ended practice. "Let's end on a good note, boys. Big game tomorrow."

♦

Mom had a big dinner waiting as I stumbled in the door. We always ate as a family, except if I had a game, then I ate earlier by myself. I never ate a lot before playing. But after a grueling practice, I was starved. Even in the winter, we had great vegetables my dad canned from the summer garden. Plus they made bread in the winter, perfect for sopping up the rich gravy from the roast beef. Mom cooked the potatoes and carrots with the meat, so the gravy had extra punch. Normally, I carried the conversation at dinner, the gabber in the clan. But tonight I was quiet. Dad looked at me, "You must be whipped, I've never heard you so quiet."

I raised my head, "You mean you never NOT heard me this quiet."

He chuckled, rapped me on the noggin. "That's my boy. It worries me when you're not incorrigible."

I came from a very bright family but never did that great in school. Actually, I was a B student but my older siblings had been straight A's, gifted. I looked mediocre in comparison. But my parents never made me feel I was being compared. The comparison's came from teachers who taught my siblings. Part of the problem was most courses didn't interest me. Drum and I had that in common. Except, Drum excelled at Math and Science, always taking great joy in correcting the priests if they gave a faulty solution in Chemistry or Physics.

The only subject I liked was English. But most of the mandatory books were pretty dry so I didn't push myself. I mean, who gives a shit about Thoreau hanging around Walden Pond? Why didn't the lazy bastard get a real job? I got the reading gene from my dad. He kept a dictionary and thesaurus beside his reading chair, proudly used obscure words he was trying to memorize. That night he turned to me after dinner, asked me how I was doing in school this semester. I hesitated and before I could respond, he said, "I was worried you were becoming a mooncalf." He saw my puzzled look, grabbed his stomach in laughter. My dad was his own best audience. Come to think of it, I had the same quirk. I went to look up what mooncalf meant. Turned out WC Fields used the term a lot in his skits for people who were simpletons. Interested, I read about lots of other funny terms WC used. Next night, I greeted dad as he came in from work. "Dad, good news, I did well in a Chemistry test today, aced it. No need to worry about the mooncalf problem." And as I walked away, "But I might be a jobbernowl or a la dee da."

STREET FIGHT

We took the bus to St Joseph's after school. If it was an inner city game, the Catholic League played Friday games early so visitors didn't have to be out late at night. St Joseph was in a tough part of the city. It was best to be cautious, especially if we kicked their butts. Nut and Hank drove to the game separately. Mrs. Delaney didn't come to the game. "She has bingo tonight. She's the reader. Kind of the big shot of the show," Truck told us.

So I sat with him, reminded him that this team would probably bait him, trying to get a technical so he'd be ineligible for the playoffs. "So, break your normal pattern, try to play smart for a change."

He swatted me, "Just worry about yourself. I got the reputation but you're just as bad when you get wound up." He had a point, I did have a fuse that wasn't short but if you found the right spot, I'd go after you. Coach Gallagher liked my grit. "I always know if you get pushed, you'll push back harder," he told me that my sophomore year. I never got a technical but was always good for hard fouls each game. It was how we played at the courts. If you lost you sat a long time. You play to win.

We started the game like we practiced during the week—lousy. As expected, the St Joe players were physical. If you drove the lane, you got hammered—no cheap fouls with this bunch. Truck played his normal ferocious way but with two guys hanging on him, he was getting frustrated. St Joe's alternated players a lot, not caring how many fouls they got. I watched Truck closely to see if his

232

fuse was lit. Smartly, they left me alone and guarded Truck and Fran. I made all my five shots and no one else scored for us. The 1st quarter ended 10-10. Coach huddled us, "Keep pushing the ball to Truck. Pretty soon, they'll run out of fouls and we'll get free points at the line. We might win ugly, but we'll win." He looked at Truck, "Stay cool."

As we walked on the court, Drum moseyed over to Truck. "Me and Dylan will back you up. Let us pound somebody if we need to, okay?"

Truck grinned, "We'll see." That worried me.

We did as Coach wanted, kept working the ball in the middle. Truck found his rhythm and began scoring, even with two defenders hanging on his arm. Fran Philips got more open looks and made every shot. Scoot stripped the guards a couple times, sailed in for easy buckets. True to our word, if somebody nailed Truck, Drum or I made them pay for it on the next possession. We pulled away quickly, going up by 15 points at half. But Drum had collected three fouls and we felt liked we'd just been in a football game. Coach was happy but he noticed how gingerly we were walking into the locker room. He looked at us, "That was about the best quarter you played all year. It doesn't matter if it's pretty, this will be a great win." He paused, looking at each of us. "You'll be sore when this is over, but remember, you'll be ending an undefeated season in the Catholic League and trust me gentlemen, you'll remember that for the rest of your lives. That warm bath will feel nice. Let's get out there and kick some hinny."

I found myself wide open again and began raining uncontested jump shots. Truck was a monster again, grabbing every loose ball, scoring relentlessly. Most times he got fouled and ended with three point plays. You could see the St Joe players were getting frustrated as we took a 30 point lead early in the 4th quarter. But they didn't give up. They called time out. You could hear their coach berating them. With renewed vigor, they started guarding us like it was a tie game, fouled us on every shot—hard fouls. I saw Truck had smoke coming out of his ears. Before I could get to him, a St Joe player came driving down the lane and Truck was there to greet him. As he went up to shoot, Truck's elbows came down on his shoulders with a thud. The St Joe forward dropped like a sack of doorknobs. The ref blew the whistle but the didn't call it flagrant because he saw we'd gotten hammered the whole game. The kid took a long time getting up. He finally rose, limped to the foul line.

That's when all hell broke loose. When the ref handed the kid the ball to shoot foul shots, he grabbed the ball, darted down the lane and threw the ball at Truck's head. As Truck was protecting himself, another husky St Joe player punched him in the gut. Tough as he was, Truck coughed out air and doubled over. When I saw what happened, I ran at the sucker-puncher and walloped him in the ear the way Jimmer taught me. Trouble was, I still hadn't mastered the technique. My palm ended up giving just a hard slap. The guy looked at me like I was crazy, swung at me. Wrestling with Nut for all these years had taught me how to move in a fight. I averted the punch, grabbed his arm, threw him hard to the floor. By then, the refs were blowing whistles and our coaches had plowed in to restore order. That's how I got my first technical and game ejection. Coach Gallagher sat Truck after he shot his

234

technical foul shots. We won the ugly game with most of the starters on the bench. I expected Coach Gallagher to ream us out. He stood over us a few seconds before saying simply, "League Champs and you did it the old fashioned way—a street fight." We all cheered.

Nut and Hank were waiting for us as we exited the gym to get in the bus. Nut had a big grin on his face. "Great game guys. Best one of the year. You have to admit that team didn't quit."

Hank chimed in, "You should have seen Nut when the fight broke out. I had to hold him with both hands to keep him from jumping in." Just then a gang of rabid St Joe fans came around the corner.

Coach Gallagher looked at them, said sternly, "Get in the bus. Now." He began herding us inside before the mob got too near. Hank and Nut moved off to the side as the crowd started yelling and throwing whatever was handy at the bus. Hot dogs, soft pretzels and french fries pelted us.

The taunts were imaginative but mostly laced with profanity. "Buncha faggots from Drexel Heights. Like fuckin' monkeys with those long arms." But most of the noise was unintelligible. The bus took off, we watched the last of the hotdogs hurling through the air as we sped away.

I looked at Truck. "They have a point. You do look kinda look like a silverback ape." He grinned but I could see he was still wound up from the battle. The ride home was subdued. The fight left our nerves raw.

But we soon regained our joy after getting back to Conner High, made plans to meet. The industrious Scoot signed up to work the night shift at The Deli since we had an afternoon game. We wanted him part of the party so we met there to celebrate. Nut and Hank joined us. Nut came over, put his arm around me. "You need a lot of work on the ear slap but your arm toss was almost perfect."

That made me laugh. I finally said, "That guy looked at me like I was a psycho. Like his girlfriend probably slapped him that way when he got fresh. He didn't know what to do, laugh or fight"

The owner of The Deli, Vito Scarlotti, was there and let Scoot join us for free hoagies and cheesesteaks. As Vito took our orders, "Least I can do for the champs. Never got ta play much ball as a kid. Been working in this damn deli since I was ten. My old man said sports was fer rich kids. Nice ta see ya grew up to be somethin' special. Youse kids been hangin' here since grade school. Wasn't sure you'd amount to anythin'. Proud a ya." He went behind the counter to make the sandwiches.

But our fun was short-lived. A brawny group of guys barged through the door. The three biggest moved to the front, St Joseph football jerseys announcing whom we were dealing with. They had followed us from the game. A super-sized lineman shouted, "Looking for the pussies who sucker-punched our guy. You don't pull that cheap shot without paying for it."

I was sitting beside Truck. He put his hand on my shoulder, pushing me back in the bench. As he started to rise, Nut moved around him, approached the St Joe thugs.

In a very soft voice, almost a whisper, "Why don't you back out of here gentlemen. Look, it was a hard-fought game, tempers flared. Let's just put it behind us. Okay?"

The lineman smirked, "How about me knockin' your teeth out and puttin' those behind us?" His gang chuckled.

That's when Nut did what only he could do. Most people stand their ground as a mob appears. Nut started moving slowly forward, talked even softer. He pointed at the leader, "If you take another step, I'm going to break your nose. And you're not that that pretty to start with." He pointed at the next guy. "And you, I'm going to kick you in the groin. Were you planning to have kids? You might want to think about that." And then to the third punk, "While you're looking in amazement, I'll sweep your right knee. Maybe it will break. I'd make new plans if you were you planning to play ball next fall?" You could see the three bullies thinking. But they made a mistake, started moving at Nut. And then he did exactly what he said. The fight was over in five seconds. The three leaders were groaning on the floor, the rest of the gang hustled outside. After a few agonizing minutes of reccovery, the three mangled wise guys crawled out behind them.

Vito comes from behind the counter, shook his head in disbelief, looked at us, "Holy shit." After a few seconds, "Tastykakes on me."

◆

Mom and dad were asleep when I got home. There was a note on the refrigerator, "Congratulations. There's a turkey and gravy sandwich inside if you're hungry." My parents typically went to bed early. Even if the Pope stopped by for a surprise visit after dinner, they'd still slip off to bed by 9 pm. I turned on WIBG when I went to my room. The music was a nice companion. My older brother had severe asthma when he was younger. We used to sleep together but he was off to college. I had gotten used to hearing his labored breathing each night. He didn't know it but I faked being asleep till I heard his wheezing settle into a peaceful pattern. That was my signal to stop worrying.

But now the Philly radio stations were a more serene background noise. I had a hard time nodding off. Maybe wound up from the game. Or was it the fight? Bobby Vee's "Devil or Angel" came on the radio. People who didn't know him well probably wondered that about Nut. Only a devil could annihilate enemies that easily. But I knew the angel side. He took no joy in fighting. He was struggling with a living devil. Those were my last thoughts as I nodded off.

◆

Mom made a special breakfast for me next morning. "Anything you want champ."

I shrugged, "How about scrambled eggs, dilly bread toast and your famous 'Crapple'?"

She shook her head, having heard my joke for the millionth time. "You mean, 'Scrapple,' son. Trying to be funny again?"

I feigned innocence. "After dad told me what it's made out of, I think 'Crapple' is a better name. Don't you?" She chuckled, went off to make my feast. I read the Bulletin description of our game, was glad my ear slap mishap wasn't mentioned. I knew that would bring lots of comments from Jimmer if he learned I botched the move.

My dad wandered in, rubbed my head as his way of praise for the championship, poured some coffee, pulled out the puzzle section and began his wordsmithing. That made me remember Digger's code. I told dad about the code I was trying to solve, asked his advice. Told him that Drum and I were having a competition. Dad knew how smart Drum was so it didn't surprise him. He didn't answer for a few minutes. He said succinctly, "The trick with puzzles is you see it, but you don't *see* it." I waited for more. He clarified, "The answer is usually the most obvious. The simpler the answer the harder the solution. So, making sure you don't over-complicate things is the trick to most hard puzzles."

I went and got the codes I'd written in my book, showed them to my wily dad. He looked at the 3 sets, 609633-C-7058-19#, 410267-B-1397-1# AND 302149-W-0890-9#. And then he covered them to look at each one individually. He crinkled his eyebrows, "First thing that pops to mind is telephone numbers. Usually my first reaction is my best. I don't know what the letters have to do with it, maybe some other meaning beside the telephone numbers. And then I remembered going to basketball camp in New Jersey last summer. The area code was 609.

I looked at dad, "What's the area code for Baltimore?" He grinned, "410. Maybe the B stands for

Baltimore?" He was born in Baltimore, most of our relatives still lived in Maryland. I didn't want to tip my hand too much about the real puzzle. So I said, "I think you cracked it, pop. Now I can tell Drum I'm smarter than him. He'll cringe. Don't rat me out that you helped."

Later that day when alone, I went to the telephone, dialed 609-633-7058. After a short ring, "Hello, Fast Eddie's Pawn Brokers."

I smiled, "Can you give me direction to the shop?" I got directions to Fast Eddie's in Camden, N.J. And then dialed the next two numbers. Both were pawnshops in Baltimore and Wilmington. I blew air out contentedly, whispered, "Got ya.

THE POP

After my miserable attempt at the ear slap on the St Joe thug, I dropped over Jimmer's house after Sunday breakfast. The older brother John let me in, so I avoided any small talk with Jimmer's parents. Not that the Kielmanns didn't like me, they were just kind of serious, made me do all the work at being sociable. Hard to believe they had a son like Jimmer, a natural storyteller and iconoclast.

When I went to the basement, Jimmer was playing a catchy folk music album. He turned as I descended, "Ever hear of Cat Stevens, Dylan?" I shook my head. "He's a new dude from England. He's writing some powerful stuff. Might have named you "Cat" if he'd been around when you were a kid." He stopped talking; seem to ponder that. "Nah, I still like Dylan better for you. Better irony. You do move like a cat, so it would almost be complimentary. We wouldn't want you getting cocky, would we?"

I responded, "Cocky doesn't play well in this neighborhood. Puts a bigger target on you." Jimmer nodded approval.

I got to why I was visiting. "Speaking of not being cocky, did you hear about my ear slap in the St Joe game?"

He grinned, "Nut was here for lessons yesterday, he filled me in. He said you need some work."

I was glad Nut didn't go into detail but decided to come clean. "The kid looked at me like I was swatting a bug off his head, like I was working for Terminix or something."

Jimmer laughed, "Let's get to work."

We went to the heavy bag. Jimmer took my hand, slapped the bag firmly. "Listen to that pop, Dylan. When you hear the pop, you have it right. That slap sends off an explosion inside the punk's head. Once you get the feel, it's easy. Like riding a camel, tricky at first, but once locked in, you'll never forget it. Just takes lots of practice." I was going to ask about the camel riding but knew that would take us off on a long story. Instead, we went at it again. After an hour, I started to get the feel of it. For the next ½ hour I heard the beautiful pop sound. Jimmer beamed, "You have it." I walked home proud of myself. But I knew I had to do it in real life before declaring victory. Practice was one thing. Would I be able to do it when I needed it?

SHILLINGTON SHUT DOWN

I hadn't heard anything from Vernon Herbein, the postmaster in Reading. So I called to see if there were bites on our "Wanted Poster" about Truck. When I reminded him who I was and what we wanted, he stayed quiet. I could almost hear him thinking. "Sorry, we got no response." And then added, "We had to take the sign down. We had a postal inspection, the inspector wrote me up for a breach of protocol." When I asked if he spoke to the clerk Lester about the German lady, he hesitated a few seconds. "Er, sorry, can't help you. Er, have to go now. Got customers lined up." And he hung up abruptly. I stared at the phone for a couple minutes. What happened to the helpful man who seemed interested in breaking rules to help? And why did he seem so nervous? I thought about that all day at school. I continued to call for Herbein over the next few days but my calls were unanswered.

Truck had been bugging me for an update. As we walked out of practice, I filled him in on the weird exchange with Herbein. I could see him get agitated. "But why all of sudden does the guy clam up? I mean, he really seemed interested in helping."

I didn't share my true thoughts. Instead, "Might have got his ass handed to him by the postal inspector. Drum said those pricks love to stick it to the post offices in the boonies. Let them know who's the boss kind of thing." Before he could get too wound up, "Let's take a drive out there tomorrow and snoop around. If Herbein won't see us, we'll look for the clerk Lester.

Truck said, "I can't believe you remember that guy's name."

I smiled, "It's easy. I made a little jingle up to help me remember. 'Lester the molester from Lancaster.' My dad taught me the mnemonic trick years ago."

Truck grinned for the first time that day. "You are a sicko."

The ride to Reading next Saturday morning was quiet. I used the silence to formulate a way to get Herbein to start helping again. But I had a nagging worry. I wondered if he had called Truck's house, got Mr. Carr by accident, got an earful about staying out of family business. That would explain the change of heart. Just then we passed the barn with "GOD IS LISTENING" on the side. I silently began my favorite prayer, the Twenty Third Psalm. "The Lord is my shepherd, I shall not want... You prepare a table before me in the presence of my enemies... Yea though I enter the Valley of the Shadow of Death, I will fear no evil... Surely goodness and mercy shall follow me all the days of my life, and I will dwell in the house of the Lord forever." I had been saying that beautiful prayer to myself for weeks. I snuck a peek at my troubled friend. I hoped we weren't walking into that ominous valley of death.

I told Truck we should try to find out who Lester was before approaching Herbein. That way, we could get some better information on the German lady before Herbein shut him up. "Might as well take no chances." Truck nodded, liking the approach. I went in first to reconnoiter. The picture of Truck was gone. Just the usual wanted posters and bunches of new postal regulations. I went back out and told Truck to wander in after I got in line. Told him to watch out for Herbein while I found out who Lester was. There were 2 clerks working the line. The older guy was the one we talked to last time. The other was much younger, tall and lanky. To myself: Kind of looks like a molester from Lancaster. When I got to the front spot, I saw that the older clerk was going to be my helper, so I asked the old man behind me to take my spot. He eyed me warily; like he was worried I'd pickpocket him. To relieve his puzzlement, "The older clerk doesn't like me. Thinks my taste in stamps is inferior." He scrunched his eyes together, wondering what the hell that meant.

I saw Truck moving around, antsy. Finally the young clerk got free. I moseyed up, "You wouldn't by any chance be Lester, would you?"

He looked surprised but nodded assent. "How'd you know?"

I went into my routine, "Mr. Herbein told me about you the last time I was here. Said you knew a German lady that was giving Pennsylvania Dutch lessons. I'm interested in taking them myself but didn't know her name."

He got a funny look on his face, like he was trying to remember some instruction that he couldn't quite place. "I don't know her name, never ended up taking the course. I just know her face. She comes in here each Monday morning to mail her letters. She always says, 'I don't trust those mailboxes. I like the old ways.' The first time she said it, I picked up on the accent. After a few visits, she mentioned the class she ran on Pennsylvania Dutch."

As I was about to ask what she looked like, Herbein came storming out of his office, eyes wild. He seemed to compose himself as he got to us. "What's going on here, Lester?"

Before he could answer, "I was asking Lester if he came from Lancaster. Was about to ask if his parents were into rhyming. That's when you popped up. I was going to stop by your office next." He looked at me funny, sizing me up before responding. But then he told Lester to go take a break. Lester wandered into the back of the mailroom.

Just then Truck walked up. Herbein seemed to soften. "Sorry, we couldn't help you out, Carr. Rules are rules. The postal inspector doesn't allow exceptions."

Truck nods as if understanding, said, "I understand. That's why we want to talk to Lester. He seemed to know who the German lady was."

Herbein's demeanor changed, got flushed, "That's not allowed either. We can't disclose information about other customers. It's against federal rules." As I was about to rebut, he said, "You'll have to leave now, you're holding up the line." He looked around me to the growing line of mailers, waved, "Next."

Outside, Truck had flames coming out of his eyes. "Fuck that guy, I'll show him about rules when I smash his face in. The prick knows something."

I had the same thought but knew I had to calm Truck down. "I think we got enough information. Lester doesn't know her name but he did mention she comes on Mondays to mail her letters in person. How about we camp out here next Monday?"

Truck said the obvious. "We'd have to cut school."

In response, I faked a cough. "Might have a cold coming on. How about you? Bet it hits full force by Monday."

Truck grinned, feigned a scratchy tickle. "Damn, those bugs sure do travel fast." On the ride home I wondered how Herbein knew we were in line. His office had no windows. Did another clerk call him? Odd. And then I thought about how to spot the German lady. There had to be more than a few tall blonde ladies in the area. I mean this was a heavily German area. In Italian South Philly, she'd stick out. But not in German populated Reading.

FAST EDDIE

We didn't start playoffs for another week, so we had a lighter practice schedule. Coach Gallagher wanted us to recover from our sore wrists, ankles and assorted problems while we had the chance. So, I went to Upper Derby, watched Nut during wrestling practice. It was fun seeing him throw everybody around. Before he found wrestling, I was the one getting tossed most times. The wrestling coach knew our history, so when he saw me he yelled. "Hey, Frazier, want a shot at Nut? He needs someone to test him a little."

I waved back, "No thanks, Coach. I just look like I'm stupid." He waved like he understood.

After practice, when I told Nut I'd cracked Digger's code, he stared at me a few seconds. "Son of a bitch. Now that you said it, it looks so obvious. Why didn't we spot it right away?"

In response, "Why don't we take a ride to Camden on Saturday? I'm anxious to see what Fast Eddie really looks like. Any bets, he's not named for his track skills?" The week flew by.

On the Saturday ride to Camden, I filled Nut in on our Reading postal episode. "How'd Truck take it?"

I shrugged, "Like a Brahma bull that just had his giant nuts kicked. He was about to explode but I calmed him down fast." I told Nut about our plan to cut school to see if we could meet this mysterious German lady.

He listened intently, eyes getting bigger. "Wish I could go with you but we have the makeup meet that was postponed earlier. If I miss school, they won't let you compete that day. If we win, we got the league championship for the 3rd year in a row. That would be a school record." Changing the topic, I asked how things were going with him and Reneé. Without taking his eye off the wheel, "Maybe too good. I'm starting to feel guilty not telling her about my Green Beret enlistment. She keeps asking what school I'm going to." He paused a few seconds, "She wants to go where I go so we can continue to go out." That didn't surprise me much. They were both incredibly talented people. And both were serious and driven, both exceptional students.

I told him what he already knew. "If you tell her, your secret might get out. You should wait till the last moment." He just shook his head, saying nothing.

We rode quietly for the next few minutes. This route to Camden was the exact way my dad took as a shortcut to avoid traffic as we went to Cape May for our annual summer vacation. It brought back recollections of my childhood. Dad never mentioned it but he was also looking for a way to avoid toll roads. My thrifty dad would drive 50 miles in the wrong direction to avoid a 25 cent toll. His theory was, "It's un-American to charge you to drive on the roads. What are our taxes for? The founding fathers should have added another Amendment—Freedom of Movement—to the Constitution. Don't you think, Kate?"

Mom smiled as she responded, "I'll pay the 25 cents

myself if it will shorten our two hour trip that takes you four hours. Do we really need to drive through the most violent crime area in New Jersey to save a quarter?"

His answer was always the same. "It's the principle."

To distract her, dad always talked about the history of Camden. "It used to be the boat building capitol of this country. New York Shipbuilding based their operations in Camden to save money, cranked out more naval vessels than anyone during WWII. Prior to that, Camden was just a sleepy suburb of Philly for a long time. But with all that money being made, politicians moved in and wanted a piece of the action." He would pause for dramatic effect, "And then like any good politician, they fleeced the voters." I had heard this all many times before so much of it stuck. Dad would also talk about how The Victor Talking Machine Company that eventually became RCA Victor. And that corporate giant General Electric bought RCA and then Camden started having more problems. "With all those workers, people didn't want to travel far so neighborhoods got built and suburbs started to grow. And if you add in how Campbell Soup started to explode, then you've got a thriving community." Another pause for drama, "But then the economy goes bust, people get laid off and gangs start to take over. Chaos ensues my friends, bleak and utter chaos."

My family trip memory stopped as Nut and I crossed over the Walt Whitman Bridge, made a quick right on the first ramp, meandered toward 4th and Pine, the location of Fast Eddie's Pawn Shop. Camden smelled terrible. The combination of urban blight, the murky Delaware River, dead fish and Campbell's Soup factories made for a nasty brew. Years ago Campbell's gave away free tomatoes in early May, before the gardening season. The catch was you had to go there in person to get the seedlings. Usually as punishment for tormenting my siblings, dad would drag me along to carry the freebies. He would whisper to me, his fellow conspirator, "Campbell's Soup isn't a match for your mom's porridge but those are the best damned tomatoes in the world." And he was right; our garden tomatoes were the envy of Shady Lane. Jealous neighbors would ask dad his secret. He would nod sagely, "The secret is my compost pile. Put all your egg shells, oat meal and coffee grinds with the other leftovers and you have a natural wonder for fertilizer." And year after year his tomatoes were the best. He never mentioned the pest-proof Campbell's tomatoes.

That pungent smell brought back those funny memories. But Nut broke my reverie, "Where the hell are we? This looks like a bomb zone in Nam. Do people really live down here?"

I looked around. "Not anybody I'd like to hang out with. I think we need to make a right on Pine and that should get us near 4th." After making the right, the street got more civilized looking, small shops dotted the street. But half the stores were boarded up, covered with graffiti. I pointed a clever one to Nut. Painted in black spray paint over the front of an old five and dime store, "Beware ye who enter these doors. Your ass is grass." As I chuckled, we neared Fast Eddie's, rolled past it cautiously. It was a big shop that looked like a military bunker. Steel bars lined the window and a thick metal gate guarded the massive front door. The entire building was brick. Fast Eddie was prepared for an assault. As we pulled to a stop farther down the street, I said to Nut, "Looks like a real welcoming place. Did you bring one of your M-16s?"

I had researched topaz in our family's Funk and Wagnall's Encyclopedia last weekend. My dad claimed he forked out the expense for encyclopedias because he sensed I would be a struggling scholar and might need an edge. His quote was, "You displayed an early predilection for tomfoolery."

I always responded, "Is that why you named me Tom?" And he always laughed. And so I learned that topaz was a mineral found in various parts of the world. In the United States, there was a huge deposit in Utah. And going back to ancient times, topaz was valued for its dazzling beauty and use in jewelry for royalty. Much of the information was too technical but I saw clearly that colored topaz that occurred naturally was very rare and valuable. I didn't know if my half-baked knowledge would be useful but I wanted to be prepared.

We had rehearsed our approach with Fast Eddie. Nut was a planner, a very precise guy. He looked at me sternly, "Try to behave. None of your funny business." I put my thumbs in my ears, wiggled my hands in response. He cuffed me on the head, "Behave." The store was surprisingly neat and ordered. A few customers were ambling among the aisles of assorted merchandise. I was trying to find the jewelry section when I spotted who I thought was Fast Eddie. As suspected, Fast Eddie was an ironic moniker—he was about 5' 7" and a bulbous 300 lbs.

The portly proprietor was haggling with a woman, pointing at a picture on the wall. "I can't prove it but the original owner says it's an Andrew Wyeth. She got it before he became the cat's meow." He pointed at a smudge in the corner of the portrait. "If you look real close, you can see the AW scrawled there."

The old lady strained but shook her head, came out with a classic Philly response. "Could mean A and W Root Beer for all we know. I need proof this things for real."

They continued the debate as we hunted for the jewelry section. Over the past few weeks, Nut and I had discussed the problem of proving Digger stole the jewelry from the corpses. It was our word against his unless we could document it. We needed verification that he pawned the merchandise and collected the money. We suspected he stashed the money, never paid taxes on it. Nut had given it a lot of thought. "He's a very careful man. If he paid taxes on it, it would be reported as income and he'd have to list how he made that much money."

When I looked befuddled, he elaborated, "Reneé's father is a CPA, so she knows everything about taxes, she helps out during the busy season. Her dad made her learn how to do their yearly income taxes. She's looking at going to Princeton, to be an Economics major. She explained the whole taxable income stuff to me. The IRS could audit Digger if things looked fishy. There's no way he takes that chance." So we concluded Digger probably sold the jewelry under a fake name or maybe some other illegal way. If he was stealing, he wasn't paying taxes. But we wanted to verify that Fast Eddie was part of the scam.

After that, we'd have to figure out what to do.

At the farthest part of the store, we found the long jewelry counter. All the goods were encased in a sturdy glass case brilliantly lit to show the wares. To Nut, "Smart guy, he puts the valuable stuff as far away from the door as possible. If you broke into the case, you have to run a gauntlet before you reached the front door." I glanced around the room. The ceilings were high. There was a series of elevated offices on this side of the room. From there you had a clear look at the whole shop. My bet was someone was eyeballing us right now. "Don't make any weird moves, Nut, I bet we're on Candid Camera right now."

He followed my glance. "You're the one who makes the weird moves. So far I'm impressed with your behavior. Stay that way." Just then the corpulent owner came bounding our way.

"What can I do for you young lads? We don't get many your age shopping in our fair community." Fast Eddie was breathing hard from the brief walk.

I started, "Are you Fast Eddie?"

He bowed, "At your service." I went to shake his hand but my extended paw went unanswered. He shook his head, "Nasty habit, shaking hands. That's how germs get passed."

I restrained from commenting, plowed on. "My friend here is looking for some nice jewelry for his girlfriend. She's a rich girl, probably out of his league, if you ask me. But anyway, he's trying to impress her. We heard you have the best stuff in the greater Philadelphia area. And at a fair price." I could see Nut staring at me, wondering what was coming next. He was fidgeting like a bug on a hotplate.

Fast Eddie took the line. "You've come to the right place. We have some lovely baubles that will win the fair maiden. And nobody beats our prices."

He waddled to the case, pointed at the rings. I shook my head. "That would be too strong a signal. Don't rings connote going steady and serious relationships? My large buddy is just trying to crack the door open, so to speak, not trying to run all the way to the altar. He's afraid he'll scare her off if he's too forward. Isn't there an old saying, 'You can't get pearls from swine'?" I heard Nut exhale like he was trying not to laugh.

Fast Eddie continued without pause. "How about a bracelet? Or maybe a necklace? I have some beautiful pieces down in the next case." This was also a long counter. While Fast Eddie blathered on, Nut moved ahead quickly, trying to spot Mrs. O'Callaghan's stolen topaz necklace. I kept asking inane questions to allow Nut time to search. From the corner of my eye, I saw Nut freeze. Fast Eddie noticed it too, shuffled past me, moving much faster as he sensed a sale.

Nut pointed at the brilliant blue necklace. "Ah, your large friend has exquisite taste. That is the rare blue topaz. Topaz is a silicate mineral of aluminum and fluorine, is mostly colorless. Topaz gets their tint from impurities, is most often yellow, pale gray or reddish orange. But every once in a while nature works a miracle and the elusive blue color appear in flawless beauty. That specimen is the finest piece I have ever seen. It is a true masterpiece." I was remembering him haggling about the Andrew Wyeth painting so I wasn't sure how much was bluster or if this necklace was really rare. Based on my Funk and Wagnall research on topaz, his story matched what I'd read. But the article did say the blue color could be induced by a special treatment. Was this real or a fake?

And so I asked, "How can you prove this is the real blue or just one that was tinted?" Not wanting to insult him, I added, "I believe what you said, I'm just curious."

He stared briefly, "Ah, we have an expert, do we?" He pulled out a jeweler's eyepiece, explained that only pure blue topaz had no tinting or clouding. He asked me to look myself. I looked through the magnifying piece and saw no stains or murkiness. The beautiful stone was crystal clear—even I could see that.

As Nut looked, I asked. "How much are you asking for that?"

Fast Eddie smiled, "I don't even need to look. That's a relatively new piece. It's a steal for six-thousand dollars."

I said the first thing to pop in my head. "Holy mackerel, Andy."

Fast Eddie nodded, "Indeed."

Remembering our practiced routine, I asked. "Where do you get a piece like that? Does someone just walk in here and pawn it? Or do you go out hunting for rare stuff like this?"

I figured correctly that Fast Eddie loved to talk, liked to flaunt his knowledge. "Sometimes I go to estate sales, rummage through someone's treasures that greedy relatives just want to get rid of for cash. Other times, I deal with professional hunters, people who spend their whole day going to flea markets, garage sales and the like. And every once in awhile these hunters hit pay dirt; like someone left granny's prized possession in an old hat box. Or maybe, granny hid the treasure in an old suitcase and died without telling anyone." I was about to ask another question when he added, "And sometimes you find a dedicated customer who has access to these rare gems."

I figured Digger fell into this latter category. But this was the tricky part, so I played the naïve shopper some more. "If somebody walks in here with a piece like that, do you just buy it or do you sell it for them?"

Fast Eddie frowned, "My, my, you do have lots of questions, don't you?"

I smiled as innocently as possible, "My mom said I came out of the womb asking what we were having for dinner." Nut chuckled. Pretty soon even Fast Eddie guffawed. I hadn't told Nut an idea that occurred to me right before he picked me up. And then I forgot to mention it on the ride to Camden. I sensed that Fast Eddie was getting cautious so I pulled the surprise from my jacket. When my grandfather died, he left his pocket watch collection to my dad. And one day a few of them would go to me so dad explained their age, history and value so I'd have some appreciation. The watch I snatched from my dad's dresser was an old Elgin, circa 1880. It was solid gold, had been used by a railroad engineer to keep a precise schedule for his train route. Somehow, my canny grandfather bought it from him.

Fast Eddie's eyes got wide but he recovered quickly. "Let me see that young man." He took out the eyepiece, inspected the Elgin carefully. "I'm not sure this is a real Elgin. There were lots of scalawags doing cheap imitations once they got so popular. And this gold, might only be plate, not solid 14 carat."

I trusted my dad; this was the real thing, very valuable. I asked, "What would you give me for it?" He breathed in deeply, seeming to have an internal debate. "Maybe a $100, but I'd have to inspect it further. Even if it is a fake, some of those were well made."

I made my best crestfallen face, "Gee, my dad told me it was worth over a thousand. Sounds like he was way off, huh?"

Fast Eddie shook his head benignly, "We all think our family possessions are treasures. Sometimes sentiment clouds our judgment. This is what I do for a living so I have to be an expert. What does your father do for a living? Not the jewelry business, right?"

I hesitated briefly, shook my head. "He works for Campbell Soup. He's a plant biologist, an expert on tomatoes." I could see Nut starting to squirm. Unable to help myself, "Dad identifies the sexes of the tomato plants. Makes sure there's an equal mix of male and females used.

Apparently that's a big deal when the bees go to pollinate. Can't have too many males, throws off the whole formula. Like what happens when hillbillies inbreed."

For the first time during that visit, Fast Eddie was at a loss for words. I was preparing to ad lib an answer on how dad spotted the male from female tomatoes when Nut jumped in. "Can we get back to the necklace? I can't afford this one but if I find one, do I buy it from you or are they on consignment from the owner?"

Fast Eddie pointed at the topaz. "That piece is on consignment. I display it and take a fee when it's sold. The less pricey ones are mine."

I jumped in, "So, if I wanted to put my Elgin on consignment, what would your fee be?"

Fast Eddie threw up his hands, "Depends. An expensive piece like this necklace, I'd settle for 20 percent. Your watch, if authentic, I'd want 40 percent. The value of the item drives the fee. I have all the overhead charges, the risk of break-ins, things like that."

Nut asked, "So, if he sells the watch, you give him 60 percent of whatever you get. Does he get a receipt?"

I could see Fast Eddie starting to wonder. I added, "My friend is studying to be an accountant. He's very anal. Freud had him in mind when he described that type; know what I mean? But, is there any way I could sell this watch without all the paperwork? I mean, I don't want my dad to know about it. He's kind of a stingy bastard."

Fast Eddie got a stern look on his face, said to my surprise, "I do everything on the up and up. My father ran this store for 40 years, never had a problem with the police. You don't stay in this business long if you don't have precise records. I can tell you every transaction I've had since I took over the business 20 years ago." By his expression, I knew he was serious.

I wanted to throw up my fist and cheer. We hoped for a clear paper record of what Digger sold to pawn dealers. We now knew Fast Eddie was a stickler for the rules. Probably not from an innate nobility; probably because he could only survive by being meticulous with the numbers. We got what we wanted. I decided to close this down. "Well, you've given us a lot to think about. I guess I'll keep the watch until I can convince dad I need an early inheritance. How about you, Nut, find anything interesting?"

He had wandered back to the ring counter. Pointed at a ring with a green gem. "How much is that one?" Fast Eddie walked behind the counter, unlocked the case. "That my friend is a fine piece of jade. I got this from a Marine just back from Vietnam. He bought it as a gift for his girl. Sadly, the young lady found solace elsewhere while he was away, wanted no parts of the soldier. Quite a shame. I can let you have this for twenty-five dollars." And then, "And that's only because you seem like a nice lad." To my surprise, Nut bought the ring.

As we headed for the Walt Whitman Bridge, Nut started to whistle. He looked at me, "That was outstanding. I believe that guy. I think he'd have records of everything he got from Digger. We could prove he stole jewelry from dead customers and sold it. Damn, that's perfect."

I agreed with his joy but had a nagging doubt. "What if Digger used a fake name? We'd only have records of Fast Eddie selling the goods to some fictitious character."

Nut slapped the steering wheel. "Then we'll just have to drag Digger down here and have Fast Eddie identify him." Nut seemed to calm down as he said, "And then we'll have him for using a fake identity to sell stolen goods. That has to be even worse."

I could picture Nut dragging Digger in front of Fast Eddie, making him squeal. I slapped the dashboard, "Can I help drag Digger?"

We crossed over the famous bridge that connected New Jersey to Philly. "Do you think Walt Whitman would approve of this bridge being named after him? I mean, it's bulldog ugly. I'll bet he wouldn't find it all that poetic."

Nut grinned, said nothing. Something was bothering me. "Why'd you buy that ring?"

He didn't answer right away. "I'm going to give it to Reneé when I tell her about the Green Berets. That it's a sign of our friendship. Something nice to remember me by while I'm in the Army."

That caught me off guard. "Don't you think that might be sending her a signal that you want her to wait? Is that what you want? I didn't know things had gone that far."

Nut looked ahead. "I don't know what it means. I just want her to remember me." And then, "She's the first girl that really meant anything to me. Other girls were just a distraction. Reneé, I just like being with. She's serious like I am. But she makes me feel comfortable. Weird, huh?"

I said nothing. Finally, "I'd have to say she'll take that as more than friendship, Nut. You're not exactly the mushy kind of guy and she knows that. Maybe she takes that as some unspoken pledge. Plus she's the type that can't keep from saying what's on her mind. She'll probably come straight out and ask you if you are asking her to wait. Are you ready to answer that?"

Nut shuffled in his seat. "The truth is I don't know. Well, I guess I would like her to wait but I know that isn't fair. I mean, we are just eighteen."

I said what had been bugging me all along. "That's how I feel about you going into the Green Berets and then to Nam. You're just a God damned kid. Why not wait until after college. Go in then if you still feel the same way. Maybe that will give you time to sort things out with Reneé. That sounds like a much better plan."

He shook his head, looked at me with utter determination, "I'm destined to be a Green Beret. I think that was why I was born."

We road another fifteen minutes without talking. As we past the Scott Paper factory, I broke the silence. "Did I ever tell you the story about my Uncle Oscar?"

Nut shook his head, frowned. "Do I really want to hear this?"

And so I started, "My Uncle Oscar is pretty crazy."

Nut shrugged, "Big surprise."

I threw out my hands, as if annoyed, "Anyway, he worked for the State of Maryland, in the Sanitation Department. Every Thanksgiving he'd tell long stories about how little work he did, how he had the easiest job in the world. Plus he'd brag about his high pay grade, great pension, that kind of crap. The stories were dumb as shit, even I knew that as a kid. Anyway, last Thanksgiving, I came back from practice and Uncle Oscar was sitting in the car by himself, engine running. I asked if he was all right. He looked at me, 'your father is a real pain in the ass.' Then he rolled up the window. As I get to the front door, Aunt Marie comes flying out. I asked her what happened. 'Ask your father.' " And she got in the car and they drove off.

When I went inside, everybody was laughing hysterically. There were rolls of toilet paper scattered everywhere. I asked why Aunt Marie and Uncle Oscar left so early. That started a new round of laughter. Soon mom said that Uncle Oscar told one of his preposterous stories about dumb jobs he made people do to keep them busy. Uncle Oscar said he found that the state was using two-ply toilet paper in the roadside rest stops and he came up with an idea to save the state a fortune, that he had become a big hero for his creativeness. I still didn't get it. "What was the idea?"

Dad started chuckling again, regained his breath and then said, "Oscar said he found a way to unroll the two-ply toilet paper and then reroll it into one-ply rolls. That was what he claimed made him a big shot." I opened my hands to say continue explaining.

Mom started laughing, finally got out, "Dad went and found a two-ply roll upstairs and made him prove it could be done." She pointed at the mess. "Obviously, he couldn't do it. So dad got another roll when he said our paper was defective." She laughed harder. "He couldn't do that one either and we all started to laugh when he said our paper was cheap. When we couldn't stop, he stormed out saying dad was an asshole."

Nut said the obvious, "That's why you're like this. You really do have an odd family."

PLAYOFFS

We had to win two games to become Catholic League champions. Up first was Eastern Conference champ, Friar Judge. Most of the players for Judge came from St Matt's parish. One of the cultural things about Philly was how Catholic it was. When you met people, you asked, "What parish did you come from?" Even the Jewish people identified themselves that way. Hank Greenberg said without thought, "I'm from St Tim's." So, when you played Judge, you knew you were playing against kids from the powerhouse CYO team of St Matt's parish.

Our St Tim grade school team played St Matt's for the city championship in 8th grade. We beat them soundly but they had gotten even better during high school. Whenever we bumped into them during summer leagues, they always mentioned the 8th grade loss and that they would get revenge when it counted. We had won every game since then but all the games were close.

Coach Gallagher knew our history with Judge, warned about overconfidence. Drum made it worse when he summarized his scouting report with, "Since we are genetically superior, the outcome is inevitable—another ass-kicking for Judge."

Coach Gallagher shook his head, "And that is what I'm worried about." He pointed at us. "Play your best game or you'll lose. This team has three great guards who can each have a big night at any time. It's the only team in the league that can match Fran and Dylan. And Scoot has to play Lynch, who's 6'3' and might be the smartest player in the league. Even Scoot won't get the ball away from him. And the big kid Smith doesn't score much but he'll give Truck a fight on defense. Smith is the only kid last year who held Truck under double figures. He's a warrior." Coach looked at us seriously, "Other than that, I'm not worried about them."

All the playoff games were at the legendary Palestra, on Penn's campus. The Palestra held about 9,000 rabid fans in bleacher type seats. All the Big-5 games were played in the Palestra and each of us watched the city's best college players make history here every year since we were little kids. I had dreamed of being one of those college heroes since age ten. That's what I thought about as I warmed up. Strangely, we were very quiet as we did layup drills. Coach Gallagher noticed it too but didn't say anything to rile us up. I wondered what he was thinking. Most games we yapped like a pack of dogs—me being the loudest. I mentioned this to Drum, he grinned, "Don't worry, Dylan, that's the fury building up inside." And then he took his layup turn and savagely dunked the ball.

As usual, Drum was right. We destroyed Judge. Truck had the best game of his storied career—35 points and 30 rebounds. He made the rugged Smith look like a tinker toy. And Scoot literally tormented the normally flawless Lynch—stripping the ball five times for easy layups. The whole Judge team looked befuddled. Fran Philips scored 30 points and I had a quiet 16 but didn't miss a shot. Drum didn't score much but was a maniac on the boards. He blocked out so expertly that Truck was often alone to scoop-up the many errant Judge shots. We were up 46-18 at halftime. Coach Gallagher's halftime speech was short.

"Don't get cocky." And we didn't. If anything, we did better in the second half. There were no plays taken off. We went full tilt, ended winning 100-64. The Bulletin headline next morning said, "The Best High School Game Ever Played?" We were on our way to the Catholic League title game. On my walk home that night, I thought how silly I was to worry that Mrs. Delaney might have a bad effect on Truck.

BACK TO READING

Since there was another week before the title game, Coach gave us Monday off. I hoped that would happen, agreed with Truck to use that day for our trip to Reading. Our plan to skip school had some weak points. If you were sick, your parents had to call in before 8:00 am to explain the illness. Otherwise, the school called your house to find out where you were. But I had an ace card. Scoot worked in the school office every morning, was the one who delivered the notes to the various classes telling teachers who had a legitimate absence. When I asked Scoot to help with our alibi, he was nervous. "What if you get caught? Then my ass is grass, too."

I was honest with him. "If you don't do it, Truck will beat the piss out of you." When he got a worried look, "Just kidding. But this is really important to Truck. It's a family problem that he needs help with. So, don't worry, I've thought it through. The plan is solid."

When we told Nut about the trip, he surprised us. "No way, I'm not going. You'll need all eyes to spot Truck's mystery woman." I mentioned his makeup wrestling conflict but he said they weren't going to do it since the other team forfeited. "They didn't want to get spanked again." And then I mentioned the sick call problem and the way we got around getting caught at Conner. Nut snapped his fingers. "I've got an in. Reneé runs the attendance program at Upper Derby. She got them to use the intercom system to eliminate the paperwork. I'll tell her what's up. It won't be any problem."

We met Monday morning at 6:45 am outside the Deli for the trek to Reading. Truck was driving. Nut and I arrived separately so it wouldn't be too obvious we were together. Truck thought I was paranoid but Nut liked the idea. His opinion, "You can't ever be too cautious. Words to live by." The post office opened at 9 am, so we figured that gave us a little leeway for the hour and a half trip.

I used the time to tell Truck about our adventure at Fast Eddie's Pawn Shop. One of Truck's good qualities was being a good listener. Maybe that might be because I talked so much; the airtime was scant. Anyway, when I got done the tale, Truck said, "Sounds like ya nailed him. If the fat guy identifies him, he's dead, right? They've got to throw him in the slammer, right?"

Nut seemed less confident. "We think so but it all centers on Fast Eddie having records that show Digger selling him stolen goods. It gets more complicated because we have to get verification from the victim's family that the piece was theirs and it was supposed to be buried with the relative. That could get messy. What if the relatives don't want to press charges? Do we have to get the bodies exhumed? Don't we need their permission to do that?" He exhaled, as if gathering strength. "What I'm saying is there are lots of unknowns to button down." An uncomfortable quiet settled on the car for the next half hour.

Not liking the gloom, I break the silence. "Nut, whatever the obstacles we find, we're going to break them down. I was just thinking, got a good idea. At least I think it is. The idea is to head back to Fast Eddie's this weekend and snap a picture of that necklace before it gets sold. That way, if it gets sold, we have a record. My dad has a nice Canon, 35 mm camera. It takes great close-ups. That will be at least one solid piece of evidence." Nut didn't look any happier but I wasn't done. "Plus, the other diamond ring he stole went to the shop in Elkton, Maryland. That's not too far a drive. After we hit Fast Eddie's, we'll shoot down to Elkton to see if the ring's still there. Snap another picture as evidence. Most likely the ring's still there, what did Digger list the value? It was like two-thousand bucks, right? I doubt they sold it that fast. It was only about two months ago. While we're there, we'll sniff around for how the guy keeps records. Let's hope he's as meticulous as Fat Eddie, er, I mean Fast Eddie."

Truck looked back at Nut, gritted his teeth, "We're gonna nail the bastard."

Out of nowhere, Nut started to laugh. Not expecting that reaction, Truck asked, "What's so funny?" Nut told the story of me telling Fast Eddie my dad worked for Campbell's Soup; that he was a plant biologist who identified the sexes of tomatoes. Nut started to crack up, had a hard time completing the story. Truck started to chuckle. Finally, Nut asked, "What would you have said if he asked about how your dad could tell the sexes?"

I shrugged, "Have to admit the minute the words left my mouth, I knew I was in trouble. I was deciding whether to say male tomatoes had a little bulge under the lowest limb, like a wiener. Or would it be more believable that females had two little knobs, like…" And then we were all laughing. I looked out the window. My favorite barn sailed by, "GOD IS LISTENING."

Nut noticed it too, got a serene look. "I hope that's a good omen." Truck exhaled, didn't say anything but liked the thought.

Within two minutes, traffic ground to a halt. This section of the Morgantown Expressway was wide open and rarely had much traffic. As we inched along, I saw the exit for Flying Hills was the problem. A tractor-trailer had flipped as it made the sharp turn up the exit. My dad always moaned about ghoulish rubberneckers. Dad's theory was, "Everybody loves an accident. It makes them happy they're on the right side of the dirt." He had a point, there was an ambulance crew working diligently to extract the driver from the mangled cab. I thought about Nut's omen comment. I hoped this wasn't the real sign.

Once we got past the snafu, traffic cleared but we had lost our time edge with the post office. I could see Truck was nervous. "What if she already got there and we missed her?"

He drove like a madman into the Shillington section of Reading, we got there at 9:15 am. Nut said, "I'll park the car, you guys run inside. I'll wait out here."

When we got inside, there was already a long line ahead of us. I pointed to the wall near where the line started, told Truck we could see everyone from there. A forlorn look on his face, Truck asked, "What if we missed her?"

Even though I was thinking the same thing, I said, "Doubt she got here at the minute it opened. I mean, who needs to be the first in line as the post office opens?"

Truck looked at me, "You would be the type. Face it; you like to win at everything. You're kinda crazy that way."

He was right, I did get a kick from meaningless contests. I had a gift for occupying myself with useless things, like imagining what people were like based on how they dressed or walked. For instance, I was watching a young guy in line with bib overalls, a baseball cap spun sideways and huge, muddy boots, like you'd see a clown wear in the circus. I pointed at him, "Truck, what do you think about that kid. Maybe headed for an audition at Barnum and Bailey after he mails his psycho, hate letters?"

He grinned, "Please shut up and pay attention."

About five people had moved through the line, nobody of interest. My buddy Lester was one of the clerks on duty. Since I didn't want him alerting his boss and risk Mr. Herbein kicking us out, we tried to stay hidden at the back of the line. I told Truck to stay put. I wandered to the bulletin board area to see if Truck's picture suddenly reappeared. It didn't but I gazed at the detailed map of Shillington to kill time. As I scanned the 'Most Wanted' list, I saw a tall, blonde woman near the front of the line. Was she our mystery mailer? I went back to Truck, told him what I saw, said I would wander up inconspicuously to see if this might be the one we were looking for. The trick was getting near enough without Lester spotting me. I was pretty sure he would remember me; most people did after one of my inane escapades. Plus Mr. Herbein probably tore him a new rear-end for giving up too much information. Lester wouldn't be happy to see me.

I sidled up along the edge, not wanting to draw

attention from other customers who might think I was jumping in line. Nobody likes line butters. As I neared my suspect, she turned towards me. When I smiled at her, she blinked a couple times, like she was trying to decide if she knew me. But she smiled back. It was a nice face, brilliant blue eyes. She turned back, watching as the line moved forward. I wasn't great guessing ages, but I thought this woman was around fifty years old. And that would make her the right age for a relative of Truck's mom who for some reason was reaching out. Truck was almost a year older than me, almost nineteen. He was held back for another year because of adjustment problems after his mom's death. Over the past few weeks, we figured Truck's mom would have been maybe forty-five to fifty. So her cousins or maybe a sister or friend would probably be somewhere in that age range. This woman fit our description. I looked back at Truck. He was eyeing me closely. I decided to risk a move, would ask her a question to see if she had a German accent.

I stayed close to the line, out of Lester's sightline. I got beside her, she noticed me. "Excuse me ma'am, you wouldn't happen to be a Pennsylvania Dutch teacher, would you?"

I got another nice smile, which made her weary face look younger. "Why yes, young man, I do give German lessons, why do you ask?" Her accent was slight but I could detect a "v" sound instead of "w" when she said "why." I had found our elusive mailer. As the line moved up, I followed her forward.

To keep the conversation going, "Well, actually, I

have a friend who you might know. His name is Robbie Carr, do you happen to remember him?" The blonde woman's face froze. Her eyes got wide. She started to blink nervously. She stood motionless, hardly breathing. And then she started fidgeting with the letters in her hand. Just then, I felt Truck move up behind me. When our mystery woman saw him, she sucked in a short breath. And then tears fell from the startled blue eyes.

But she tried to recover her composure, turned away. I saw her take a deep breath, started to move toward the open spot when Lester called "next." In her haste, she fumbled the letters, dropping them to the ground. I stooped to help, grabbed a few, but she had already rushed to Lester forgetting the letters I held. She seemed to throw the pile at Lester, said, "Please mail these-but said "zeez" as she lapsed back to German. Covering her face with her right hand, she rushed away.

I yelled, "Ma'am, you forgot these." She ducked her head, ran out the door. I ran to Lester, looked at the letters again, and then put them on the counter. "Lester, she dropped these. Just mail them with the others." He had a puzzled look on his face but I didn't have time to explain. I needed to catch our escaping mystery lady. As I turned to leave, I saw Truck staring, completely stunned. His face was ashen, totally drained of blood.

A GHOST

Truck watched Dylan trying to be inconspicuous as he inched up the long line in the Shillington Post Office. That made him grin. Dylan liked making people laugh so being subtle wasn't his strong point. He thought about his boyhood pal, who seemed to get funnier when the situation was at its worst. That trait drew him to Dylan after moving to St Tim's parish after 8th grade. When they met trying out for the freshman basketball team, Dylan looked at him, said, "Do you always look pissed off or do you need to take a dump?"

Those were the worst times for Truck. He was still confused about his mom dying, then Sue and Liz had recently moved in. It didn't take long before Liz started experimenting with him. It was exciting at first. He didn't know what hit him. And then he couldn't wait for her to slip into his room each night. But then she started toying with him. Weeks would go by when she ignored him, made him feel like he was bothering her. Just when he started to adjust, the visits started again. She drove Truck nuts. He had a hard time concentrating. His schoolwork suffered, and he took out his frustration on the basketball court. And then he got big. And then became a star. The only time he was at peace was playing basketball. He could hit someone.

But everything started to change when those letters came last year. He started feeling angrier with Liz. But he didn't know what to do. Should he tell Sue how her daughter was messing him up? Would she believe him? Would that cause her to move out? Would his dad hate him then? But the worst part for Truck was that his dad shut him out from knowing about his mom. The more he wanted to know, the more his dad withdrew. His dad had always been his closest friend. Truck could talk to him about anything: Except his mom. He eventually gave up. He realized the memories must be too painful.

But that last letter changed everything for Truck. When he told Dylan about it, Dylan helped him dig back into it. He didn't feel it was as hopeless. And when he told Dylan about Liz, everything seemed to drain out. All that guilt slipped away. Dylan said aloud what Truck never realized; Liz was a sex maniac. It wasn't his fault. For the first time since his mom died, Truck felt like he was okay. What helped him the most was when Nut told him about his problems with Digger. Nut's dad was beating the shit out of him since he was a little kid. Truck stopped thinking that he had it so bad. At least he had a dad that loved him. Plus, it made him realize he wasn't the only one with problems. Nut had it worse.

All this raced through Truck's mind as he watched Dylan studying the map on the wall. He was sure Dylan would come back with some weird quip. When he did come back, Dylan said he spotted an older blonde woman, that he would check it out first. Truck's heart began to race. He really thought the letters were coming from his mom's family, maybe a close friend he couldn't remember. He thought it would be great to meet someone who really knew her, someone who could fill in the gaps. Ever since she died, he tried to keep her face in his memory. It was getting harder for Truck, but he still had a murky image. He noticed Dylan seemed to be excited–gabbing away, like he was having a nice talk. Truck decided to move close so he could hear. He stopped breathing when he heard the German accent. He moved beside Dylan. When the woman turned toward him, the murky face he tried so hard to keep alive was staring right at him. Tears came pouring down her beautiful face. Truck was looking right into the face of his mom. And then she started to run away! Dylan looked at him; sensing he might pass out, couldn't talk. Finally Truck choked, "I think that's my mom." Dylan's eyes got huge.

ROAD TO NOWHERE

It took a few seconds to grasp the magnitude of what Truck said. Finally, "That doesn't make any sense. Maybe it's a sister or cousin that looks like her." Truck was still holding his breath, didn't answer me. And then he turned, ran toward the door, after who he thought was his mother.

I sprinted after him, found him standing near the curb, scouring both directions. He was frantic, "Do you see her? I can't find her."

I looked all over but she was gone. A car came pulling up, Nut jumped out. "What's going on?" He looked at Truck, saw his ashen face, watched his head darting left and right.

When Truck didn't answer, I did. "Truck thinks he saw his mom. That the blonde woman was his mom."

Nut's eyes got wide. All he could say was, "What?" I filled him in on what happened inside, that when the woman saw Truck she started to cry. And that she hurried off before we could ask her anything.

Truck moaned, "This can't be real. I find my mom and she runs off. Jesus Christ." I tried to console him but he kept repeating. "God damn, this can't be real."

But then I remembered the letters. "Truck, I saw the return address on the letters she dropped. It was such a weird name, "10 The Road to Nowhere."

He spit out, "What good's that gonna do. We don't

know shit about the area."

I needed to get him calm quickly; he was getting more furious. I had seen that too many times. The next person he bumped into was going to have their face reworked. "Truck, there's a map of Shillington and Reading inside. I was staring at it when I was trying to avoid Lester. Let's go find it."

We went inside, studied the map and sure enough, not more than a few miles away was the "Road to Nowhere." As I memorized the route, Mr. Herbein, the postmaster, came out of his office, rushed up to us. "Didn't I tell you not to come back here? Do I have to call the police?" He turned without waiting for a reply, rushed back toward his office like his pants were on fire. What had turned this guy against us? I felt Truck moving after him when Nut grabbed him, held him in a bear hug so he didn't smash Herbein's face. Nut herded Truck outside to the car, into the back seat, said he would drive so Truck could help me navigate this rural area.

As we drove to the mystery woman's house, I hoped her odd address wasn't another bad omen. Were we headed on the road to nowhere? But I rekindled my enthusiasm for Truck's sake. "Settle down, Truck. If that was your mother, you don't want her seeing you like a psycho patient, do you? Settle down. We're going to find her, get this figured out." He was still breathing fast, like a bull about to charge. To distract him, "One thing we know for sure. That woman knows you. Her face froze when she saw you." I heard Truck starting to breathe more regularly. "So, if it isn't your mom, it has to be some close relative.

Maybe she has a twin sister or something. Anyway, we'll find out soon. Here's a big intersection coming up. What's that sign say?"

Truck said his first coherent sentence in fifteen minutes. "Says "Road to Nowhere," a quarter mile on the left." We were getting close.

We followed the sign, made the left from the sleepy farm road and suddenly were on a four-lane highway. Truck said what I was thinking, "What the fuck?" We entered the highway and drove slowly, looking for house signs. There were none. And there were no other cars on this big road.

To Nut, "Maybe they weren't being ironic when they named it? I mean, we seem to be in the middle of nowhere."

Truck said, "Stay alert. There has to be a house here, right?" We continued to scan the wooded farmland to the left and right, nothing there.

After about ten minutes, the highway narrowed and the single lane farm street continued. I saw Truck getting fired up. To settle him, "Nut, let's turn around, go slower this time. I'll focus on the right; you guys look left. We must have missed it. Maybe it's just a number sign pointing down a long dirt road or something." I heard Truck breathing steadily again. After about a few minutes, I saw the #10 signpost, partially obscured by mountain laurel bushes. "Got it, slow up, Nut. We've got to back up about fifty feet." I looked behind us. "All clear, Nut, nothing behind us." As we started down the dusty lane, I thought:

Doesn't look like they want company. You couldn't find a more isolated spot. But I kept that to myself. After a half-mile or so, we came to a clearing. A small white Cape Cod home was perched on a hill. There was a small barn behind it. There were no plowed fields or any indication this was an active farm. Weeds overgrew the fields; the nearby woods seemed to be winning the battle for control. There was no indication of a car. Was the barn used for a garage? As we got nearer, we pulled past the house. I noticed a large garden outback. My dad's garden was a piece of art, so I knew a good garden when I saw one. This was a good one. Weird, the front yard was almost overgrown but the backyard was perfect.

Before I could finish my thought, I heard a loud noise from the driveway behind us. Nut spoke first, "Looks like we have company." He added, "Let's park, get out and knock on the door before they get here."

As we piled out, I thought: This isn't good news coming. A dark sedan came around the last curve, roared into the driveway. Nut changed the plan, "You guys go knock. I'll greet our visitors." And he then added, "If they try to stop us, Dylan, move back toward me but about twenty feet to my right."

I didn't know why he thought they'd charge us but wasn't about to argue; he had a 6th sense for trouble. Truck had been quiet, eerily calm. I pushed him ahead, "You knock. I'll stay right behind you."

Finally, "What do I say?"

The poor guy looked lost. I said what came into my

head, "Ask her if she's your mom."

You should have seen the smile beam from his face. He nodded, "That's what I'll do. God damned, that's just what I'll do."

The approaching car came to a dusty stop beside Truck's old bomb. Three huge guys threw open the doors, came at us. The lead guy yelled, "Stop where you are." The other two stayed back, moved farther apart, like they didn't want to be bunched too close.

Nut said quietly, "Identify yourself." The big lead man got a funny look on his face. He wasn't expecting that. But he gathered himself, "Never mind that. This is government property. You need to leave."

I watched, stayed quiet, letting Nut do what he did best, deal with bullies. Nut shook his head, "It doesn't work that way. How do I know who you are? There are no signs to indicate this is government property. You could be burglars for all I know. So, show me some ID or we don't move."

The guy moved fast, went at Nut, thinking he'd catch this young punk off guard. He came in low but Nut pivoted, swept his feet from under him. Like a cat, Nut climbed on his back, pinned his arms, said, "We can do this all day but you still need to show me ID."

The thug grunted, "Inside my jacket, top right pocket. Agent Larsen, FBI." And then the other guys charged Nut.

I yelled to Truck, "Get moving." I ran to help Nut.

◆

Truck walked onto the porch, stopped still. When Dylan told him to ask if she was his mom, he suddenly felt better. He heard Nut talking to the three guys but didn't really pay attention. He still felt like he was moving in quicksand. Self-doubt took over. He thought: Maybe I'm afraid of knocking on that door and finding out this wasn't mom. He hesitated and thought:. Am I so anxious to solve this mystery that anyone would look like mom? Did I even remember what mom looked like? It had been almost fourteen years. What could a five year old remember?

Truck shook his head, trying to break the trance. Slowly, he moved to the door, knocked. When the door opened, a man in a dark suit peered at him. But then the stranger lifted his eyes, looking around Truck. We both became aware there was a fight going on. The man in the dark suit shifted his glance, like he was deciding to stay with Truck or join the fray. Truck looked at the hesitant man, "I'm here to see my mom." Behind the man, deep in the house, he heard a gasp.

The man made a decision. He slammed the door shut and ran right past Truck. And then Truck turned to see Nut fending off two guys. Dylan was moving to avoid his adversary but trying to get over to help Nut. Everything still seemed to be slow motion. Truck watched Dylan slam his palm at the guy's ear who was grappling with Nut. The guy turned, punched at Dylan, the blow glancing off his forehead, but knocking him back. And then the third man got to Nut, tackled him from behind. But Nut wasn't done. He spun, ear slapped the tackler, who squealed in pain. But the other two men piled on top of Nut's chest and legs. But Dylan was now on his feet, diving at the one holding Nut's legs. This freed Nut enough to curl his legs on the one pinning his chest. Truck watched as Nut hurled the big guy backward. He stood there motionless, like he was watching a movie.

Everything changed when the fourth man from the house entered the contest. Nut had to fight three men; they all seemed skilled. Dylan held his own with the other but was losing steam fast. Nut did his best to avoid a rear attack but he couldn't defeat all three. And then Truck watched Dylan fall to the ground. The big man jumped on him, slamming his forearm into Dylan's neck. Watching his best friend getting hurt snapped him out of it.

Truck darted off the porch to help. As he plowed into Dylan's assailant, all his anger and frustration exploded. He hammered at the man's exposed back with a shot to his rib cage. The man fell away from Dylan.

Dylan gazed at Truck through glassy eyes, mumbled, "Bout time you showed up. Were you waiting for a limo or what?"

Before Truck could react, somebody hit him in the head. He was seeing stars, stumbled down beside Dylan. Two big figures loomed over them as they heard the gun shot.

♦

Everybody froze. Our four assailants got to their feet, stared at the porch. The blonde woman from the post office was standing there with a pellet rifle pointing at the sky. She said simply, "That is enough. There will be no more fighting." She had a German accent. She pronounced "that" like "zat," and "there" like "zer."

But then the pissed-off man beside Nut threw a sucker punch at him. It didn't seem Nut was paying attention but his hand rose like a snake about to strike, grabbed the thrown fist, twisted it so the man was thrown off balance. To make sure he stayed down, Nut delivered a quick kick to his stomach. All I heard as he fell was "ooph." The man from the porch yelled to his team, "Stand down. This is over."

The big lug next to me looked at Nut, turned to me, "Who is that kid?"

I looked at him, nodded, "A freak of nature." The lead man said firmly, "We are federal agents and you are trespassing." He pulled out ID showed it to Nut.

I didn't know what to say but didn't need to. Truck said loudly, "I don't leave till I speak to my mom."

I shifted my glance to the blonde woman. Her shoulders were shaking, face flushed, tears streaming from her eyes. Without asking, Truck moved toward the porch, slowly climbed the steps. The blonde woman was taking short breaths, like she was suffocating, desperately needing air. The lead agent followed behind Truck, like he was protecting the lady. She put out her hand toward the agent, "It's alright, Fred. We need to talk." And then Truck put his huge arms around her, gently pulled her toward him; she breathed deeply, rested her head on his bulky

285

shoulders. She raised her hands to the back of Truck's head, started to pat him, like she was soothing a baby. They both sobbed quietly, shoulders quivering. When I walked over to Nut, my ferocious friend looked at me. Both of us were welling up. I never imagined The Road to Nowhere would lead us to a miracle.

Truck and his mom walked inside with the head agent. Trying to mend fences with these federal agents, I said, "So, nice weather we're having today, huh?"

The big agent looked at me like I was a lunatic. But then he started to chuckle. "How old are you kids? I mean, we can't let it get around that a few high school kids kicked our ass. Keep this to yourself or I'll throw you in jail. Okay?"

I pointed at Nut, "Don't feel so bad. Nut here is the next Olympic wrestling champ, if he tries out. The toughest wrestlers in the state have gone at him. He throws them around like he's Johnny Weissmuller messing with the baboons."

The other agent walked up to me, frowned, "What were you doing when you slapped me in the head?" Nut started to laugh as I explained my ill-advised attempts at the paralyzing ear slap.

Pretty soon they were all laughing—except the agent Nut had kicked. He pointed at Nut, "Next time I take you out. No more playing around."

But the friendly agent intervened, "Settle down, you heard Fred. This is over." And then he looked at Nut; "I got a feeling he took it easy on us. Even money says we'll be reading about this kid one day." That simple sentence hit me hard, made me think about Nut's dire plans for Digger. I hoped that wasn't what this agent would read about.

Trying to shake that idea, I asked the congenial agent, his name was Sam, why this was federal property. He shook his head, "We can't disclose that." He pointed at the house, "Fred will have to decide what we can tell you." He looked concerned, "This was not supposed to happen this way. I still don't know how you found this house Maybe you ought to think about joining the FBI. That's pretty impressive work."

Not one to be put off that easy, "How about me guessing what might be happening. Like we're playing 20 questions. So you didn't tell me, I just guessed. That way you're not in trouble."

Sam never answered, looked at Nut, "Is he always like this?"

Nut grinned, "He's just warming up."

Sam looked back at me, said succinctly, "No more questions."

I shrugged, "Can we sit down on the porch while we wait. I gotta admit my butt hurts from that fight." We moved to the porch.

As I was sitting there, I remembered my somber thought about Digger. To Sam, "Can I ask you a question that has nothing to do with this? It might seem weird but it's a project I'm working on, I need a professional opinion."

Sam eyed me warily, "Why do I think I should say no?" I smiled at Sam like an innocent moron. He rolled his eyes, "It's against my better judgment but go ahead."

I proceeded to ask if someone stole jewelry in Pennsylvania, then sold it in another state, would that be a federal crime or a state crime. Sam shook his head, "You shouldn't be stealing jewelry at all. Despite our trouble today, you seem like decent kids."

I waved my hands, "Believe me, it isn't us. But this is a something I need to know. Come on, just give me an opinion."

Sam was quiet for a while. "It would be a federal crime. Moving stolen goods across state lines becomes a federal crime. The law goes a long way back. That's how Elliot Ness got involved with Capone, moving booze across state lines." He paused, "They finally nailed him on income tax evasion of all things." I wasn't sure where I was going with this idea but I wondered if we could get Digger committing a federal crime. I was having nightmares thinking about Nut rotting in prison for killing his father—even though he deserved it. I sat still, turned my thinking to what Truck was doing inside.

♦

Truck didn't want to stop hugging his mom. At least, he was pretty certain she was his mom, at this point. When they moved inside, the agent named Fred looked at her and said, "Be careful what you say."

She reached out, patted Truck's cheek, looked at Fred, "This is over." There was a glow on her face as she added, "This has gone on long enough." She looked back at Fred, "With things as they are, it really doesn't make any difference."

Fred lowered his eyes, said softly, "I understand." She took Truck's hand, moved them to a couch. They sat close together. Truck couldn't take his eyes off her. Her eyes blinked rapidly as she sat there thinking. He noticed that her hair was perfectly blonde, not a hair out of place. He thought she was the most beautiful woman in the world.

What she told Truck was a story out of a Hollywood movie. He sat and listened, mesmerized.

A WAR-TORN LIFE

After all these years, Gert couldn't believe she could finally hold her dear Robbie again. He had gotten so big. Strong like his father—but his face was like hers. He had the strong Heydrich jaw, the blue eyes, that intensity when he looked at you. She never thought this day would come.

She wondered how she could begin explaining why his own mother had left him? She thought for a while, finally deciding the truth was the only way. Would it be better for him to go through life thinking his mother deserted him or thinking she left to protect him? She thought even if she put him in danger, the truth was now better; things had changed. She had thought that same problem through before leaving years ago but decided enough time had passed, it was safe now. And with her condition, she might not have another chance. Yes, she concluded, she would start from the beginning. Her Robbie needed to know his mother loved him, who left to save him from harm. She breathed deeply, started.

Reaching out, she took Robbie's strong hands. "This is a long story but you must hear it all or it won't make sense. But first of all, yes, you are my dear boy who I love with all my heart." She leaned in, embraced him like she'd never seen anything so precious, kissed his forehead before she continued. "You know that your father and I met in Germany, at the end of the war, at the Nuremburg trials. Your father was an MP, assigned to protect witnesses against the Nazis. What you don't know is that I was a witness for the Allies, for atrocities during the Holocaust." She watched her sweet boy's eyes grow wide.

She patted him again. "During the war, I worked in the office of Reinhard Heydrich, who was my uncle. I had always been good with numbers. In the beginning, I had what I thought was an accounting job. Keeping track of materials Germany acquired as they invaded other countries."

She sat back a little, took a deep breath. "I came to learn my uncle worked for Heinrich Himmler, the Reichsfuhrer of the SS. Himmler was one of the most savage men in history but I came to learn my uncle wasn't far behind in cruelty and inhumanity. Adolf Hitler called my uncle 'the man with the iron heart.' My uncle was so brutal that the Czechs and Slovaks sent a special team of assassins to murder him." She saw her son's look of shock but continued. "They were successful, killed my uncle on the first attempt. But even after his death in 1942, I continued to work in the office of accounting."

After a brief pause, she gathered herself. "My first knowledge of what horrors my uncle masterminded was reading about "Kristallnacht" on a report he wrote afterwards. That was a program he organized against Jews in Germany in 1938. Not only was it mass extermination and arrest of all Jews in Germany, it was also a confiscation of valuable archival material and treasures from the synagogues. Our job in accounting was to track stolen treasures and assess the value. There was an attempt to hide that Jews were being targeted. The term used was "inferior races" or "enemies of the Reich." But after awhile it became clear to me. When I spoke of this horror to co-workers they denied what I was saying as propaganda from the Allies. Finally, the office supervisor spoke to me. 'There will be no more of this wild talk or you will be reported to the SS. Even your famous uncle's name can't protect you now.' It was then I began planning my escape."

She could see Robbie was slightly overwhelmed. She looked at his blue eyes and reminded herself that he needed the whole horrible story to help him understand what she had to do. She continued. "I began to keep records, to search for proof of what was happening to the Jews. It was dangerous but it was my only way out. And when my uncle was assassinated, I knew the time had come to act. I began a systematic collection of damaging reports. As with all organizations, there were careless people who forgot to use the sanitized terms. It took months, but I had clear documentation of the genocide. I did this by using extra carbon copies and concealing the documents in the lining of my dress when I left for the day. Co-workers thought I was diligent, wanting to be the last to leave each day." She smiled at Robbie, "I was just being cautious." Robbie seemed to be holding his breath, so she reached out again, "It's okay dear. I had it all planned."

She looked at Agent Fred, "Can you be a dear and make us some tea? I want to keep my sweet boy calm. This is a hard day for him." Turning back, "The hardest part was how to disappear. I was an only child and my parents were dead. Papa was killed early in the war and Mama died shortly afterwards." She softened her eyes, "Just as you have been these years, I had no mama." She exhaled deeply, composing herself. "So with no close family left, I had to make a story that would be believed. I told my co-workers I planned a short holiday to Salzburg. It was easy for Germans to enter Austria since the invasion. But what I really did was take a train the opposite direction to Kehl, which is just a short journey from the French city of Strasbourg. It was on the German border and many people spoke German. Since Germany already occupied France it was a simple matter of crossing the Rhine on a foot bridge. I had forged papers, thanks to my access to proper documentation. Once in Strasbourg, it was easy to assimilate. I found work as a bookkeeper and soon made contact with the French underground. No one came looking for me. I guess they thought I had been killed or captured on my trip to Salzburg. Anyway, from then, it was just a matter of waiting out the war."

Fred, the federal agent, interrupted the dialogue as he delivered the tea. Truck drank tea with Dylan's mother when he visited, so he knew how he liked it. When he said, "Just a little milk and sugar," his mom beamed. "That's just how I like it Robbie." Her smile helped him settle down, he began to breathe normally, even though this story was starting to overwhelm him. He sipped at the tea; the warm fluid relaxed him almost immediately. Her tale continued. "And so, when the Nuremburg trials began, I was one of the key witnesses. My precise documentation and credibility as an expert were key pieces of evidence. And the family relationship to my sadistic uncle made me highly believable. That is when I met your father. He guarded me night and day. We soon became friends." Here she smiled again. "And then we became more than friends. When he asked to marry me, I hesitated for a while but then realized I had no family left. Why not start over in America?"

She sipped her tea, paused to collect her thoughts. "And then you were born, my life had meaning again. For those early years, all was wonderful. I loved America, felt safe again. No more looking over my shoulder to see if I was followed."

And then Agent Fred spoke, "And then I showed up." Truck watched them exchange a long, seemingly sad look. Fred continued, "Witnesses started to die. At first it seemed random. Then patterns developed. Any German who testified against the Reich was being targeted. And then we realized we had to protect these brave people. Why that never occurred to the brass before is beyond me. I think they thought the Nazi's had been devastated, that they had run for the hills." He shook his head sadly. "That was a mistake. We soon learned that Hitler and his gang had prepared for the possibility of defeat. They had a plan to rise again. But they wanted revenge first. Anyone they thought betrayed them must die. And that is when the FBI stepped in to form the Witness Security Program for anyone who had moved to America."

Truck watched his mother's kind expression. "Fred showed up at your dad's shop, told us the incredible story. My name was on an assassin's list the police caught, after he murdered a witness in Baltimore. I was to be eliminated next." Truck had already begun to put the puzzle together as she confirmed. "So we planned my death. It had to look real or you and your father would both be in danger."

She had hit the point that bothered him. Truck, in almost a whisper, "Why didn't we all go together? Why did it just have to be you?"

Truck's mom swallowed hard, seemed to be thinking as Fred answered. "It wouldn't have been as believable. It was hard enough to make her death seem real. A whole family dying isn't easy to fake. Too many loose ends." Here he delayed a few seconds before adding, "And your mom didn't want your life to be ruined. She was brave enough to walk away from her family to keep you safe." He added, "And it worked." But he started to shake his head, "At least until you three came driving down this forgotten road."

DIGESTING

Truck was quiet on the ride home. We asked a few questions but he wouldn't do anything but nod. Finally, "So, is she your mom or not?"

Without looking at me, "I can't talk about it." He looked shell-shocked, so I let him be. I hadn't gotten much from the FBI agent Sam, but it wasn't for lack of effort. I shut up when Sam said, "Don't you know it's a crime to harass a federal agent?"

About halfway home, Nut started talking. It was more like a speech he rehearsed before the mirror. He wasn't looking for responses, more like spouting facts, checking to see if he was missing something. "I've studied all the federal agencies in preparation for the Green Berets. I wanted to know who the competition was, know how they interacted, if you know what I mean."

I didn't and said, "No clue what you're talking about."

He laughed before going on. "The FBI's main job is to protect and defend the United States. Some of their top priorities are counter terrorism and preventing foreign intelligence activities. But they also fight against organized crime." He paused. "So, what these guys are doing here is probably one of those things." I looked at Truck. He lowered his head. Nut ended with, "Which means, we better be careful who we screw with." And then Nut reached over, grabbed Truck's arm, "But we're in this with you." Truck exhaled, lowered his heard further.

As we got near home, I told Nut to drop me at the courts. It was only 2 o'clock, I didn't want mom wondering why I got out of school early. Truck kept a ball in his car. "Can I borrow your ball, want to practice something." Truck nodded, I jumped out. To both, "We'll talk later." It was late February but the weather was beautiful, one of the mildest winters in years, almost 60 degrees and sunny. Since school was still in, no one was there. I went into full-court layup drills to work up a sweat. I needed to clear my mind, sift through the mess we walked into. On the bright side, I think Truck found his mom. On the dark side, why was she was being guarded by the FBI? What was that all about? Was the Mafia looking for her? And what about his dad? How was he involved in this? After about ten minutes, I was dripping wet; the exercise took control. I shifted to jump shots. Remembering Laura's advice, I tucked my elbow, the shots swished. The world became simple again.

But then a strange question came to me, ruined my serenity. Why doesn't my mental peace ever seem to last? Is it my insatiable need to button things down? Before I could ponder that, out of the corner of my eye, I saw Nut vault the fence, head toward me. When he got near, "I thought you could use some company. Maybe between the two of us we can figure out what Truck's gotten into."

I threw the ball to him. "Let's talk while we shoot. Okay?" Nut took a long shot that clanged on the rim. I shook my head, "Lucky you're monkey strong. You sure had no future in hoops." He didn't answer, lofted another shot that missed even worse. I opened my hands, "If the wrestling or Green Berets doesn't work out, maybe you

297

can be a blacksmith." He threw the ball at me. We settled into a quiet rhythm, didn't say much. It was nice to have company; both worried about our buddy. We continued to shoot, comfortable with the silence.

But then we heard Truck's car come rambling up the street. He walked around the fence, came at us slowly. He had a peaceful look on his face. That surprised me. As he got near, "Do you shit-heads want to hear a crazy story?"

I threw him the ball. He dribbled up, "But this has to stay with us." He got a serious look, "This is too much for me to handle alone. I need your help." But then I saw the first look of pure joy on someone's face. Truck beamed, "I found my mom."

We did the only thing we could. We screamed, "Yes!" Then went over and hugged him. I could feel the big lug shaking. After we separated, he told us the story of how his mother had become a witness after WWII and then how her life became a nightmare. He still wasn't clear on exactly what she said that made the Nazi's start hunting her but we figured it had to be bad.

When he got finished, Nut summarized our thoughts, "Holy shit."

I nodded, "Well, maybe unholy German shit would be more accurate."

It was quiet for a few minutes, when Truck asked, "What do I say to my dad?" I didn't say what really puzzled me: Why did his mom suddenly reveal herself?

We agreed we would go with Truck when he talked to his dad that night. "He works late on Monday nights, doing the books, so Sue won't be there." Nut told Truck he needed to be direct. Tell about getting the letters, tracing them to Reading and by dumb luck finding her.

I liked the approach, added, "Maybe leave out the part that this was my detective work. He might be pissed, just as soon have him think I'm a good influence on you."

Nut chuckled, "You lost that battle years ago. Even Digger thinks you're dangerous." Truck laughed for the first time that day. We shot hoops until it was safe to head home without raising suspicion. Nut hoisted another long shot that missed by a mile.

Looking at Truck, "I was telling Nut that with his touch, he would probably make a great brick layer if the Green Beret thing falls through." Another ball got thrown at my head.

◆

After dinner, we met at the courts, jumped into Truck's old bomb. I felt a little weird about being there when Truck talked to his dad. We were almost to the butcher shop when I surfaced my doubt. Truck looked panicked, "I can't do it by myself. I don't know why, I just want you there. I might chicken out."

Nut looked at me, nodded. I turned to Truck, gave him a thumbs up, "We're in." Parking behind the store, we trudged through the refrigerated area on our way to the office. I looked at the hanging carcasses. "I hope that isn't a harbinger of things to come." Truck frowned confusion. "You know, we end up dead meat?" Truck shook his head, said nothing, but that seemed to break his somber mood.

Mr. Carr heard us coming, was standing at the office door to greet us. He sensed something was up. "Why do I think the Three Musketeers showing up unannounced isn't good news?"

Truck was so nervous. I thought he'd explode. So, I filled in the dead space, "Mr. Carr, you better sit down."

We piled into the office. Truck began the story. At first, when Truck started the tale of tracing the letters, Mr. Carr got furious. "I told you to let that be. Your mother is dead and buried. Let her rest in peace!"

Truck started to swallow hard, couldn't get out anything. I took a risk. "We know the whole story, Mr. Carr. We know about the Nazi threat, how you had to fake her death. We found her today when we cut school and drove to Reading."

His face changed from fury to utter shock in seconds. His shoulders slumped. He sank into his chair. Truck had calmed down, explained that mom was living outside Reading, being guarded by the FBI. Mr. Carr regained his composure. "How in the world did you ever find her?"

Truck turned toward me, deciding whether to rat me out. I beat him to the punch. "My fault Mr. Carr. Those letters upset Truck so much; I just kept digging. Pretty soon we got lucky. Even the FBI agents seemed amazed. Everybody's good at something. I guess I'm good sticking my nose where it doesn't belong."

Mr. Carr raised his eyebrows, "Now that is an understatement."

We offered to leave, to let Truck and his dad work things out. Mr. Carr shook his head, "Stay put. We need to discuss how this secret can't leave this room." A slight delay before, "Ever." Another pause, "I don't know why your mother put herself at risk after all these years but what's done is done. Now we have to make certain no one else learns about this." He turned to Truck, "Not a word about this to Sue. It might put her at risk." And then mumbled, "Plus, I don't know how she'd take it, me being technically still married." He seemed to drift for a while. "When we did this years ago, the FBI said I was free to remarry, that I was legally a widow. They even hinted it might be better for the cover story; that I had moved on." Truck didn't answer, had a vacant look.

I looked at the sad father and son who seemed shell-shocked. But one thing kept bugging me, I couldn't shake it. Like an uncontrollable itch, I fought from asking the nagging question. Why did Mrs. Carr suddenly risk being discovered? Truck broke the silence, said he planned to return to Reading next Sunday. His dad shook his head, like he understood. Out of nowhere, Truck dropped the bomb. "Dad, didn't it drive you nuts knowing mom was so close by?"

That was our cue to leave, the answer to that was too personal. I got up, "Got to take off. Nut and I are due at CCD tonight. Monsignor Pugh will give demerits if Nut skips classes. We don't want our star to get a venial sin,

301

blemish his perfect reputation. And don't worry, Mr. Carr, we'll never say a word about this, to anyone."

Mr. Carr said succinctly, "Your life depends on that." There wasn't anything to say after that. Truck didn't argue for us to stay. I think he was comfortable finishing the conversation alone.

When we got outside, Nut stared at me. "You forgot something, Einstein."

And then it dawned on me. Truck had driven us to the shop. We were without a ride. I laughed, "Stay out of the way when I start to thumb. If a driver sees a big gorilla like you we'll never get picked up. Shrink down some." Nut smacked my head. We ambled toward Darby Road.

As we waited for a kind soul to stop, Nut said, "Did you notice the look on Mr. Carr's face when Truck asked that last question about having his wife close by?"

I hadn't, said so. Nut answered quietly, "He looked scared."

CCD

We were late getting to CCD. I apologized to Monsignor Pugh, said we had car problems. The benign priest frowned, "You only live 4 blocks away. Why drive?"

I said, "I mean Truck had problems. We were helping at his dad's shop when we got stuck, had to thumb it here. Sorry, about that."

Monsignor Pugh processed that, started to ask more, but decided it wasn't worth the verbal battle. He pointed at Hank Greenberg, "Are you sure you want Dylan as your sponsor? He might not be the best influence on your trek towards Catholicism."

Hank grinned. "I'm sure Monsignor. I mean, compared to Dylan, I look like a solid citizen, don't I?"

The whole class laughed. I raised my hand. "If I take this kidding silently, will I get a partial indulgence out of it?"

Monsignor Pugh never batted an eye. "Okay, ladies and gentlemen, let's get started. Our topic tonight is timely." He paused for affect, stared at me for a few seconds. "Can the devil take earthly form?"

LEAGUE CHAMPIONSHIPS

There had been so much going on with Truck that I hadn't had time to worry about the Catholic League championship Friday night. Coach Gallagher was very careful about staying with our same practice routine. We had played Bishop Wood last year, barely won. But this year, they had two sophomores starting for the new stars who graduated a year ago. But these young players were the stars. The sophomore center, Sam Stone, was 6'8" and solid. He looked like he was still growing, a scary thought. And he had guard skills, shot from the outside mostly, didn't get a lot of garbage underneath. That would mean Truck would get pulled from the hoop, if he had to guard him. Coach Gallagher didn't like that idea, planned to have Drum guard Stone, keeping Truck under the boards. The weak point to that was Stone was much taller. Could Drum stop him? Coach Gallagher had thought of that. "If Drum has trouble, we rotate Dylan next. If he can't do the job, we try Philips. The key is to contain him, let Truck dominate underneath."

The other star for Wood was Geno Riley. Geno was a big guard, 6' 4" but slender. But he wasn't weak, more a wiry type. Coach had a plan for Geno, who was a great talent at a young age, a future superstar in the Catholic League. "Scoot, I want you to hound the kid full-court. They like having him bring the ball down. The kid's a magician with the ball; so you might not get any steals. But what's most important is to wear him out. By the second half, you'll be able to pick his pocket."

I would be Scoot's backup, if Coach saw him getting

winded. But if Drum had trouble with the center, Stone, I would have to guard him and not be able to help Scoot. So, the strategy depended on Drum. Coach asked if we had questions.

I did. "Coach, Drum isn't a very good defender, kind of a lard ass. I think Stone will eat his lunch. Got any better ideas?" Just as Drum was about to explode, I waved him off. "Just kidding, Drum. Trying to motivate you."

The Palestra was hopping. I was worried that Truck might lose his edge now that he found his mom. But in practice, he had been his old ornery self. We had agreed not to talk about his mom except when alone. With our practice schedule, we hadn't had any time. He looked focused as he barreled in for layups. As I went by him, "Kick ass tonight, big guy. This is what we've been dreaming about."

He nodded, "No prisoners."

Next I watched as Fran Philips slithered in for his unorthodox but lethal drives. He shot the ball high off the backboard. The ball seemed to be sucked through the basket. I had asked years ago, how he did it. I remember his answer well. He said indifferently, "I just do." Fran never seemed nervous. That was part of his strength. He played the game the same way regardless of circumstances. It wasn't complicated for him. He just happened to be a natural. And lastly, I thought about myself. Was I ready?

The game started ugly. Not mean or intense, just sloppy. Scoot pressed Geno from baseline to baseline but never got close to stealing the ball. But Stone seemed reluctant to shoot from outside. He looked confused that Truck wasn't guarding him. For the first few possessions, Geno got him the ball for clean shots but Stone drove to the basket, trying to get Truck to foul him. Drum knocked the ball away from him and we went down court. Unfortunately, we weren't much better. I missed a couple wide-open shots, Fran couldn't get his feathery drives to fall in and they double-teamed Truck. Coach called time out. He looked at us calmly. "Settle down. Keep shooting; we're getting good looks. Truck will start to get some garbage points and they'll forget to double-team him. Plus, your defense has been great. Keep letting Stone force the drives. That's not his game." He looked at Scoot. "Keep hounding Geno. Dog him."

We started to click. I made three open jump shots and Fran's shots started to fall. Their defense had to pay more attention to us and Truck got rolling. Anything we missed, Truck grabbed and put in, most times after getting fouled. His three point plays started to mount. By half, we lead by 15 points. Coach Gallagher looked nervous. "They haven't played their game yet. Be ready for something different in the second half. Stone will start to shoot every time. Stay in his face, Drum. Don't let him get a rhythm. Scoot, Geno isn't even sweating yet. Keep at him. Make him work harder. They will come at us, trust me." I loved Coach Gallagher but I thought he was wrong, kept thinking: We haven't played well ourselves. Next half we eat them up. I wasn't being cocky. I just knew our team.

But that's why I wasn't the coach. The 3rd quarter they ate our lunch. Stone made five long shots in a row and Geno flew past Scoot for one drive after another. If

Scoot stayed too far off, Geno drilled a mid-range jumper. We were down two points entering the final quarter. Strangely, Coach wasn't panicking. He smiled at us in the huddle. "We got them right where we want them. I know Stone and Geno ate us up last quarter. But what they don't know is that they are running on fumes now. I can almost smell the tank on empty. Scoot, dig down, push harder. Make him eat up the whole ten seconds getting the ball over half court. Drum, overplay Stone. Make it harder to get him the ball. I don't care how far out he goes, stay with him. If he gets by you after he has the ball, Truck will be waiting." He stepped back, smiled at us. "And gentlemen, have some fun out there."

It didn't go exactly as Coach outlined right away. They scored the next two times. We were down five points. But then the plan worked. Scoot stole the ball off Geno twice, went in for uncontested layups. The next time, he forced a pass to Stone; Drum stole it and sailed in for an easy hoop. But that was when Truck earned his legend. He scored every time he got the ball. Using both hands, he lofted short hooks, totally faking out Stone. Soon Stone got frustrated; started fouling. And that made Truck more intent. Truck got the ball at the foul line, pump faked Stone into the air, and then slid in for one basket after another. It was fun to watch. When I looked at the scoreboard, we were up by 20 points with a minute to play. The rest was a blur; we were Catholic League champions. It was only the second time Conner had won the Catholic League in school history. Now for the city championship; which Conner had never won. Since I was ten years old, this was my dream.

After the game, we went to the Deli to celebrate. The owner, Vito, had been to the game, threw his arm up in the air when we walked through the door. "My boys, youse made me proud. Hoagies and steaks on me." He looked at the crowd with us, "Only the players, youse other bums gotta pay."

I pointed at Nut and Hank, "That means youse." We piled into the open booths. I ate my dripping cheesesteak in bliss. Washed it down with a cream soda. I watched Truck slam down a huge bite from his hoagie, Genoa salami hanging from the sides. Again, I saw that look of pure joy. It wasn't just the championship, finding his mother alive had rejuvenated him. Just then he looked over at me, seemed to read my thoughts. He winked, his way of telling me thanks. I had to drop my head; afraid I might choke up. As that happy picture played in my head, I looked over at Nut. He was having a good time, happy for us, but I could tell he was thinking about our trip the next day. Would we find anything useful to trap Digger?

FLIGHT OF WHIMSY

Truck picked us up around 10 am. We went to Fast Eddie's first. I had my dad's camera, would use it to take a picture of the topaz necklace. I had called ahead, told Fast Eddie we wanted to take a picture to show to Nut's girlfriend. Fast Eddie laughed, "Where are you young kids going to get that kind of money?"

I responded, "A lot of people pay me to be their friends; the cash keeps piling up. I told Nut I'd loan him the cash." He chuckled as he hung up. After that was done, we'd take the Jersey turnpike toward Wilmington, wind our way to Elkton. Everything went as planned at Fast Eddie's. The topaz was still there. Fast Eddie let us take it from the counter to get a good close-up.

Fast Eddie looked at Truck and Nut; turned to me. "Are all your friends this enormous?"

I nodded, "My dad feeds them bioengineered tomatoes from Campbell's, like lab monkeys. They're the first in a series of giant genetic mutants." Fast Eddie looked puzzled as we exited the shop.

Elkton was a small, sleepy town on the border of Maryland and Delaware. It was famous as a place that allowed young couples to get married; hence the nickname "The Elopement Capital." My dad made a yearly trek there to buy his supply of liquor. Unlike Pennsylvania's punitive liquor laws, there were no state taxes on booze and overall prices were cheaper anyway. My dad would drive to Timbuktu to save money even if the gas costs ate up the savings. With dad, it was the principle. As I got older, I became his travel companion for the hooch run. I was the only kid in the neighborhood who knew the difference between Woodford Reserve and Maker's Mark. I started to tell Truck and Nut about dad's theories of small batch versus single barrel brands when they begged me to shut up. I pretended to be offended. "You guys really are lab engineered gorillas. Maybe I wasn't lying to Fast Eddie. Tell me again why you deserve my friendship?" We spent the rest of the journey down Route 40 planning our approach at the pawnshop, "Flight of Whimsy."

I was surprised how nice the place was from the outside. These owners obviously had a buttoned-down approach to the whimsical. Made from green serpentine stone, the shop was formerly a big colonial house, beautiful and immaculately landscaped. We were also amazed how many cars were parked in the orderly rear lot. Inside was just as nice. Most of the store was full of furniture. There were dining room tables with matching seats, old lamps, tons of wooden chairs and coffee tables in the main room. Everything was brightly polished, wood ranging from tiger maple and white pine to red oak. It took us a while to find the jewelry counter, which was neatly organized by sections—rings, bracelets, necklaces and broaches. A big diamond ring jumped out. Digger's ledger described it as a Marquise cut, two-carat diamond in a pink gold setting, $2000. We had looked up what the Marquise cut meant and the pink gold was obvious. There it sat in all its pink glory, valued at $2500. Nut beamed. "That's got to be it."

We would take a picture as last resort but hoped the

owner would have accurate records, not play fast and loose with the paperwork. I wandered around, leaving Truck and Nut by the counter. I found an angular man near the cash register, asked if I could speak to the owner. He bowed politely, "Lemuel Pilgrim at your service."

I liked his unusual colonial name, decided to restrain myself, saved my thoughts for later. Instead, "I'm interested in the diamond ring, can you tell me more about it?" We wandered over. Lemuel started a bit when he saw my burly friends. I nodded at him, "We get that a lot. We're basketball players. Big is good in that sport. Now if we were trying out for the Olympic luge team we might be in trouble."

He had a good sense of humor. He said wittily, "Unless you were on the huge luge team." We all chuckled at that, pretty good quip for a guy named Lemuel.

I don't know why, maybe it was the pristine condition, but I decided to play it straight with Lemuel. This seemed like a high classed place. He wouldn't be dealing with stolen goods knowingly. And so, "Can we go to your office. We have a story to tell you that you might not want overheard."

Lemuel looked surprised, but led us to his office. As with the rest of the place, his office was neat as a pin. Without any hesitation, I told him the tale of how a dishonest man pilfered valuables from the deceased, seemed to be selling it through pawn shops in different states to avoid detection. I left out Digger's name, his sadism and other details intentionally, waiting to see how he'd react. I was surprised at his answer. "I knew that damned O'Hanlon was shady. I should have listened to my instincts, something about him was off." You should have seen Nut's face, utter shock.

Next, I hit him with the punch line. "Will you help us put him behind bars?"

It turned out that Lemuel was a very honest man, a cagey judge of character. I was surprised he knew Digger's name, said so. He got a smug look. "I've been dealing with him for a few years. He said he was Jonas Finn, an art collector from the Philadelphia Main Line. At first, everything was smooth. But one day about a year ago, I heard from a customer he tried to sell her earrings directly. He spotted her looking at my collection, tried to do an end-around to save my consignment fee. Unlucky for him, the lady happened to be a regular customer, didn't like his manner. She told me immediately. So I called a state trooper I know, asked him to run his license plate. I never fully trusted the guy, jotted down the information in case I needed to hunt him down."

He frowned, "People are always making liquor runs to avoid Pennsylvania tax and the state troopers occasionally hassle them when Pennsylvania complains." I thought about dad's forays, got an incredulous look on my face, acted like that was a tasteless bit of larceny, lifted my eyebrows in sympathy. Lemuel continued, "Anyway, I found out the guy's real name was O'Hanlon, apparently he's an undertaker." Lemuel still hadn't answered my question about helping us. I asked again. He got an exasperated look, shook his head. "I'd like to but can't do it. It will kill business if it gets out I don't keep deals private. Reputation is everything in this business."

We spent the next ten minutes trying to persuade him. He didn't budge. But he let us take a picture.

On the drive home, Nut was dejected, didn't say much. But then he broke the gloom. "We can still get a family to corroborate the theft." He thought some before adding, "But that might be tough. I mean, they might not even remember what jewelry was supposed to be buried or have proof of ownership. Again, it might get down to our word or his."

I liked his positive attitude but since I never expected to get this much evidence, I already had another idea. But didn't want to explain it till I ironed-out some things. It was a long shot. To Nut, "You're right, we have some work to do. But just think how far we've come. In the beginning it seemed hopeless, but now, it's possible, right? Let's keep plugging away." Nut didn't brighten much. Not wanting to lose momentum, I added, "Don't quit on this, Nut, we have a chance. We never thought it would be easy to put Digger away." I could see Nut processing that, hatred oozed from his pours.

As we crossed from Maryland to Delaware, I saw a sign for Braddock Heights. "Did I ever tell you guys the story of my uncle Fenton and aunt Fentress?" Neither one answered, probably hoping I'd stop. "Well, I'll take that as a no. Aunt Fentress and uncle Fenton were identical twins on my father's side, the hillbilly clan in Western Maryland. Apparently the twins had a falling out when they got older, never spoke to each other. Uncle Fenton stayed local, so my parents saw him a lot over the years. He lived near my grandmother. Often dropped by when we visited. Pretty neat old guy, swore a lot, I liked him. Anyway, after the sibling fight, aunt Fentress moved away, no one saw her for 25 years." I paused to make certain they were listening. "I forgot to say that uncle Fenton was not too good-looking. Big, WC Fields nose, bug eyes, flushed complexion, wiry white hair. But he was real funny, always cracking jokes, the life of the party kind. What I'm saying is he made up for the lack of looks with a huge personality."

Without taking his eyes off the road, Truck said, "Is he where you got your looks?"

Nut finally grinned, added, "And maybe the odd personality."

I feigned hurt but forged on. Glad my pals were thinking about something besides their imminent troubles. "Anyway, all of a sudden, uncle Fenton died. We went to Baltimore for the wake. My parents weren't the type to shield their kids from reality. Well, I go through the line at the funeral home and kneel in front of uncle Fenton to say my goodbyes.

As I'm walking away from the coffin, I hear a big uproar in the back. Old ladies are screaming. People are fainting left and right. When I get back there, I see my dead uncle Fenton standing in the midst of all the mayhem. I'm wondering to myself, 'Did uncle Fenton fake his death, just for a joke?'

But then I looked closer. Uncle Fenton had a dress on. And then I noticed the big knockers. I couldn't ever remember uncle Fenton with boobs. And as I'm figuring this out, someone yelled, 'It's Fentress! She's back for the funeral.' And that's what it was. You know how some women look like men as they get old? Well, aunt Fentress and uncle Fenton had become dead-ringers for each other."

It was silent for a few seconds. Truck turned, "You made that up, didn't you?"

I shook my head, "No lie, totally true." But then Nut started to laugh. Pretty soon we all were howling, a nice break from the madness.

That night I lay awake for a long time, listening to the radio. Hy Lit was jabbering in the background. The noise relaxed me. I had to admit that Nut was right. We had to get more proof. I looked at dad's camera I used at Fast Eddie's and Lemuel's. I'd take the film to get developed the next morning. Hank Greenberg was working at Solomon's Drug Store, could get a rush job done.

Thinking about the pictures, gave me an idea. I'd need some information from Nut but it would be worth a shot. I also thought the plan might backfire if I didn't handle it right. That was when I decided to do this on my own. Not involve Nut until I worked out my strategy. Had to get the wrinkles out. I thought more about Lemuel. He really seemed to dislike Digger. Gave that some more consideration. Hmm? In the background, I heard Lee Andrews and the Hearts singing, "Try the impossible…" With that encouragement, I fell off to sleep.

ROAD TO NOWHERE PART II

Truck begged me to go to Reading for his next visit. He got me when he said, "For whatever reason, it helps to have you there, that you'll talk if I freeze." Since it was Sunday, I went to 9 o'clock mass, prayed to St Anthony, the patron of lost causes, ate my mom's belly bustin' breakfast and met Truck at the courts. I was still trying to solve Nut's problem about getting convincing evidence on Digger. Shooting hoops always helped me think. Maybe the mindless repetition cleared the cobwebs. After I shot for a few minutes, my wild ass idea was starting to make more sense. Maybe I could pull it off. Nut was unable to come with us since he had a rare Sunday practice as they prepared for state wrestling finals. He felt bad about not going, wanted to see Truck before we left. So I wasn't surprised when he vaulted the fence, ambled toward the baskets. I swished a long jumper as he came up. I threw the ball to him. He tossed it back, "I don't want to get taunted about my shot. I'll just feed you."

I caught the ball, "Good decision. Watch how it's done." I drilled another long one. We turned as Truck's old car chugged to a halt outside the fence.

I jumped in. Nut went to Truck's side window, said simply, "Sorry I can't be there." Nut reached through the window, cuffed his head. Truck nodded, he understood. There wasn't anything else to say so we pulled away. I watched Nut staring at us as we rounded the corner, a tough kid with a soft heart when it came to friends.

We stopped at Solomon's on the way. I ran in, told

Hank I needed this film done right away. Hank winked, "I'll put it in the overnight batch. I'll get it to you late tomorrow or the next day. Fast enough?"

We began the quiet journey to meet Truck's mom. Truck hadn't told me what else was said after we left his dad. Had to admit I was curious. How could you leave your wife and kid? I couldn't picture my dad surviving without mom. My parents had quiet strength. They didn't need to yell much. You did what they told you. They were the type you wanted to please. I always thought of mom and dad together, a single unit, a team. So when Truck asked that question about it driving his dad crazy with his wife nearby, I couldn't put it out of my mind. As we neared the turnoff to the Road to Nowhere, Truck ended the silence, like he'd been reading my mind. "Dad said it was the only thing he could do, that keeping me safe was their only concern. To try to disappear as a family was too hard. The FBI couldn't guarantee our safety."

I didn't know what he wanted me to say, mumbled, "I don't know what I'd do." And then mentioned something else he needed to clear up with his mom. Truck gave me a funny look, didn't say anything about my suggestion. Not wanting to push too hard, I let it rest.

We pulled down the long, desolate driveway. The agents knew Truck was coming, so we didn't have the same reception party as last time. Fred and Sam were standing on the porch, watching us park. Fred looked back to the car. "Where's the other big gorilla?"

I raised my hands. "They don't let him out of the zoo on Sunday. He's a huge draw for the kids, the big moneymaker."

Fred smirked, "I can't say I'm disappointed." And then pointed at me. "Mrs. Carr wants to speak to Robbie alone. You can stay outside with Agent Roberts."

He looked at the guy I knew as Sam. Before Truck could argue, I looked at him, "You'll be fine. I'll be right here. Just yell if you need something." He looked worried but turned away, moved toward the door. Agent Fred followed him inside, shut the door firmly.

Agent Sam rolled his eyes toward the chairs. "We might as well get comfortable. Take a seat, funny man." Without Nut being there, I was able to discuss my crazy idea about nabbing Digger with Agent Sam.

I figured he was an FBI agent. He must be trustworthy, right? Looking at Sam, "I need your help with something. I'm going to tell you a story about that big guy who was with us last time. We call him Nut. Based on your interaction with him, you probably figured that's fairly accurate. But what you don't know is what a shitty life he's had. What I want help with is my idea for turning things around. Getting the rest of his life back to normal." I could see Agent Sam was intrigued. And so I told him the story of Digger's brutal abuse of wife and kids. How Nut overcame it by becoming the fearsome weapon he saw in action last Monday. And then I told my idea. How I needed his help if what I suggested made sense. I didn't mention I knew Nut might kill Digger one day.

The congenial agent listened attentively. When I was done, he voiced the same worry of getting solid proof.

That without that proof, nothing was certain. I went into detail about our visits to the pawnshops. How I was certain there was a paper trail but that the owners might not cooperate. I told him Lemuel's concern about privacy. And then I told him my next steps if the owners clammed up. He smiled as he heard what I would do next week.

Sam broke the silence, "We did some research on you clowns after you left. Don't you have a championship basketball game coming up? When will you get the time to do all this conniving?"

They had checked us out. Not surprising since they would want to know our backgrounds thoroughly after we blew their cover. "Our game isn't for a couple weeks. The public schools have a different schedule than us. I'll have a few days off. I'm the kind of kid who needs to stay busy. The nuns say, 'An idle mind is the devil's workshop.' "

Sam grinned, sat back. "If you get that far with the evidence, then I can help you. This bastard sounds like he should rot in jail." He scratched his head, seemed to be weighing something. He waved me closer, gave me some elaborate advice for how to get the pawn dealers to be more cooperative. Being a hard kid to surprise, my eyes got wide.

♦

When Truck got inside, he told his mom and agent Fred about his discussions with dad. Fred looked apprehensive, like he still couldn't believe this bunch of basketball players ruined their operation. But Gert smiled, "How is your dear dad?" She already knew about Sue well before their discussion last Monday.

Fred told Truck that his dad had kept them informed periodically over the years. They knew Sue and her daughter lived with them. Getting those reports from the FBI was how Gert knew that he had become a basketball star. So Truck told her about their latest discussion, that dad was angry at first but settled down when he heard the whole story. Truck looked at mom, "I think he might be relieved. It must have been hard for him to lie to me. I never could figure why he wouldn't talk about you."

Gert reached over, grabbed his hand. "Your father is so strong but inside he's very gentle. That must have been hard for him to push you away." She squeezed harder, "It was to protect you." That made Truck feel better, it was just what his dad said.

He believed that his dad was shielding him from harm, but now wanted to get at what was really eating at him. Dad had hesitated when he asked him how hard was it to have his wife so close. Mr. Carr eventually answered but it didn't sit right with Truck. He had tried to discuss it with Dylan on the ride up, but never got out his real feelings.

Dylan wasn't good at faking it. He knew there was more to the story but didn't want to be too pushy. But, Dylan did ask him one question that he hadn't thought about: Why had Truck's mom risked sending him letters after all those years? In all the excitement, it hadn't hit him as unusual. But if his mom and dad were so scared of protecting him, why did she chance it? Truck was tired of not knowing the real story. Gathering courage, he told his mom what was worrying him, unloaded the two questions that needed answering: Was there another reason they didn't go with her into hiding? And what had changed that caused her to risk contact?

Truck watched his mom's eyes get wide, blink rapidly. She caught her breath. After a few seconds, she turned to Fred, said softly. "Can you give us a few minutes alone, Fred?" You could see the concern on the agent's face. But mom said, firmly this time, "Please, I need to talk to my son privately."

Reluctantly, Fred rose from his chair, ambled into the kitchen, closed the door. Mom moved closer to him, held his hand. "You are a smart boy, Robbie. I will tell you the truth. Fred knows about the one reason but the other is a family matter." She exhaled slowly. "When your father first asked me to marry him, I said no."

She saw Truck's reaction, patted his hand. "But your father was persistent. I was truthful with him, told him I didn't love him, that it wasn't fair to him. But he told me I would get those feelings with time. That he loved me enough for it to work. After weeks of pleading, I agreed. But I was always honest with him."

Gert lowered her eyes for the first time since she began talking. When she looked up, "And then we moved to America and you came along immediately. I took it as a sign from God that he meant us to be a family." She looked at him intently, "But I never did develop those feelings for your father. I did love him. He was a wonderful man. But the love was like you had for a protector. The reason I stayed was you. It was never really fair to your father." She sat quietly, gathering her words. "And when the FBI came and told us of the danger, I did the only fair thing. Protecting you was the most important thing." After a brief pause, "But it also gave your father a chance for true love. He deserved that. I told him when I left it was the opportunity to have true happiness. Your father is too fine a person to tell you this himself. When I heard about his girlfriend Sue, I took it as another sign from God."

Truck's eyes started to blink real fast. He couldn't talk. What his mom said knocked the wind out of him. He had asked for the truth but hadn't expected this. But as the information raced through his head, he realized his mom was right. His dad wasn't the type to blame anyone else. He would take responsibility, would never badmouth her. And it clicked why he never wanted to talk about his mom. It had to be painful knowing your wife didn't love you.

Truck was still struggling to absorb this disturbing tale. And then he thought about his dad and Sue. You could tell Sue worshipped him. His dad had finally found the happiness he never had with Gert. Truck choked up as he thought: I've been such an asshole to Sue. And dad never said a word. What a shithead I've been.

The storm of thoughts swirled. These shocking revelations made Truck realize he needed to fix things fast. The relationship with Sue had changed for the better recently. He resolved when he got home to tell his dad to get moving with the marriage. Actually, he thought he better tell Sue first. She'd been waiting for him to accept her. He felt like a dickhead, but he promised himself he would fix that fast.

Gert grabbed his hand again, snapped his reverie. "I have another thing to tell you. About why I risked exposing myself after all these years." He watched her hand go to her head. She lifted the perfect blonde hair up, exposing a bald head. She let him stare awhile before replacing it. Truck had stopped breathing.

She caressed his cheek, told him to breath. To his wide eyes, she said quietly, "I have breast cancer. They have me on a new form of treatment called chemotherapy. One of the side effects is losing your hair." To his troubled look, "Don't worry, it will grow back they say."

He stuttered out, "But you'll be okay?"

Gert blinked a few times. "I have a chance but nothing is certain. One of the benefits of being under FBI care is getting the best treatment. The doctors say this form of chemotherapy has shown great promise." And then she finished. "And that's why I started making contact with you. I had to deceive the FBI but I hid your letters with my other mail. Eventually, I would have been more direct but I wanted to go slowly, not shock you." She started having trouble speaking. "I needed to see you again." A long pause, "In case." She stopped again, voice cracking, "In case I didn't make it."

That's when Truck lost it.

♦

Truck was quiet on the ride home. I thought he'd be

excited and happy, he found his mom again. Instead, he was strangely still. But I knew he was going after the missing information about why she started writing him. I mean it was a long shot that we found her. And yet we did, because she started writing those letters. Truck didn't react when I brought that up on the ride there, the sudden start of communication. But I could tell it hadn't occurred to him as odd, hadn't asked his mom about it. I looked over at my sullen pal. Maybe the answers he just got weren't what he expected. All that ran through my relentless mind. I forced myself to shut up.

As he had last time, Truck would start talking when he was ready. To occupy my time, I thought about the discussion with agent Sam. I intentionally gave him minute details of Digger's abuse. I wanted to get him engaged. When I mentioned Digger broke Nut's ribs in grade school, I thought he was going to drive back with us to arrest him. But his advice motivated me. Maybe my half-assed plan could work. Truck never said a word the rest of the way.

ANTICIPATION

Practices got to a new level of intensity. Truck still hadn't told me what went on with his mom. It was eating me up, but I said nothing. To distract myself, I practiced even harder than my normal manic way. I was playing better than I ever had. I felt ready to play. It was tough waiting. Coach Gallagher took us to the Palestra to watch the Public League championship. Drum sat next to Coach, I sat on the other side.

Eastbrook and South Philly both had 20-4 records. Before the game started, Drum was watching the warm-ups closely. Without being asked, Drum said, "Eastbrook looks loose. South Philly's tighter than an Eskimo's sphincter. I'll pick Eastbrook by 20."

Coach didn't bother correcting Drum's colorful vulgarity. He knew that was useless. But when I watched closer, Drum was right. South Philly's team was almost silent, no yapping encouragement to each other as they warmed-up. The game was over by halftime. Eastbrook won by 25, made it look easy. As we walked from the gym, Drum said, "We'll kick their ass, we just have to play our normal game. They have no answer for Truck." He was right. They had a nice team, but were no match for Truck or Fran Philips. One more game.

A TIGHTER CASE

That night after dinner, I secretly grabbed my father's camera, headed out the door after telling my parents I was working with Nut at a funeral. My plan to help Nut involved another trip to Digger's funeral home. Truck agreed to drive me there. He still hadn't said what went on with his mom. I hoped our time alone might open him up. Nut let it drop yesterday that Digger had another funeral tonight. His shop would be deserted. From previous trips, I knew where they hid the key. I was keeping Nut in the dark in case my plan backfired. He could deny any involvement. But I told Truck what I had cooked up. At first he frowned, "You're crazy." But then he drove some more, turned, grinned, "That's pretty cool. It might work." We got to the funeral home a few minutes later. Truck stood guard. I slipped inside, made my way to the hidden ledger, took it to a bright place, snapped photos of all the pages. I also took pictures of the hiding spot. The more evidence the better. At least that's what I hoped.

Truck was just as quiet on the ride back. Unable to restrain myself any longer, "Ever hear the phrase, 'A problem shared is a problem solved?' Well if you want to start keeping secrets from me, that's all right but why not talk it out?"

He turned his head, looked at me, continued driving. I continued, "But you've been telling me everything for the past few months and I have to admit you seem happier. I mean, it's not like you're an amusing guy or anything. But for you, you almost seem normal. Less of a brute."

Normally, he'd laugh at my jabs. This time he looked over at me; started talking in a low monotone. He told me about his mom's breast cancer. That she had a chance to make it but nothing was certain. He was going to spend as much time with her as possible. And then, in a whisper, "I just found my mom. I don't want to lose her." I found myself biting my lip, trying to think of something encouraging. All I could do was pat his massive shoulder.

I asked Truck to drop me at Solomon's Drug Store. Hank was working again. I needed another rush job. Truck said as I got out, "Do you want me to wait?"

I told him no, I would walk home. Needed the time to think. Before he left, "Truck, I know this sounds like bullshit to make you feel better, but I feel like your mom's going to make it. I just can't believe you beat all these odds, just to lose her." I pointed at him, "She's going to be fine. Believe it."

He stared a few seconds before, "It's what I've been telling myself the past few days. Somehow she'll beat it. It's been keeping me going." I asked him if he wanted company when he visited this weekend. He shook his head. "No, I can do it alone now. I was thinking of bringing Mrs. Delaney. Fred will shit but I keep thinking she might help mom recover, best friends and all. Plus she's got no family. And I know you have work to do for Nut. I'm sorry I can't be around to help, but I can't waste the time." And then very softly, "Nothing else seems important, except mom."

I nodded, "Like the Mrs. Delaney idea. Kinda wish I could be there to see Fred crap out a brick." He finally chuckled, drove off. Inside the drug store, Hank handed me the 1st photo batch, promised to get this new one done fast. I ripped open the pack, the pictures of the stolen jewelry were clear. I walked home alone with my thoughts. A lot to do.

CONFESSION

It was the beginning of March. Lent was starting. Lent was the time of abstinence before the holy day of Easter. Jesus had given up his life, was crucified brutally on the cross so he could be resurrected to save mankind. In the spirit of this immense sacrifice, the Catholic tradition was to give up something you liked for the entire six weeks of the Lenten season. I thought back to my childhood. As kids, there was always an unspoken contest for whom would make the greatest sacrifice. One time my 7th grade classmate, Gerald Lewaski, who had a giant head, said he wouldn't wear a hat no matter how cold it got. When I protested that was kind of a chintzy sacrifice, he pointed at his huge noggin. "With a melon like mine, that is some serious pain if it's freezing out." He had a point.

When he asked if I could top that, I thought a bit. "I'm going to do nothing but have nice thoughts about people."

He scoffed, "That's pretty weak. How hard is that?"

I looked straight in his eyes. "It's murder for me. For instance, up until now, every time I looked at your giant bulb, I wondered how you'd ever get a football helmet big enough to fit. But now that you told me your pledge, I'll look at you and think about your huge frozen head." I wonder if Gerald still thinks I'm an asshole?

That's what I was thinking about as I marched to St Tim's that beginning week of Lent. There would be confessions held every night instead of just Saturday. Over the years, I learned which priest went into which confessional booth. Monsignor Pugh was my target tonight. I would need his help to pull off the miracle. It was Wednesday night. Church was almost empty. I pulled back the confessional cloth, entered the box, knelt down and began the ritual. "Bless me father, for I have sinned. It's been a month since my last confession." I hesitated, and then began. "I'd like to get something straight before I start. Anything I tell you is private, right? What I mean is, if the cops or maybe the FBI ask you about what I said, you gotta clam up, right? They can't force it out of you?"

He was silent for a few seconds. "Dylan, this isn't one of your pranks is it? Confession is a holy sacrament so none of your foolishness."

I paused, "I thought I was supposed to be anonymous in the confessional box. How'd you know it was me?"

He chuckled, "That devilish voice is burned in my soul. Now go on with your confession."

I began slowly, not wanting this story to seem too crazy. "Monsignor, I'm going to tell you a story about one of the pillars of your church that will be hard to believe. But I've brought pictures and some other proof that what I'm telling you is true." I waited before adding, "I swear this is true on my mother's soul. And you know how precious that little lady is to me." I heard Monsignor swallow deeply, like he wasn't looking forward to what I had to say. And so I started. "James O'Hanlon has been beating his wife and kids…"

When I was finished, I could hear Monsignor Pugh sit back in his chair. After a deep breath, "And you have proof of this?" I told him what I had and then passed it under the thin veil that separated us. While he was reading the material, I thought how I would say the next part, asking for his help.

I heard him move closer, "This is incredible. Dear God Almighty, those poor people." And then added, "What can I do to help?"

I explained that without witnesses, this was his word against Nut's. We couldn't count on Mrs. O'Hanlon to testify. She was probably too beaten down. But I told him about the pawn dealers and my hope we could get their testimony. And then I told him my back-up plan, which was where he came in. He didn't hesitate, "I'll do it. I'm sure I can get their support."

I wasn't surprised by his answer, more relieved. After a deep phew, I ended the confession, "For these and all the sins of my past life, I am sorry."

ROAD TO SOMEWHERE

The big game against Eastbrook was Monday night. We practiced lightly Saturday morning, we felt ready. That afternoon, while Truck and Mrs. Delaney visited his mom, I got a rare gift from dad—he let me borrow the car. He was in a great mood because of our pending city championship and couldn't come up with an excuse about building up my stamina by walking.

My plan was to hit both pawnshops, use the gift Agent Sam gave me. I went to Lemuel's shop in Elkton first and then to Fast Eddie's in Camden last. Both times I got the same negative response initially, "Bad for business if our customers get thrown in jail." But when I used the card agent Sam gave me, both owners started immediately to stutter their change of heart. "No need to get the FBI involved, son," was how they babbled their new willingness.

I smiled at both, "Thanks for your cooperation. You've renewed my belief in human kindness." Both dealers looked puzzled as I left, a spring in my step, with all the information I needed. As I sailed over the Walt Whitman Bridge, I hummed "Wouldn't it be nice…" by The Beach Boys.

As soon as I got home, I went to the rectory, visited Monsignor Pugh before he sat down for dinner. He looked at me, "You look like the cat that ate the canary."

I faked to the left, squared-up and hurled a fake jumper —holding the documentation I had pulled from my pocket, yelled, "It's a desperation heave from full-court—what?—it swishes to win the game!"

I showed this kindly priest the evidence. He beamed, "I never would have believed it, Dylan. I kept thinking that maybe you were exaggerating this story. I knew you believed it but I thought you might have gotten ahead of yourself." He studied the papers before him. He looked up, "But I have to admit this is very convincing."

I nodded, "But you still have to visit those families, Monsignor. We need a ton of evidence. We can't take a chance here."

He looked at me, shaking his benign head, "I'll do it this week. You can count on it." And then we called the number agent Sam had given me, reported what I had just gotten from the newly cooperative pawn dealers. That night, I slept like a baby.

♦

While I was gathering evidence against Nut's dad, Mrs. Delaney was beside herself with happiness on the ride to Reading. "You're not fooling me are you Robbie? You promise me your mom is alive?"

Truck had told her some of the story about being in danger after testifying in Nuremburg, that the FBI was protecting her, but he never mentioned the cancer. He looked at his mom's best friend, "The FBI will be really angry about this, so be ready for a lot of yelling."

She looked at him, a sweet look on her aging face,

"For a chance to see Gert again, I'll take a little yelling."

It was time to fess up. Truck looked at my his mom's dear friend, "Mrs. Delaney, I didn't tell you the bad news about mom. She has cancer." He watched her eyes get big. "Apparently, they caught it in time and are doing some special new treatment. She looks pretty good but you might notice her blonde wig. It looks real unless you get close but I just didn't want you to be surprised. Sorry, I didn't say something sooner. I thought maybe that cancer part was too much."

She patted his shoulder, "Not to worry. I'll take good care of Gert."

He explained a little more about what he remembered about his mom's treatment, but Mrs. Delaney just nodded, taking it in. As they entered the Road to Nowhere, he said, "Dylan has renamed this the Road to Somewhere. He said since we found mom here, it deserved a promotion."

Mrs. Delaney laughed, "That Dylan is some special friend you have. Always making the jokes." But she shook her head and added, "But like a brother to you. "

Truck thought about that, "I think of him as my brother. Him and Nut, the brothers I never had." And then added, "Don't tell him I said that, he doesn't take flattery well. He'll turn it on me somehow."

She sat quietly for a while. But then, "Your mom and I were like that. We would sit in your backyard sometimes for hours. Just telling stories, laughing. Like we knew what each other was thinking." Truck heard her take in air, "I can't believe she's back in my life." Truck's eyes started to tear up, so he looked straight ahead.

Fred was expecting him but Truck could see him get agitated when he saw Mrs. Delaney. He looked at him hard, "What's going on here kid. What part of 'don't tell anyone'–don't you understand?" Get back in the car and come back without any surprises."

As Truck started to protest, his mom came outside. He was shocked how pale and weak she looked. Before he could say anything, she spotted Mrs. Delaney. Mom gasped, looked like she saw a ghost. Without asking permission, Mrs. Delaney veered around Truck, gave Fred a look that made him hesitate and continued till she got to her dearest friend. She moved in tight, gathered her in her arms and said softly, "My dearest Gert, you never looked more beautiful."

Gert lowered her head, almost sank into the soft shoulder of her best friend. Mrs. Delaney wrapped her right hand around mom's head, kept repeating, "Don't worry, Gert, Rose is here to take care of you now. Everything will be alright." Gert started to cry softly. As Truck was about to break down, mom turned, "Robbie, come over here, join us." He walked around the bewildered Fred, reached both arms around the sobbing women. And finally broke down. He looked over at Fred, who had tears in his steely eyes.

CITY CHAMPIONSHIP

I never got a chance to talk much with Truck, find out how the Mrs. Delaney visit went. He got back late Sunday night; when I saw him in the hall before school, all he said was, "I'll tell more you later, but it went great. Mrs. Delaney's gonna stay with mom till she's done her treatment. After school tomorrow, I'm gonna get her clothes and other stuff." Truck had a look of pure joy on his face. But then the bell rang, we ran to homeroom.

The championship game was that night. Coach's plan was to meet right after school, walk through our scouting report and strategy one more time and have team dinner before boarding the bus to the Palestra. Coach wanted us there about two hours before tip-off. Wanted to keep us occupied, not let us overthink the pressure that awaited us. Could we be the first Connor team ever to claim the slippery title of city champs?

•Eastbrook was already there when we got to the Palestra. We heard balls bouncing as we walked on the floor but there wasn't much noise. They weren't talking at all. Drum sidled over, "They look scared. Like their butts are sewed tight but they got diarrhea. Know what I mean? Ready to burst."

I shook my head, "Not the image I want in my head walking into the big game, Drum. Can you spin a prettier picture, please?"

He patted my head, "Don't be a pansy, Dylan. Toughen up. Big night ahead." But Drum was right, the other night Eastbrook looked loose, played like it. Tonight they looked like the pressure was hitting them. Liked that. I scanned my teammates, everyone looked calm. I glanced at Truck. He looked almost serene. It must have gone really well with his mom.

Coach Gallagher was all business. As we were about to go out for warm-ups, he gathered us. "Gentlemen, we've worked hard all season to get to this moment. Tonight's game should be no different from any game this season. We always walk on the floor knowing we can win if we execute on offense and play stifling defense." He paused for effect. "But tonight will be the last time you play together as a team. I want you to think about that if there's a loose ball on the floor. Did I give everything I had for my teammates who fought with me for the past four seasons? Did I hesitate when hustle was demanded?" Coach turned his back to us, and then spun around suddenly, "I want this so bad for you boys. This is the game you will remember till the day you die. Give it all you have, and you will have a memory that will last a lifetime." He turned his back again. This time he turned around slowly, pointed at us, "Crush them!"

We stormed on the court, adrenaline flowing. Just as we suspected, Eastbrook was tight, clanged their first few shots like barbells. But Fran Philips was on fire. He slithered through Eastbrook like they were walking in sand. When they sagged off Fran, I was wide open, made four long jump shots. Scoot pestered the Eastbrook guards, getting two backcourt violations, clearly rattling their guards. And Drum got every missed shot. He scored six points easily on offensive rebounds. After the first quarter, we were up 22-6. Coach Gallagher was calm in the huddle. "Great quarter, guys. But keep up the pressure. They'll loosen up this quarter, so be prepared for a comeback." As we were walking back on the court, I heard him say to Truck, "Let's join the party, Truck, you look like you're watching the game, not playing in it." And he was right. Truck had done nothing so far.

That flashed through my head as the 2nd quarter began. Just as Coach had predicted, Eastbrook settled down. They beat our press, got a few baskets in a row and we went cold, reducing the lead to 22-14. Coach called time out. He looked at us in the huddle, "Don't let them score another easy point. If they come down the paint, make them pay. I don't want any sloppy fouls. But if you do foul, make sure they don't score. Make them earn points on the foul line." And then he said aloud, "Truck, snap out of it. You look like a zombie out there. Let's get some juice going." And we did settle down. Fran Philips took control again, built our lead almost singlehandedly to 30-14 before a late flurry by Eastbrook narrowed the lead at half to 32-20.

As we walked into the locker, I realized Truck hadn't scored a point. I got up beside him, "You alright, Truck?"

He smiled at me with a look of sheer contentment, "Perfect, just perfect." And that's when I started to worry.

Coach was great at half. He told us we had them where we wanted them. He never mentioned Truck's lousy performance. He focused on what we needed to do, not what we had done wrong so far; stressing that defense would win the game. Keep our intensity and Eastbrook would fold. From the corner of my eye, I watched Truck. He was smiling, not really responding to Coach's words. As we walked back on the court, I got up to Truck, said casually, "You can take over the game anytime you want. I won't be pissed that you hog the glory. I mean I would like to outscore you in the biggest game of our life so I can taunt you forever. But it'll be okay if you go nuts and just kick some tail."

He blinked fast a few times, grinned again. "You're trying to use psychology on me, right? But I'm wise to you, Dylan." Looked at me funny, "Let's get this game over."

♦

When I looked back at that game years later, I wondered if there was anything I could have done. We lost to Eastbrook on a last second shot, 53-52. When they realized that Truck wasn't himself, they switched to a box and one on Fran Philips; held him to six points the second half. It wasn't his fault; they had two men guarding him at all times. He made all three of his shots but he just had no daylight. I had the best game of my life, was high scorer with 20 points. But we lost. Truck didn't score a point. Coach tried relentlessly the 2nd half to shake him out of it. But to no avail. Truck had lost his fire. He was sleepwalking the whole game. Even during our somber end of game huddle, he still had a smile on his face. I was worried about him, asked to ride home with him. It wasn't till I got him talking about his visit with Mrs. Delany, that I understood. Basketball was no longer important to him. He kept repeating, "I think my mom's gonna be alright, I really do." He looked like a bright-eyed little kid on

Christmas morning. He had his once lost mom back. Nothing else mattered.

BACK TO REALITY

The whole school was somber the next day. A few people congratulated me for a good game, said Truck must have been sick or we'd have won. I just nodded. But mostly kids ignored me, like they were embarrassed for me. I remember thinking: No parade for losers. I got more bad news when I returned home that afternoon. As I walked in the door, mom said, "Monsignor Pugh called, asked for you to call when you got home." She looked at me funny, "Not in hot water with the Monsignor are you dear boy?"

I grinned, "That's always a jump ball situation, mom. When she frowned, added, "But no, he's helping me with a project. You should be proud of me, hanging around with the priests. Kind of like your dream come true, right?"

She shook her head, "Now you really have me curious."

I went over, hugged her. "Thanks for the faith in me." She swatted at me as I scampered to the phone.

After a short delay, Monsignor Pugh came to the line. He got right to the point, "Neither family is willing to get involved in this mess. Even when I showed them pictures and laid out the whole scheme, they just shook their heads."

I let that sink in. "Did you mention this same creep beats his family? That we need their help putting him away?"

I was getting mad. Monsignor sensed my frustration, "Let's say a prayer for them, Dylan. I'll go at them again, maybe they'll soften."

I thought to myself: How about I pray for them after I give them a swift kick in the balls? Instead, "Thanks for trying, Monsignor." I hung up. Back to square one but I wasn't about to give up.

Almost every day after school, Truck drove to Reading to visit his mom. After a few days, trying to shake off my basketball gloom, I asked if I could go with him. He smiled, "I'd like that. Mom would love to get to know you." And then he asked, "Are you still pissed-off at me? I know I cost us the city championship by playing so lousy."

I told him the truth. "For the first couple days, I wanted to kick your ass. I kept thinking: How could Truck just quit on us like that? I mean, it was the biggest game of our lives. Something we'd worked for and dreamed about since we were little. How could he just not give a damn?"

He was staring at me, shocked by my blunt answer. And then I added, "But then I realized that after all those years of thinking your mom was dead, you suddenly found out she was alive. And just as suddenly, you learned she had cancer and might lose her. And if that wasn't enough, you start to really believe she's going to be okay the day before the game." I smiled at him, "When I thought about that, I realized it was a miracle you could even walk. So yes, I forgive you." I took a deep breath, had a hard time getting out the next few words. "I hope you can forgive me for not being a better friend, understanding what you were feeling." Neither one of us could talk for a while.

The ride to Reading was fun. It was just Truck and I. Nut couldn't go because he was at a ceremony honoring him as the only kid in Pennsylvania wrestling history to win the heavyweight title three years in a row. He didn't mess around in the final match. He pinned the guy in thirteen seconds, a record for the title match. I went to the match, saw Nut slaughter the guy, filled Truck in on the details during the drive. He was visiting his mom that day, didn't see Nut crush the guy. "You should have seen the other guy prancing around the mat, snarling at Nut, trying to intimidate him. It was great, Nut just grinned at him. When the ref started the match, Nut exploded at the guy, lifted his left leg and threw him like a sack of potatoes. And then Nut springs on him, pins the guy's chest and jams his shoulders to the mat so hard his eyes were bugging out. Afterwards, Nut complained that he didn't pin him under ten seconds." We both laughed.

And then I filled him in on something big Nut just told me that morning. His discussion with Reneé. "He swore her to secrecy but told her the Green Beret plan. She was pestering him about what college he would go to for wrestling. Said she'd go wherever he went. So, he finally spilled the beans."

Truck turned to me, "How'd she take it? I mean, based on how they look at each other, I'm pretty sure she's thinking wedding bells someday."

Nut had told me she took it hard. Tried to talk him out of it but finally gave in when she saw his mind was set. I then told Truck what I really thought. "I think Reneé feels that was the first round, Nut won. But I'm thinking she has some more fight in her. That's my read." And then I told him the bad news about Monsignor Pugh's talk with the families of the dead people Digger robbed.

He shook his head, "Shit." But he looked over at me, asked, "What are you gonna do next?" But before I could answer we were driving down the dusty road to the FBI hideaway.

I couldn't believe the change in Truck's mom. Now I knew why he was so optimistic. Her skin color had returned, she had gained some weight, just looked much healthier. And Mrs. Delaney looked ten years younger. Finding out her best friend was alive was a fountain of youth. Even agent Fred seemed resigned to his blown mission. He looked at me, "I thought bringing Rose here was probably your idea but Robbie says you're innocent."

I threw open my hands, "As I always tell my dad when falsely accused, 'Blessed are the pure of heart.' "

He laughed, "You should go to Hollywood. They need more comedians." And then he asked how the case with Digger was going. I gave him the latest. He pointed at me, "Don't give up on it. After what Sam said this guy has done, I'd love to help you throw him in jail. He sounds like a real piece of scum."

I assured him I wouldn't quit. But secretly, I didn't see a happy ending. But I shook off the dour thought then sat back and enjoyed watching Truck take care of his mother. She brought out the softness he never showed. And then I realized that was why we lost the championship. The fury that made him great was gone.

Not wanting to revisit that loss, I shook off the negative memory. Settled in to watch Truck lather his mom with the affection so long buried in his tortured soul. Mrs. Delaney fixed a great dinner that night, my first taste of sauerbraten and red cabbage, unbelievable. And we chatted amiably about the weather and other mindless topics. It was fun being normal again.

DEVIL OR ANGEL

Nut had called the night before, asked to meet him after school. He wanted to catch up on our next steps, figured we could have some privacy as we walked home. I was surprised he was free, said so. "I'm supposed to see the councilman for Delaware County this afternoon but I'm cancelling. I'm getting sick of being paraded to all these political bigwigs that don't know the difference between a Full Nelson and Ricky Nelson."

I chuckled, "You're getting a sense of humor in your old age, Nut."

He shrugged, "Hanging around with you has warped me, I guess."

As we neared his house, we finalized our next move with Digger. The plan was to wait some more, give Monsignor Pugh time to wear down the families. Agreed that their testimony would slam the door shut. And then I asked about Reneé. Nut exhaled, had a peaceful look like he had just slammed an opponent to the mat. "She said she's waiting for me." I hadn't seen such a happy look on his face for months. That made me content. Some things were working out well.

I hadn't seen Mrs. O'Hanlon for weeks so I decided to stay with Nut. As we walked up the driveway, Nut stopped sharply. "I wonder why Digger's car's home so early?" He wasn't looking for an answer, he was thinking aloud. As we rounded the corner of the driveway, near the backdoor, we heard a muffled cry. Nut never hesitated, he knew what that meant. I watched him vault the steps, rushed into the kitchen. Seconds later, I ran after him. As I got to the door, I saw Mrs. O'Hanlon slumped on the floor, blood dripping from her temple. Digger was standing over her, like a lion taunting his prey. Nut had come to a stop, glared at Digger and then at his injured mother. I didn't know what Nut would do next, but expected the worse. But surprisingly, he seemed to control his rage, brushed Digger out of the way, stooped down to care for his mother.

And that's when it went to hell. Nut pulled a towel from the counter, mopped the blood from his mom's brow. That was a mistake. While Nut was busy tending his mom, Digger moved to his left, grabbed a heavy frying pan with both hands and moved in. Before I could yell, Digger swung the pan, connected full on the back of Nut's skull. I felt sick as I heard the dull thud of bone against iron. I watched as Digger moved closer, lifted the pan over his left shoulder, got ready for another blow. Operating on pure anger, I closed on Digger and delivered a crushing smack to his right ear. Unlike my numerous failures, this was world-class. Digger went rigid, his knees buckled, he crashed to the floor like a ton of rocks. He groaned in agony. I went to Nut. Sure he was dead. But he was still breathing, seemed to be coming awake after I mopped his head with a cold cloth. Mrs. O'Hanlon had revived enough to call the police, asked the dispatcher for an ambulance. The rest was a nightmare.

The police came in as the ambulance arrived. By then Nut had gotten to a chair, was sitting but was clearly dazed. Digger was still on the floor but was conscious. The medics gave him smelling salts that seemed to jolt him alert. He started screaming that Nut and I attacked him and his wife, that we were the cause of the trouble. Nut still wasn't too lucid and Mrs. O'Hanlon seemed in shock. Before I knew it, the police were handcuffing me, putting me in a cruiser that followed the ambulance that contained Nut, his mom and Digger. As the ambulance headed toward the hospital, we veered off toward police headquarters. I kept babbling that they had it all wrong, that Digger was an abusive father, that he was beating Mrs. O'Hanlon. That was why I hit him. The police officers nodded, they had heard this stuff before. We got to the police station. I was read my rights, processed as a criminal, charged with aggravated assault.

It's funny how weird things hit you in traumatic moments. I was hungry as hell, starving. Apparently, I had arrived at jail shortly after dinner so I went to bed hungry. I tried to amuse myself with optimistic outcomes to this mess, but failed. I kept thinking: I'm screwed. Lights were out by nine pm. I had a troubled sleep. When I awoke early next morning, I thought about finally delivering a perfect ear slap. My pride was dampened as I realized it got me thrown in the slammer. And then I analyzed my situation. I had to admit, Digger played it perfectly. It was our word against his, two big guys against a smaller old man. Who would believe our story? Plus the guy's the pillar of the church, a big shot in the community. And then I thought how this ruined our plan to get Digger jailed for stealing jewelry from dead people. Who would believe us now? I shook my head. Screwed. I turned on my side, tried fruitlessly to lift my dour mood.

♦

Hours later, I heard the jingle of keys just as I was drifting off. I saw my parents and Monsignor Pugh stride through the door with the jailer. Monsignor had a smile on his face as he said, "Given your penchant for mischief, I can't say I'm shocked to see you behind bars." Mom laughed and just as I was about to protest, he raised his hands as if giving a blessing. "It's okay, Dylan, we got this all straightened out. I was just having a little fun with you. But I guess that's not truly in the Christian spirit, is it?" He turned to the jailer, "Let's get him out of there." The three of them pulled me in for a big bear-hug.

Just like that everything changed. On the ride home, I learned that Mrs. O'Hanlon had called him from the hospital, needed his moral support to finally tell the truth. Digger screamed and hollered but Mrs. O'Hanlon purged her demons. The police put her under protective custody and put a guard on Digger until he recovered from his broken ear drum and concussion.

But Monsignor Pugh wasn't done. He had called agent Sam and the FBI was on their way to arrest Digger for transporting stolen goods across state lines—a federal offense. He had been able finally to sway the deceased family members to prosecute, after hearing his impassioned story of family abuse. This latest incident cinched their help. Agent Sam told him Digger would be locked up for at least twenty years, maybe more if the family-abuse charges were proven. Monsignor Pugh looked at me, an incredulous look on his face, "Your crazy plan worked, just as you laid it out to me."

But there was no time to celebrate. I was worried about Nut, asked how he was. "Other than a big egg on his noggin and a headache, the doctors said he should be fine." And then, "It might have killed a normal person, but that young man isn't normal." After a pause, "But if you hadn't stopped the next blow, I doubt he'd be alive."

I looked at the Monsignor. "I have to admit that felt good, smacking Digger senseless, watching him collapse." He laughed when I added, "That's only a venial sin, right?"

♦

Everything settled down after that horrible day. We were nearing the end of our senior year. Truck's mom was doing better; the prognosis was optimistic. He hadn't played basketball since the championship game. Despite the horrible championship game, he had loads of scholarships. Word from the scouts was "Truck was sick that night," was still a major talent. When I asked where he'd play ball, he shrugged, "Somewhere near here, near mom." But then wistfully, "If I play at all. It doesn't seem that important anymore."

I didn't argue with him, he had never been happier. And best of all, Digger had been found guilty of both federal and civil crimes. He would be in jail for at least forty years, a feeble old man by the time he was released. Nut's brother Jimmy was running the business with Mrs. O'Hanlon as the bookkeeper. She was going to counseling, it would take a long time but her fear was melting, her smile had returned. She was healing. Nut and Reneé were inseparable, true love if I ever saw it.

I thought about all this as I walked to St Tims. The things I had worried so much about last November had turned out well. Westminster University had offered me a scholarship, but it was contingent on making the team and maintaining a C plus average. My marks were mediocre, the coaches worried I might struggle with the college curriculum. Funny, I wasn't worried. It was just a matter of taking schoolwork seriously. Which got me thinking about basketball. I was having a difficult time shaking off our championship loss. I had worked so hard, put my soul into it and yet failed. Where's the justice? I fought off feeling sorry for myself, hated that I couldn't shake the gloomy, self-absorbed thoughts. I even blamed God for not listening. He had abandoned me at the most important moment of my life.

That was why I was going to confession. I needed help chasing my gloom. I entered the sacred confessional. "Bless me father for I have sinned, it has been one month since my last confession…" I unloaded my self-pity to Monsignor Pugh.

He listened quietly before commenting sagely. "We all have doubts about prayer, Dylan. It is normal for you to feel angry after losing something you worked so hard for. But let me ask you this. If God had granted you three wishes, where would you have placed the basketball championship in comparison with helping Truck find his mother and saving the O'Hanlon family from their torment?" I was about to answer when he added, "Because of you, your best friend's lives have been forever changed. What you did there was truly a miracle. If I had to guess, I'll bet basketball would have come in last. Am I right?"

Before I could answer, he finished with, "So if I had to say, I think God did a pretty good job of listening to your prayers." I had a peaceful walk back home.

ABOUT THE AUTHOR

TOM FAUSTMAN is a retired Senior Vice President from a Fortune 100 company. Born in Maryland, Tom spent the rest of his youth in Drexel Hill, PA where he divided his time between playing pick-up basketball on the neighborhood courts and making the Catholic school nuns shake their heads. An English Literature graduate of West Chester University, Tom is also a Vietnam Veteran, a lover of family, fine wine, books, humor, and sports, He pens a monthly newsletter, WineLore, and is the author of *Chameleon Skills*, *Dylan's Monster and Dylan's Nam*. He lives with his wife on an orchard farm in South Glastonbury, Connecticut, where they are surrounded by their three children and six astounding grandkids.

www.ingramcontent.com/pod-product-compliance
Lightning Source LLC
Chambersburg PA
CBHW051327250626
47155CB00007B/2487